IMAGE
DECAY

Library and Archives Canada Cataloguing in Publication

Title: Image decay / Mark Lisac.
Names: Lisac, Mark, 1947- author.
Identifiers: Canadiana (print) 20200159739 | Canadiana (ebook) 2020015978X | ISBN 9781988732893 (softcover) | ISBN 9781988732909 (EPUB) | ISBN 9781988732916 (Kindle)
Classification: LCC PS8623.I82 I43 2020 | DDC C813/.6—dc23

Board Editor: Douglas Barbour
Cover and interior design: Michel Vrana
Cover images: iStockphoto; spxChrome, LoudRedCreative, g-stockstudio, MarioGuti, Simon Herrmann. psdbox.com: Andrei Oprinca.
Author photo: Ellen Nygaard

NeWest Press acknowledges the support of the Canada Council for the Arts, the Alberta Foundation for the Arts, and the Edmonton Arts Council for support of our publishing program. We acknowledge the financial support of the Government of Canada.

NeWest Press wishes to acknowledge that the land on which we operate is Treaty 6 territory and a traditional meeting ground and home for many Indigenous Peoples, including Cree, Saulteaux, Niitsitapi (Blackfoot), Métis, and Nakota Sioux.

NeWest Press
#201, 8540-109 Street
Edmonton, Alberta T6G 1E6
NeWest Press   www.newestpress.com

No bison were harmed in the making of this book.

Printed and bound in Canada

1 2 3 4 5 22 21 21

To Ellen

IMAGE DECAY

Mark Lisac

NeWest Press

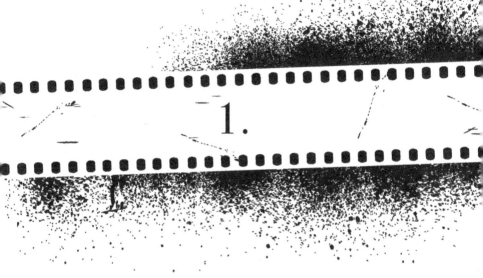

1.

THE RIVER SLID UNDERNEATH HIM. THE WATER WAS NEARLY clear over the gravel bars. Over the deeper hollows and channels it folded in slowly undulating ribbons of olive and light brown. The surface looked like camouflage fabric with something alive underneath it. Some of the greens bordered on dirty blue but all the currents had the tint of suspended mud or dead leaves.

It did not look like it was flowing hard. Random twigs floated by faster than his normal walking pace, passing out of sight under the bridge. There was still laziness to it.

Not like the Niagara, which he remembered as cold, blue, and terrifyingly muscular.

The light was not the same either. In the early September sun, the air here had lost the diamond hardness of midsummer and had taken on the clear, washed-out quality of faded jeans. Not the soft haze usually visible around the Great Lakes. Not the faint golden promise of the air in California. He could have lived in either of those places. He had chosen instead this pre-cast concrete city, frozen half the year, slovenly with litter and dust the other half, in denial about its nature always.

"What am I doing here?" Ostroski thought.

He stopped. Had he spoken the words out loud? He could not remember when he had started mumbling his thoughts, or when he had stopped being embarrassed about it.

His mind wandered in other ways, he knew. Faded jeans. Sky like faded jeans. Why did they have to be faded? When had they stopped making powder blue?

Sweat started trickling down his back. The sun had swung onto his side of the bridge and his jacket was now too warm but there was too much risk trying to take it off. He rubbed his back against one of the iron girders, its black paint starting to peel and rust starting to show around the peeled patches and the rivets.

He looked at his hostage. She had short brown hair, darkening toward black in a few patches. Her liquid brown eyes met his. They looked alternately nervous and angry.

He did not flinch from her gaze. If he had to, he would throw her over the railing. He had already threatened to do it once to keep the cops back. He thought he would need about one second—two at most—to send her dropping straight like an elevator into the water. It would probably take another two or three seconds for her to hit. She might survive. You never knew.

He reasoned the cops would not shoot him because there was too much chance of hitting her. But he would have to do it fast. They might try to shock him with a flash grenade or tear gas. The big plainclothes cop who had got close to him to talk might have decide to rush up and grab him.

He hoped they would find the lawyer or Adela soon. He was willing to talk to one of them, although even they would have to keep their distance. He did not want to send the girl sailing in a short arc and then straight down through the washed-out air and onto the surface of the river. Onto, not into. He guessed after a drop like that it might feel more like concrete than like water. He didn't want to do it. It had already been a tough life for her. That idiot had named her Mitzi. "Don't worry, Mitzi," he said. "I'm not asking for much. They'll see reason."

She tilted her head slightly with curiosity on hearing him talk. What he had hoped would be reassuring words seemed to have little effect. She was probably getting irritable with hunger. She was bored, too, getting squirmy. At least she wasn't drooling much. He hoped her boredom and nervousness did not slide into aggression. He didn't like the look of her pointed teeth. Her voice was snarly, too. That was even more disturbing.

"Goddamn dachshunds," he thought. The nastiest, most short-tempered kind of dogs he could think of. He would rather have been holding onto the leash of a small pit bull, or anything else light enough to lift over the edge. Just like that smug moron to breed dachshunds and think they're lovable.

Just like me to start concentrating on the goddamn squirming dog and forget how fast even a big cop could get to me, he thought as he heard shoes scratch on concrete. He felt the big cop slamming into him. He dropped the dog as a twisted and toppled to the sidewalk, scraping a knee and elbow. He lay still and tired as the shock of the collision and the fall seeped through him.

Mitzi stepped up and licked his face. She was snarly, but not one to hold grudges. It was the most physical affection he had known in twelve years.

On the ninth floor of a nearby administrative tower a grey wraith of a man's silhouette let vertical blinds drop back into place. He had looked out to check the weather and been held by the drama taking place down on the bridge walk. Disorder mesmerized him. He had spent most of his last fifty years struggling to keep life under control, keep it as neat as the files in his office and the art collections he now supervised. He looked at his reflection in the glass covering a pen-and-ink drawing of an 1880s-era homestead on the wall across from his plain mahogany desk. He saw his metal-rimmed spectacles and thinning hair and flat, expressionless mouth, but he could not see past that surface detail. Nor did he want to.

2.

GEORGE RABANI LIKED BEING A LAWYER. HE DID NOT LIKE being an informal social worker, which his practice required on certain days.

He thought people were enormously and unfailingly interesting. He saw in them a vast field of bleak self-interest interrupted by oases of compassion and generosity. He enjoyed talking to them. He found most of them a never-ending source of delightful surprise. They constantly invented quirks or stumbled into improbable predicaments. Sometimes they strode into those situations wilfully. Sometimes they wandered in as if driving mistakenly onto a road that petered out, turning suddenly to gravel and then to dirt.

He helped when he could. But he did not like dealing with people who seemed essentially incapable of understanding their situation. Jack Ostroski was on the border. Rabani knew Ostroski was smart. He was not sure what Ostroski understood and what he did not.

The previous day's incident on the High View Bridge could result in an order for a psychiatric assessment. It might be kept quiet instead, with Ostroski simply being calmed down and told to go tend to his store. Rabani thought there was too much behind the incident to go away. Who takes a dog hostage? And the episode suggested some capacity for violence.

He had walked into the office seeing his image reflected on the plate glass of the building front and the door. The pictures flickered past like frames of old movie film. He had become used to his pockmarked face and the slight muffin bulge at his beltline. After nearly two years he was almost used to seeing that image entering one of the capital's top law offices.

Saying good morning to Julia at the front desk had brought him back from doubt. He was a lawyer with a promising future. In a good firm. In a city with cheap grey buildings, and a downtown filled with panhandlers and with haggard, blank-faced teenagers catching a bus to school. But the city had plenty of money. It also had many people whose hidden needs or bad judgments eventually dragged them into law offices. The variety of their inspirations and failings promised him years of education. Mere entertainment was not enough. He wanted to learn.

Rabani was not a cynic or a voyeur. He was a student of humanity. Mostly he saw at least as much reason for hope in his clients as he did weakness. In his darkest moments he worried that he studied his clients as a way of learning about himself. People were not so different from one another. Yet they were different enough—some were lawyers and some were clients.

Julia of the perfectly coiffed hair and expensively understated dress had given him her warm but utterly dispassionate smile and handed him a large brown envelope. He saw the previous day's date and "Ostroski" scrawled on the upper-left corner. The delivery in itself was worrisome. It indicated that whatever Ostroski had thought he was doing on the bridge, he had planned it.

Rabani tore the end of the envelope neatly and slipped out a thin sheaf of paper. It was going to take some time. He stepped outside to get a cup of coffee, double cream and double sugar. He asked Julia to hold any calls, returned to his office and settled into the massive chair that he thought was one of the best perks of working at a good firm.

Then he began to read:

"I am typing this on an Underwood from the mid-1930s. I like old Royals too but this is a solid machine and has been my favourite for a long time. It's been such a long time that I can't remember. "This machine is real. You can see the action. You can see the parts move. Press the concave button with the light letter printed on a black background and the long metal arm swings up from its resting place. It curves through the small space in its assigned arc.

"The black fabric ribbon lifts and the end of the metal arm with the neatly cast letter on the end hits it. You can hear the thwack. The fabric transfers a shape of ink onto the rolled paper. Sometimes I hold the key down to keep the metal arm in place. The alloy kisses the ink-soaked cloth. It's the moment of creation.

"Yes, it's a mechanical and chemical process just like a photograph. But you choose what image to put on the paper. That makes it creation. So does the transfer of the ink. A message appears on the paper. At that moment, nothing turns into something. It stays there. It can stay for centuries. Not like an arrangement of electrons in a computer.

"I have an old Oliver too. Named after a guy from Canada. And a Remington Noiseless from 1938. They're more like investments and I keep them hidden. If I have to, I'll sell one of them to buy a bottle of good booze when I turn eighty-five. But the Underwood is what I write with. Like when I have to send a note to a lawyer once every ten years or so.

"I'm taking one of Becker's dogs hostage. It's one of his special pets. He calls her Mitzi. She may or may not still be alive by the time you read this. That's up to Becker.

"The son of a bitch won't listen to reason so he'll have to deal with a madman. That's what I am now. A mad man, which is also what I am, would steal a dog and hold it hostage. A madman would try to explain himself. Which is what I'm doing now.

"Becker stole my photos. Maybe not technically. He didn't break into my shop one night and carry off the cases. He might as well have. They said I walked off my old photographer's job with a government Hasselblad. Total bull. Manchester said I could have it. It was sort of a gold watch deal, a present for years of loyal service. But after I left they wanted it back. I'd sold it by then and was still short of money.

"Becker brokered the deal to have my photos donated to the archives. I could have sold them for a lot more than the Hasselblad was worth. He knew that, the son of a bitch. It was worth it to me then to get them off my back. I was getting worried about proper storage of the negatives and prints anyway. They last a long time but need proper care.

"But here's where it went wrong. They didn't let me cull the collection first. It was pick up the boxes and go. The lawyer in Becker's department said I agreed to sell the collection and there was nothing in the agreement that said I could take anything out. Becker's a cabinet minister. He could have let me have a look through. But no. He had it in for me for some reason.

"That was bad enough. I figured I could live with it. The photos would get stored somewhere. A few of the personal shots I took on the side when I was on government work might make it into a display case at the museum. Everyone wants to see candid photos of Manchester, that old con man, and the collection of mental dwarfs he pretended helped him run the government, right? There were some nice ones of historic oil wells too.

"That wasn't to be. I've heard someone has started snooping through the collection. I wouldn't be surprised if it was Becker himself. Then I heard someone has been assigned to look into new technology that may make it possible to transfer everything into copies on a computer. It's got something to do with changing everything from physical copies to electronic simulations, the way that's happened with turning vinyl records into CDs. Instead of chemical film or grains of silver nitrate the pictures get turned into a bunch of ones and zeros in a computer. The bright boys call this digitization, I hear. You may think it sounds farfetched but I'll tell you, when I got to Hollywood in the late 1940s television sounded like a novelty. Five years later it started destroying the movies. And once real things get turned into electricity they can spread all over. They could decide to they could decide to 'digitize' everything and put it on this thing they call the Internet. Digitize. I never agreed to that. I agreed to let the photos go into the archives.

"If they go that way, their idea isn't to preserve anything, it's to chew it up and spit it out into garbage. They want to turn silver nitrate and paper into electrons. It's a perversion. Photographs are meant to record a passing moment and keep it forever. Converting them into an arrangement of electrons in a computer explodes them. It destroys them like an atomic bomb. You can't take something meant to last through time and make it ephemeral—you didn't think I knew words like that did you? Oh yeah. When I lived in Hollywood I drank now and then with screenwriters, back when they weren't afraid of words and ideas.

"Then there's the invasion of privacy. There are photos in that collection that aren't meant to be seen, at least not in my lifetime. Why didn't I destroy them, you say? Because they happened and can't be erased. Because I could not bear to see them erased from the record of life. But I thought they would be preserved out of sight, saved but unseen until it didn't matter anymore. Now it looks like someday they'll want to put these photographs on a computer network. God knows who might see them. It isn't meant to be.

"Becker is the culture minister. He could stop it. He won't. I'm going to make him stop. He loves his dogs too much to let Mitzi die. He'd let me drop a person off the bridge but he won't let me drop a dog. That's what I'm counting on anyway.

"By tomorrow this should all be cleared away. Come and see me in my shop. If I'm not out in the front I'll be in the time machine. If I'm not there I'll be in jail, or maybe the river."

Emotional but not insane, Rabani decided. Disjointed enough to suggest a psychiatric exam. That probably depended on whether Becker chose to press charges. The cops wouldn't be happy about letting Ostroski loose but if the incident could be played as something closer to a potential suicide than to a crime, there was a chance.

He put the three sheets of paper back into the envelope and put the envelope into his private file for cases he wanted to think about more before acting on them.

"Time machine." It didn't sound good but he'd been a lawyer long enough now not to jump to conclusions.

He turned his head and looked up, as he did from time to time, at the portrait of James Vickert on the wall behind him. Vickert, now retired somewhere out amid the extravagant flowers and shrubs on Vancouver Island. He would have smiled on learning that Rabani had asked for a large print from the office portrait file and said something about not putting too much stock in heroes. Vickert had drummed into him the importance of patience, had taught him in a short year many things about the practice of law and the daily effort of integrity, had been for him a model not only of a lawyer but of a gentleman, had given him hope that his essential optimism about people could more often than not be fulfilled. The photograph on the wall behind his desk, the phantom ideal behind his own reality.

He picked up the next file. It was far simpler than Ostroski's case. A condo association wanted to know if it would be worth suing a developer for drainpipes that had cracked badly after five years. Yes, there was probably a case that the dirt had not been properly compacted. No, there was probably no way a bunch of cash-strapped families in townhouses could come out ahead in a legal fight with an established firm with millions at its disposal.

Not a social worker, he thought. But sometimes being a lawyer was like being a boxing manager. You picked the right fights and avoided the ones that looked unwinnable. That limited the upside for the clients and himself. But the downside of taking on a weak case was usually too painful to risk. Taking risks was what brought people into lawyers' offices; his job was getting them out of the office and back into their own lives. That was his life.

3.

TWO DAYS LATER, RABANI STROLLED THROUGH DUST AND rolling paper cups and scraps of candy-bar wrapper flying in the spring wind down 108th Street and looked up at the sign for Ostroski's Cameras. An image of an old Kodak Brownie decorated the upper right corner.

He opened the grainy wood-frame door and saw a woman behind the counter—not young, far from old, not suspicious when he gave his name and said he had come to see Ostroski, but gazing at him as if taking mental notes. A melody of Spanish in her voice.

She told him Ostroski was in back. Rabani walked through an open doorway and looked around at piles of boxes and a battered desk. He called, "Jack, it's George Rabani."

A voice answered him from behind a black cylinder set against a wall: "I'm in the time machine finishing some prints. Be out in a minute."

The cylinder began to revolve. It appeared to be a sliding door of sorts. Ostroski stepped out, a few centimetres shorter than Rabani but more solidly built.

"Good morning."

"Good morning, Jack. Hope I'm not disturbing you."

"You're a lawyer. That means I'm in trouble. Of course you're disturbing me. Then you'll send me a bill and I'll be disturbed again. Someday maybe your firm will hire me to take a portrait of the partners for five hundred bucks. Then I won't be disturbed."

He saw Rabani looking at the round compartment with a curved, sliding door built into the flimsy wall.

"Never seen one of those? It's a door for a darkroom. A cylinder. You turn it, there's always an opening on one side and a black surface on the other to keep the light from passing through. That way you can go in and out of a darkroom without outside light having a chance to come in. Effective and simple, just like a camera shutter. Except more simple than a shutter. A work of genius but not complicated enough to have people think so. You came to talk about what happened?"

Rabani looked out toward the doorway, where the woman was within earshot.

"Adela," Ostroski said, "it's a good time for you to walk down the block for a coffee break. Doesn't look like there will be many customers this morning anyway."

Her voice came back through the opening without her looking through it: "Yes, Jack. Would you like me to bring one back for you?"

"Thanks."

They waited until the front door closed. Ostroski said they might as well talk out front where there was more light. Rabani went first and surveyed shelves while Ostroski gathered two chairs. He saw 35mm cameras bearing famous names, two boxes full of leather cases, a few vintage Kodak Instamatics that he guessed were from the 1950s. One old Brownie. Other shelves offered filters, brushes, and other paraphernalia.

"Why do you call it the time machine?" he said as they sat down.

"You think this whole place is a time capsule, right? Nah. This is just a store for people who like working with old equipment that still does the job. The darkroom in back, that's the time machine.

Because working with photographs is working with time. You know about Cartier-Bresson's theory of taking pictures at what he called the decisive moment?"

"I've heard the phrase."

"So have a lot of people. A lot of people think they can recognize those moments and can take pictures. Well, every moment is important in someone's life. And taking a photograph is recording a moment on film, then printing the record on paper. The moment lives on for a long time. Maybe not forever, but for a lifetime. That's forever to most people. They don't care much about what comes after."

"But the moment is gone. Having a picture of it doesn't bring it back. Those prehistoric cave drawings in France can't bring back ancient horses and antelope."

"You're right, lawyer. The people in photographs are gone for good. The people they were at that moment are gone the next day, or the next hour. Even stone buildings that last for centuries aren't the same as they once were. Just ten years can add scratches and dirt. That doesn't matter. What they meant lives on. That's what photographs do—they keep the meaning alive. Hell, that's all Cartier-Bresson was talking about when he talked about the decisive moment. He thought there were times when the way things looked expressed the real meaning behind a person or a place or an event."

"Okay. What was the real meaning of you being on the bridge threatening to throw a dog off it? Because right now there's a real court and real police machinery that could end up throwing you into a real jail or mental hospital."

Ostroski looked at him, grey eyebrows raised. "I was trying to get his attention. Like hitting a mule with a two-by-four. You know?"

"You got the cops' attention."

"Don't worry. I got his, too. He doesn't care much about anything but he cares about his dogs."

Rabani looked at Ostroski's eyes. Not looking for the person inside but taking in their pale blue colour, and their unblinking frankness. Or was it playful guile? He made guesstimates and hoped he was getting them right: open and honest, but open only as far as he wanted to be; experienced and knowing about the world; capable of taking risks but preferring risks on which the odds could be calculated in advance; naturally friendly, but unafraid of fights; dangerous.

A so-so client, Rabani thought. He'll listen to reason, up to the point that suits him but maybe not after that. Co-operative, but also unpredictable. There were better clients, and many worse, and many less interesting.

"What do you want from Becker to settle everything?" Rabani asked.

"I want my photographs. The ones that are really mine. The personal ones."

"I don't know if we can do that, Jack. Ownership has been established. It would have to be a matter for negotiation."

"Well, that's what lawyers are for, isn't it? Negotiate them back for me. The ones I want are of no interest to anyone anyway."

"What if he gets stubborn?"

"I've thought about that. It wouldn't surprise me. Then I'll settle for control of what gets displayed and or put on this Internet thing for public access. Most of them don't matter. They can do what they want with all the old oil wells and politicians and stuff I collected over the years. But then I want a realistic price. Not some token to wipe out that trumped-up accusation that I walked off with a Hasselblad. Fifty thousand. Start higher and bargain down if you have to. But fifty thousand is the cutoff. They pay me or things keep happening. I'm not the only one who wants to avoid more trouble."

"You can't be kidnapping his dogs, Jack. Or throwing strychnine-laced hamburger over the fence to them or anything else. You'll end up in jail or worse. And you won't get money or pictures."

He thought he saw a glint of humour, so faint and fleeting that it was barely visible, spark through Ostroski's eyes.

Ostroski said, "Maybe there's more than one kind of dog. Maybe there are other pictures, too."

Rabani stared at him. Ostroski said, "Don't bother asking." He got up from his chair—lithe and quick for his age, Rabani noted—and half-turned toward the door to the back room. He stopped, turned his head back to Rabani, and continued, "See if you can get a little more than fifty thousand. I need it all and I'd like to have some extra to pay you."

Rabani watched him go through the doorway, got up and went out the front, leaving the wooden chairs where they were.

He walked down the street in the direction he had seen Adela take. The storefront windows needed cleaning. One had a "for lease" sign taped inside. The window frames were mostly old and made of wood, with dingy paint that had faded in years of harsh sunlight and rain. The paint on most of the frames was cratered. Older layers underneath had not been scraped smooth before being covered. Yellow and brown were common colours.

A small storefront at the end of the block had an aluminum frame window and a sign reading "Sunrise Coffee." Rabani looked inside. He saw Adela sitting on a high stool at a round table, a take-away cup in front of her, reading a paperback book. He also saw a rack of muffins and what looked like banana bread and date squares.

His mouth filled with the taste. He wondered if the reflex would ever go away. He was currently near the upper limit of the seven-kilogram swing in weight he allowed himself. Once he had gained eight kilos and been overcome by mortal fear of diabetes and, worse, of loss of control. This year he was starting the weight loss only about six and half too heavy, disturbed by no more than having to switch to his larger pants. He walked into the café and to the table.

Adela looked up, her expression neither surprised nor indicating she had been expecting him. Her colours ranged from the faint brown of her skin to the dark brown of her eyes and hair. She wore no makeup. She said, "Hello."

He would normally have sat down on the stool opposite her. Looking at her face and hearing the inexpressive steadiness in her voice he decided that he should ask first if she minded.

"For a minute," she said. "I have to get back to the store and take Jack his coffee, too."

"I won't waste time, then," he said. "I'm going to try to help him settle the business with the dog. Have you worked at the store long?"

"Nearly two years."

"Long enough to know what he's like then. Has he been acting especially nervous or depressed?"

"Jack? No. He is as you no doubt saw him." She did not elaborate.

"You're from Latin America somewhere?"

"Nicaragua. And you're wondering why my Spanish accent has almost disappeared and why my English sounds American."

He waited.

"I learned English when I was young and spent two years in New York, studying at Columbia. I thought I wanted to be an architect, specializing in historical preservation. Then I came here and found there's almost nothing old enough here to preserve and almost no interest in preserving what is old enough. And a reluctance to trust foreign credentials, which you probably know if you've ever asked foreign-born cab drivers or security guards what they did before they came here. Now you know my life story as well as everything I can tell you about Jack."

"Does that mean you don't like me?"

"I like people. I don't trust strangers. Nobody should trust strangers. But I don't tell other people how to live."

Rabani searched her face for any hint of irony, or of interest in him. He saw only honesty backed by impenetrable blackness—the qualified openness of a mirror. He wanted to see more.

She closed her book and said, "I have to get back to the shop."

He looked at the roundness of her face and the rounded curves of her body and thought about the contrast with what seemed to be an angular mind. He made a quick decision and blurted out, "Would you like to have dinner with me sometime? Or just a coffee if you prefer? After Jack's legal business is settled, that is."

She stood up and said, "We wouldn't be strangers then. Do you think that's a good idea?"

"I've never been good at predicting the future."

"Perhaps. Let's see what becomes of Jack's case first."

He let her walk out of the café ahead of him, not watching her as she turned north and headed back to the camera shop. He walked out and turned south, and then east, back toward his office. He wondered how many calories walking eight blocks would burn.

After he got the day's routine out of the way, but before rush hour, he put a file into his briefcase to work on that night, went down to the parking garage, and drove to the northeast end of downtown. It was a multitalented neighbourhood. There were poor people, some middle-class Italians and Portuguese who ran nearby businesses or just liked to be close to people who spoke their language and knew their card games. They had recently started being joined by a scattering of young professionals buying properties ten or twenty years early, before the real gentrification might set in. There were hookers and drug addicts, some trying to straighten out and some not. Once in a while there were gang outposts but the police usually closed those houses within months, sometimes a couple of years.

On the main business street there was a pawnshop with a small appliance repair annex in what had once been a garage. Rabani parked in front of it and walked across weeds, dirt, and a broken concrete pad. He said hello to a solemnly calm man wearing a blue polo shirt under a jacket and sitting on a frayed lawn chair just inside the annex doorway.

"Doing business today, Alex?"

"Not today. I had time to work on the latest model. This one has a nice rack system. I expect it to sell fast."

Rabani looked at the three other models displayed in the one-time garage. Two former freezers and a former refrigerator. He calculated that sales were still running about one a month—enough to make converting them into barbecue smokers a small, worthwhile source of pocket money for a man collecting income support for the permanently disabled.

"The apartment okay?"

"Yes, it's fine. The vacuum cleaner broke down but Jerry said he'll let me borrow any cleaner in the store once a week until I can find a new one."

"Have you been looking?"

"It takes a lot of research, George. You don't want to jump into something like that without knowing what you're doing."

"You could probably take a look at *Consumer Reports* in the library."

"Yes, I could. I've been busy on a new book, though."

Rabani pulled up a paint-stained wooden chair that had probably been someone's good kitchen furniture about fifty or sixty years earlier. He sat down to hear the newest turn of Alex's imagination.

"What's the book about, Alex? I thought you were working on the roads book."

"The roads book. It's coming along. I think it will sell when it's published. People all over the country drive on highways without really looking at them. I will tell them what it's like to stand on the asphalt and feel the local breeze. They will see the differences in the colour and granularity of the pavement. Every road has its own unique border of weeds and birds and insects. They will know the sounds. I just can't quite remember all the roads I've stood on so I'll have to do some more research. And I'll have to see about buying a camera. People will probably want to see pictures. Something more urgent has occurred to me—a long-term project. It won't require photographs. I'm going to do a books arcade."

"Sounds interesting. What's that going to be like?"

"It's going to be a collection of interesting passages from books. Some people might call it a collage. I'm thinking of something more like Walter Benjamin's arcades project, though. But it won't be random thoughts. The selections will be carefully selected and placed. The chapters will be like literary landscapes. Each one will have its own theme and own organization. I think the first chapter should have F. Scott Fitzgerald as a centrepiece. You know there's that line in the middle of *The Great Gatsby* that I love."

"No, I don't think I know that, Alex."

"I thought I'd told you about it. I read it again a few weeks ago and the sentence jumped out at me. It's in the part where Gatsby and Daisy meet face to face again for the first time and Nick tells Gatsby the sun is coming out. Gatsby is too excited by the meeting to understand at first. But then Nick writes that when Gatsby realized what he was trying to say, that twinkle-bells of sunshine were entering the room, Gatsby smiled like a weather man, like an ecstatic patron of recurrent light, and repeated the news to Daisy. I don't know why the mysterious part of that didn't strike me before. I'm sure I read the book before. What did Fitzgerald mean by weather man? There were no TV weather men in the 1920s. What did it mean to smile like a weather man? And ecstatic patron of recurrent light. Who else would write like that? You see? It's not just the language. There's a deeper meaning. He caught something mysterious and mundane. It's something evanescent yet lasting. People tend to let these things go by unnoticed, just like I did. I can make a book out of such quotations. There would be commentary, of course. The question I'm wrestling with is whether the commentary should be interpolated with the quotations or grouped in separate chapters. There's also the collection of the passages. I imagine I'll be spending a little more time in the library."

"That sounds like a good project, Alex. I'll be interested to read it. Will you show me what you've got when you're halfway through?"

"I don't know, George. It might be something that requires seeing as a whole. It's going to consist of small pieces fitted together. That sounds like you could read just the pieces. But you may not understand what I'm saying until it's all fitted together. Art is like that."

"Well, let me know when you have something you can show me."

"I'll do that, George. Jerry is still letting me use that old typewriter. I may have to find some more paper. People don't bring paper into a pawnshop. How's Mum?"

"Oh, she's fine. I went to see her last week."

"I'd like to go see her sometime."

"I think we can arrange that. Maybe next week."

"That would be good. Let me know first. I may be doing research in the library. I may have to arrange a time."

"I'll do that, Alex. I think I can find paper for you, too."

"That would be good."

"Are you eating good meals?"

"Yes. Mr. Sandro lets me have old carrots that haven't sold. And old bread. I make hamburger sometime. Peanut butter is good when you can put thin slices of carrot on it. Mr. Sandro let me have a package of raisins last week. That was so good with the peanut butter I couldn't decide whether it was an ordinary sandwich or dessert."

"You remember next Tuesday is our night out at the café?"

"Is it? That would be good, George. I like going to the café with you. You listen to my plans for the book and I always feel better about what it's going to end up like."

"Who's Walter Benjamin, by the way?"

"He died years ago. He was a German philosopher and cultural critic, but he never learned how to fit in with the society and culture around him."

"Sounds interesting. I have to go now. I'd like to give you ten dollars so you can buy some bananas to go with your peanut butter, and some milk."

"Oh? Thank you. I would like that. Thank you very much."

Rabani got up and smiled at Alex. He wondered if he was smiling like a weather man. He wondered if recurring light was the opposite of light captured once in a photograph—ongoing life rather than a memory dead and gone. He walked back to his car, waved and drove off. He thought he should visit his mother's grave sometime soon so that it wouldn't be so much like lying the next time he told Alex that he had seen her last week. He wondered if refusing to think of his job as social work came from knowing the pain of caring for others. And worse, of letting them down.

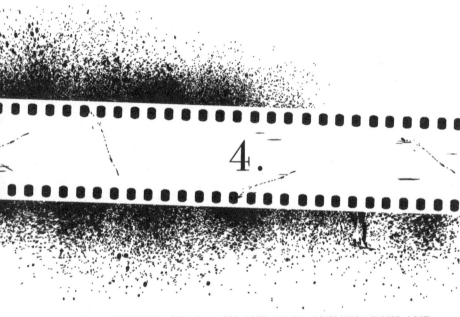

4.

BECKER FINISHED HIS BACON AND EGGS, PUT THE DISH AND cutlery into the washer, cleaned the greasy frying pan, put on his red-checked flannel jacket, and went outside into the last of the morning darkness.

He picked up the bag of dog food and opened the wire gate of the kennel. His four dachshunds and his Doberman pinscher—the "babysitter" that was actually more gentle than the smaller dogs unless provoked—milled around him as he poured out their morning ration.

The smell of dog hair mingled with the smell of dirt and morning dew. He knew the moist smell would linger until the sun rose above the row of caraganas. The fragrance of the scattered lilacs inside the caragana belt had dissipated; it was waiting to re-emerge next spring. That was fine with Becker. He liked the lilac fragrance but it was strong enough that he liked not having to smell it all year.

He turned the tap on the outside of the shed wall and filled the water dishes. He rubbed all the dogs on the head or behind the ears and patted the sides of the ones he could reach. Then he walked out, propping the gate open behind him so that the animals could have the run of the acreage for the day. He had long since stopped thinking about how he would have preferred to leave them free in the evening too. The neighbours worried about their own single dogs being attacked by a pack. He admitted to himself that their concerns were a handy excuse; he worried, too, about them possibly wandering off. He didn't like seeing them chained. He let the Doberman stay out on summer nights as a guard dog. Having the dachshunds out too might help control the mice. The owls in the trees along his property line helped some but were not consistent.

He went back into the house for his office suit. Arlene was still in bed, but awake, watching him knot his paisley tie.

"Will you be late tonight, John?"

"Probably. There's a committee meeting and that dinner with the museum people could stretch out. They probably want to corner me afterward about a grant."

"Do you really have to leave this early if you're going to be late coming back?"

"We've been through this. First thing in the morning is when I can get some work done without an endless string of people coming into the office. You'll take care of the dogs' supper?"

"Better than mine, I suppose. You know I don't like cooking for just myself. Besides, I'm not feeling well today. A little fuzzy and congested."

"Well, try to get some fresh air. It's going to be sunny."

"The dust from the leaves will be in the air. You know that bothers me."

He took his brown-checked jacket from the closet and turned to her as he put it on. "You could try a dust mask."

"I've told you, I'm not going around here looking like an invalid."

You're less like an invalid than anyone I know, he thought. But he said, "Maybe you can go into town, then. There must be one of your friends available for lunch."

She looked at him as she sat up and received her quick morning kiss. She watched him walk out of the room, telling her, "I'll try not to make it too late."

Outside, he climbed into his full-size sport utility and made his patient way to the road. It was only out there that he stepped on the accelerator hard—where she couldn't hear the engine wind up and think he was rushing to get away from her. He never rushed anyway. The quick morning talk with his wife and the slow drive out to the road had long ago become as much part of the routine as feeding the dogs. Routine had seeped into his life like summer heat. It was easy to give in. That was part of the attraction of the new admin assistant; she was not routine.

He passed other vehicles fast until the morning traffic grew thick enough toward the city that he had to slow down. The drive took him about forty minutes. There was plenty of time to think but he didn't use all of it. He pulled into the legislature parking lot still not sure how to deal with Ostroski.

He spent the next few hours on the usual run of business. At five to ten he walked out and down the hallway. It was wide enough but claustrophobic with the sense of unyielding time—the high dark baseboards on the plaster walls, the art nouveau light fixtures, the terrazzo floors that had been walked on by generations of politicians and secretaries, and by campaign supporters who hoped that encouraging words and handshakes would sublimate into a façade of friendship that could turn into a job or government grant. Becker felt he could hear the decades of footsteps. He wondered how long he could last before he started seeing smelling the wool of bulky suits that had been worn in the days before frequent dry cleaning.

He got into the elevator and rode up to the executive floor. There he walked past the portraits of former premiers and lieutenant-governors. Some looked alive, especially the early governor in an evening suit, white cuffs showing, cigarette in hand, bearing an amused expression of an Edwardian gentleman with a good income and a taste for whisky and cards—what had a man like that really been like out here at the farthest reaches of British settlement? Some looked full of themselves and stared out at the future as if it was wasting their time. Some had their eyes averted as if they knew they had not stood up to a crush of dire events and did not want the failure in their faces to be put on display for future generations. No fear of that happening with Morehead, he thought.

The premier was ready to see him. Becker had watched him long enough to know that starting exactly on time meant he took this business seriously.

"Good morning, Premier."

"Good morning, John. Have a seat."

Waschuk was there, too. The chief of staff instead of the EA. Another sign that Morehead wanted action, and wanted it fast. If he had still been in doubt, the premier's neutral expression would have told him all he needed to know. The famous Morehead grin was nowhere in sight. There was no offer of coffee.

"Do you know why I like being premier, John?"

"Must be either the pay, the adulation, or the pleasure of not having to wonder how long you'll be in cabinet."

Morehead still wasn't in a smiling mood.

"I'd have left you in Industry but it was too big a job. An American-born premier is one thing. Having an American-born senior cabinet minister as well would have been pushing it."

"Plus, I didn't back you for the leadership."

"Neither here nor there after I won. I like the job for two reasons. One, I show that a retired wide receiver can run a big organization as well as any retired quarterback. Two, the pay isn't great but it lets me buy a new car every two years.

"Here's what I don't like about it: having to get along with all the cabinet ministers. And control them if necessary. Getting along with the other guys on the team wasn't always easy. But they all had skills and were willing to work hard. They had to. They were constantly competing for their jobs. There isn't enough competition when a party's been in power for decades like ours has. Carelessness sets in. Sloppiness. That can eventually bite you on the ass. It just takes a little longer than in football. What was that business with the dog all about and has it ended or not?"

Becker knew the question was coming and didn't have to search for an answer. "Jack Ostroski has never been happy with the sale of his photographs to the government. What's really burning him up, though, is that he wants some of the pictures back. He says there are some personal ones that aren't of any historic or artistic value."

"Personal how?"

"I think they mostly involve a woman he once knew. There are probably no more than a few dozen of those. Maybe not even that many. One problem is that he won't identify them. He wants the right to go through the collection in private and take out whatever he chooses."

"Would that be so bad?"

"It would set a bad precedent. My deputy isn't happy about the idea of reneging on a sale. Letting him cull the collection in private would be worse. But now that he's come close to throwing one of my dogs off the bridge it's impossible. We'd be giving in to threats."

Waschuk cleared his throat, his way of asking permission to speak. Morehead looked at him and Waschuk started talking in his flat voice. It always sounded from his first few words as if he was running out of breath. Becker always thought the layer of fat around Waschuk's middle might be squeezing his lungs. Or maybe he had to push out the words forcibly, reluctant to let anyone know what he was thinking.

"We've had the pictures for a year. Why are they a problem now?"

"He's objecting to a possibility that the archives may plan to digitize them eventually and make them available publicly on this new Internet utility. Says he could have lived with them being stored in a filing cabinet. That way they'd be just a quiet little example of the government spending money on art that wasn't going to interest anyone in a few years. They haven't even been catalogued yet."

Waschuk squeezed more words out of his barrel-bellied frame: "That doesn't sound like it's worth kidnapping a dog. If his reasons ever get out, it will only make people curious about the pictures.

We need to know three things. Is he likely to do it again? Is there more involved? And does he have a pile of crap he can dump in front of a fan aimed at us?"

"You know the answer to the first one. He's obsessed enough to pull a stunt like he did. He might do something nuts again. The other two I don't know. Maybe something will come out that will tell us more. We're negotiating with his lawyer."

"He's got a lawyer," Morehead said. "Great. Unpredictable, probably unhinged, and with an agent. Who's we?"

"I'll work on it with my deputy. He knows the business arrangement that was made for the pictures. He's tight-assed and mealy-mouthed. He's still sulking because I won't approve his plan to commission an opera about the province. But he has a good head on his shoulders for this kind of thing."

"That's it then," Morehead said. "Keep us informed." Meaning: communicate with Waschuk. "And don't screw up. If you think anything's getting out of hand, let us know right away."

"I'll do that. We'll try to wrap it up fast."

"You know, I never liked the idea of the government taking those pictures. You start collecting art, it encourages people to keep producing more."

"That's right," Becker said. "Apparently that was the point, aside from owning the pictures themselves. We're supposed to be proving the place has culture as well as oil. Art collecting is an old hobby of the rich and famous. All the way back to J.P. Morgan. All the way back to the Medicis. Probably even before them."

"If you say so. I just had a couple of reclining chairs fitted into one of the government planes, with compartments underneath for beer. Maybe they'll end up in a museum someday. You know what? I don't care. The chairs and beer I can use. Pictures are for people who are satisfied with seeing something and knowing they can never touch it."

"Good morning, Premier. Henry. I'll get back to you soon." He had almost blurted out a specific day but he was wary of overpromising.

His own immediate agenda went in another direction. His new admin assistant was single, only moderately talkative, good at applying just the right amount of makeup, ready to make a joke but rarely a pointed one, unafraid of making eye contact but never in a way that could be read as a challenge. Better yet, she liked an occasional drink and didn't mind having one in a small bar that Arlene and her friends would never want to be seen in.

5.

OSTROSKI FELT THE PAPER-THIN BLADE BETWEEN HIS THUMB and index finger. He thought it represented the value of old technology. A device often had many uses after it was invented. It could be manipulated, reshaped for different purposes. The flat safety razor blade had that advantage. Cartridge blades had only one use and could be used with only one handle.

Ostroski was using the flat blade as a tool this morning. It was remarkable for its thinness and sharpness. He sliced slowly into a matte intended for framing photographs. This one did frame a photograph, a nice Ansel Adams shot of a moon over a stark landscape.

He made three incisions. Then he took three single frames of negative film and inserted one into each whisper-thin cut. When he was satisfied all three pieces of film were well into the matte and away from the edge, he remounted the matte and photograph into the frame. Then he moved his chair back to the wall on the side of his store and hung the photograph back in its original place. He had never thought about hiding the negatives before but the skirmishing over other pictures had awakened an instinct to be careful. After moving the chair back he opened the blinds on the front windows. Anyone who finds that deserves to have it, he thought. But anyone looking for it would never look there, he was sure, because they'd be too dumb to think any sort of art had a practical purpose—like hiding residues of violence.

It was one of Adela's days off so he stayed in the front of the shop. He thumbed through old photography magazines and dusted the displays. A good camera was worth keeping clean. He made sure his were in good shape. If they worked like new they should as much as possible look like new.

A handful of customers wandered in during the day. Potential customers. Only one of them genuinely looking for a purchase. "The place is getting to be more and more like a museum," he muttered. "I should charge admission." He wondered when he would stop worrying about talking to himself. The trouble was that when he no longer realized he was talking out loud to himself would be the time to start worrying.

At noon he went into the back for a salami and lettuce sandwich and a cup of coffee. He brought the cup out front, set it on the counter, and started reading his magazine again.

Two middle-aged men came in during the next three hours looking to sell equipment. They had decent 35mm cameras, a Canon, and a Pentax with a wide-angle lens, but there were too many of those around. One other guy was looking for a leather cover for a Pentax. Ostroski dug through his box of covers and found the right fit. That made him feel good. A good camera needed protection. He didn't talk to the guy about that; he was running a business, not a club. The lawyer walked through the door late in the afternoon.

"Hello, Jack."

"Afternoon. Just touring the up-and-coming business area? Looking for hot properties?"

"Maybe they will be hot someday. Oil prices can't stay down forever. The office work is done for the day. I got down to the take-home work and thought I'd drop in here to let you know how the talks about the collection have been progressing."

"Progressing. That means nothing is settled. Does it mean there's been progress? Must be important news to rate a visit instead of a phone call."

Rabani faced his client across the counter. He assumed it was Adela's day off if she wasn't there. He didn't ask about her. He was disappointed but he was also relieved not to have her there. He needed his wits about him when he talked with Ostroski.

"They don't want to renegotiate. They say that would set a bad precedent. They also aren't happy about the idea of you going through the collection and identifying material to be set aside. They aren't necessarily opposed to identifying pictures that could be kept private for a certain period...."

"Like until I die."

"Like that. Or they might go for an arrangement that would require permission for the photos to be viewed, and then only in person rather than on the Internet. But they want to sort through the collection themselves first. They've decided that should be something of a priority but staff are in short supply. It may take six months or so."

"What would that sorting involve?"

"Making a general classification—by subject matter and date. It's possible they might ask you for help firming up information about photos that don't have much to identify them. They said they may even be able to find some money in the budget to hire you as a part-time assistant for that."

"Buy me off for the price of a few beers, you mean."

"I know it's not what you hoped for, Jack. The issue is that the government has full ownership rights. They bought a collection and paid for it. They don't want to start paying twice for anything."

"But they're willing to hire me as a part-time assistant."

"It's a gesture of goodwill."

"It looks to me more like a gesture of worry."

"Why would they be worried, Jack? You aren't thinking of anything like another dognapping, are you?"

"Like I told you already, there's more than one kind of dog. I took a lot of pictures in eighteen years as a government photographer. Maybe I took some pictures of dogs that they might be interested in having. Maybe they're worried I'd be more interested in a business deal than in a phony part-time assistant job."

"Let's stop there, Jack. That's starting to sound like blackmail. Whether or not it is, it sounds like something you aren't explaining to me. I'm not going to represent a client who's playing games I don't understand."

Ostroski had been looking at him the same way since he'd walked into the shop, head straight up, eyebrows held with a hint of a quizzical arch, mouth verging toward a wry smile. Now the amusement flattened into an unblinking gaze—take it or leave it.

"I don't care who calls it what. I have some pictures they may want. It's not a renegotiation of an old purchase. I'm willing to do a new deal. They can have these other pictures that I have stored away. In exchange, I get to go through the collection in private— no one looking over my shoulder. Then I tell them what can be made public and what can't. And if they want to buy some more of my prints and negatives, that's on the table. I'm not making any threats, just offering a solid business proposition. They already bought some old photos from me. No reason they wouldn't be interested in buying more. But this time at a fair price."

"I don't like this, Jack. Pictures of what?"

"Told you. Dog photos. You can tell them I have pictures of an old hound and his doghouse. With poodles and German shepherds coming over to visit. Becker will be interested. He likes dogs."

"I don't care what he likes. We're talking about what I like and don't. I don't like the sound of this and I don't like representing someone in a situation I don't understand."

"It's real simple. I'd take this deal to them myself except that Becker would probably go off the deep end if he had to deal with me directly. The other thing is they can't screw me around if my lawyer is doing the negotiating and keeping proper records. They won't be able to say afterward that I misunderstood something. As for your thinking it might be blackmail, see how they react. I think you'll see they take it as a straight-up business proposition. Nothing to get upset about. Hell, I wouldn't do anything that would cause so much trouble that it might end up with me shutting this place down. Adela needs the work."

Rabani didn't let the reference to Adela slow down his response. He knew Ostroski well enough now to assume that bringing her into the conversation was a test.

"Are you a social worker?" he asked. "Is that why you hired her?" He cut himself off before he could add that he'd assumed Ostroski had hired her because she was easy to look at.

"She earns her salary, which isn't much, minimum wage in fact."

"Jack, you told me once that Becker had it in for you for some reason. I think you must know the reason. Or at least have a good idea."

Ostroski measured him. He was still looking eye to eye but Rabani had the sensation of someone looking him up and down. Neither one spoke. Hissing from the tires on a couple of passing cars intruded into the silence. Rabani took in the shop with his peripheral vision and noted that everything was in its own place, despite a surface appearance of clutter. Ostroski considered for several seconds and decided to answer.

"He used to be the industry minister. He was always a politician. Always on the lookout for information of any sort about anyone. Someone gave him the idea that I knew too many people inside the government after nearly fifteen years as a government photographer. Maybe that I knew too many things, some of them maybe embarrassing if they ever got out."

"Like a photo of a poodle or a German shepherd."

Ostroski smiled. "That's all you get, lawyer. For your own protection. Besides, you sound like you're really considerate about them, understanding about their position. You are working with only me in mind, right?"

Rabani considered his client for several seconds. He nodded without changing his expression and walked out without looking back. He walked down the street, in the litter-strewn and dusty breeze, with the fall light taking on a filtered quality and throwing long shadows. The sun was tracking now through a low arc. He felt he should drop the case. And he knew he would not. It had too much danger for him to back out, too much promise of exposure of human deceit and frailty and oddness. He walked down the street, northwest wind pressing on his pant legs and jacket, sun forcing him to tilt his gaze down, and wished he were a drunk or a smoker. It would have been easier for him to say no to a drink or a cigarette than to a new view of human imagination and folly.

About half an hour later, just before the shop closed for the day, Roberto Morales walked in. Ostroski looked at Morales's clean sweatshirt and jeans and knew he hadn't been working that day.

"Roberto. Haven't seen you in a while. How're things?"

"You know, they could be better. Not so much construction work these days. When there are no cranes in the sky, there is no money for labourers. It is good they have that food bank. Otherwise I could not even afford a beer."

"I know the feeling. When you get to my age you learn to make compromises. I drink a little more coffee now. It's cheaper."

"Yes. Many people do. Maybe I should go back to Nicaragua and find a job on a plantation."

"Don't do that. Someday people will wake up and find it costs them more to fill their gas tanks all of a sudden. Then construction will come back here."

"I found other ways to bring in some cash, Jack. But Adela, she does not want to hear about them. Big sister still worries about me. I am tired of being her little brother. I was enough of a man to carry a gun and shoot it. I want to be a man now, not a little brother. I worry about her. This trouble you have been in, will it put her job here in jeopardy?"

"I think everything will work out. Why do you ask?"

"If there is anything I can do to help."

"Thank you, but I don't think there's anything to worry about. I have a lawyer working on it. He's going to negotiate for me and I think I'm in a pretty good position. Those guys in the government want to run everything, but when you show them they can't, they're realists. Most of the time. Sounds like you're running some risks yourself. You aren't going to get into more trouble than me, are you?"

Roberto grinned, the same easy smile that Ostroski saw on Adela on the rare occasions when she could be persuaded that not everything was serious. "Life is trouble as well as pleasure. Anyway, I have seen real trouble. People here worry about small things."

"Cops and lawyers have a way of making small things suddenly look large."

"Then I will stay out of their way. Have a good one, Jack. Gracias for everything."

Ostroski watched him leave, saw the head up and legs taking long strides. His mind drifted back to when he was about that age. He remembered cockiness, fear, and disgust. Then he snapped back to the present.

6.

RABANI SPENT MOST OF HIS LIFE INDOORS. HE THOUGHT that was strange. A life enclosed by walls and focused on papers sitting on a desk was part of the deal for lawyers. He nevertheless felt he should spend more time outdoors.

The river valley running through the middle of the city was full of walking trails. It seemed there were more every year. Ravines with stub trails ran up from the valley. Outside the city boundaries there was still plenty of farmland. Most of it was in crops, but an hour's drive north took a person to the fringe of the boreal forest, the great green hinterland of the settled part of North America. Out there you could often see the northern lights.

Everything about this environment called him outside. Yet he spent most of his life inside, looking at paper and walls. During some of that time he arranged real estate deals that would produce high-rise offices or condominiums—all of them promising money but also an obliteration of the past as well as of part of the natural environment. The past belonged to hick towns, to glitter-eyed dreamers who thought they could build a small, contained world free of banks and debt and disappointment.

The future? That had yet to be built. It was constantly under construction. The future belonged to anyone who wanted something more. It was a land where people could tell themselves they were as smart and rich as anyone from anywhere.

He could understand the reaching for more. He belonged to the first generation of his family to go to university and become a professional. He wanted enough money never to be in debt like his parents had been all their lives. He also thought he would like a certain amount of status; his parents had never seemed to think about such things. Yet he was not sure he understood others' need to strive for a never-ending more—more money, more status, more pouring of concrete and asphalt over some of the best farmland in the country, more of not just escape from the past but obliteration of it.

If you wipe out the past, he thought, can you really have a present? But can you have a future if you don't let the past go? Those were things he thought about some days, less and less as time went by. His work had him dealing with real people in real situations rather than with abstract notions. He was a lawyer, not an academic. On this day, he was not thinking such thoughts at all. He was concentrating on the counter-offer that had surprised him when he took Ostroski's pitch to Becker's deputy minister, Frank Jeffries.

Now there was an odd duck. If it weren't for the bright, brassy rims of his glasses he would be all grey, the caricature of a life-long civil servant. Odd duck didn't quite cover it, though. Rabani detected patronizing in the deputy minister's smile and in his apparent certainty that anyone would agree with his point of view. His chilly charm covered a hard base of contempt, Rabani suspected. More than that. Contempt linked to connections and power and years of getting what he wanted suggested danger.

The government people still wanted to catalogue the collection quickly. That meant they were looking for something and didn't know where it was among the thousands of prints and negatives they had bought. They possibly did not even know what it was. But they had shown clear interest in something hidden in the jumble of images. They apparently had made whatever it was a priority. Offering Ostroski a chance to sort through the collection was a concession. But it was only a means to whatever end they had in mind. It was also obvious that Ostroski did not want anyone in the government to see something in the collection. Ostroski knew what that was. Becker probably knew, but might not. Rabani certainly did not know what any of the others were after; he didn't like knowing less than either of the two men he was dealing with. He disliked even more the possibility that Jeffries might have a separate interest.

The offer to sell the government other photos not in the collection had sparked only mild interest from Jeffries and vague talk of perhaps a few thousand dollars. Rabani was calculating what that meant. Ostroski clearly thought he had material for which the government would pay a fair chunk of money. That meant it was probably embarrassing to the government or to someone in the government.

Frank Jeffries was known to be a cool character. His pasty face and thinning hair of pale, uncertain colour could have been intended to blend in with any background in the manner of an octopus. His eyes were shiny and soulless behind the metal-rimmed glasses. His habit of talking in cultivated bureaucratese served as a bland front. Rabani had been in the party's university club and had heard small stories and rumours about Jeffries' sly machinations even then. Jeffries had juggled budgets and staff positions for years to keep his operation in the Culture Department going. He had found ways to bring in revenue. He had created virtual staff positions during the last spending cut by sending departmental staff to non-governmental organizations where they ended up doing much the same jobs as before, nominally off the civil service payroll but still at public expense because the NGOs operated on government grants.

It was one thing for Jeffries not to act worried. It was another for him to hint at a roundabout method of paying Ostroski. He could be stalling for time. Or he, or maybe Becker, wasn't sure that Ostroski had anything really damaging. Or they thought there might be other ways to handle the situation.

The fourth possible explanation, the one that was actually the case, didn't occur to Rabani.

Jeffries didn't much care about Becker or Becker's problems. Whatever the other photos showed did not concern Jeffries or the Culture Department. If they put the minister in some jeopardy, well, ministers came and went. He had no strong incentive to protect Becker, whom he considered arrogant and basically a philistine. Becker had given him authority to negotiate as he thought best. And he thought it best not to waste any more of the department's skimpy budget than necessary on something he did not see as important. The main Ostroski collection was safe. That was what drew Jeffries' attention. He wanted to bring something under control that he saw as far more dangerous than a potential passing scandal involving a former cabinet minister. A small number of additional photos that his minister might be interested in were irrelevant.

He would sit tight and see what happened. He reported to Becker what he'd been told about the other photos Ostroski was offering now. The description sounded like some sort of code because it involved dogs; Jeffries had searched through his mental file and thought he understood what that meant. He also reported that Ostroski and his lawyer were playing hardball. They wanted a lot of money. And they wanted complete control of the review of the main collection. They threatened a lengthy legal action on the grounds that the original sale agreement did not mention anything about digitizing photos. Becker's reaction had told him little. A more or less frozen face, but a barely noticeable brightening of complexion. Something important was at stake. Important to his minister or to others higher up in the great chain of status and authority. And important enough not to trust Jeffries with a full explanation, which was another reason that Jeffries was not eager to help Becker out of whatever hole he was in.

"No trust," he told himself. "After all these years of keeping cabinet ministers looking capable and keeping them away from dangers they were too dim to spot, no trust. Not appreciated." Especially not appreciated by John Becker—an immigrant no matter how long he had been here or whom he had married, an economist more interested in the departmental budget than in nurturing the province's culture, a minister who sent his executive assistant snooping around talking to managers in the department when he should have been satisfied with reports from his deputy, a man too close a match for himself in brains and tactical sense.

He looked down at the sleeves of his ash-coloured pinstripe jacket. The pinstripe was a classic, unobtrusive width. The impeccable white cuffs of his shirt extending a half-inch past the jacket fabric—he declined to think in centimetres unless necessary. The silver cufflinks making a subtle statement of enduring taste in an era when most men had accepted buttons. The ash-coloured vest was hiding as usual half the understated lilac tie, hiding what he was sure most men subconsciously thought of as their symbol of virility.

No. No need for primitive display. No need for obvious concealment either. Simply a statement of good taste and manners; a reassurance of life lived according to accepted principles; an expression of probity and self-confidence. His clothes spoke for him. Nothing to display except good taste, and nothing to hide. And the province would have nothing to hide, either. He would see to that. Nothing to taint its reputation. He looked at the print of the neatly built homestead on his office wall, an ideal and reassuring image of beginnings. He felt the sudden prick of memory of the real-life farmhouse where he had grown up in the 1930s—washed-out paint on the outside walls, cracks in the interior plaster, stains on the wallpaper that made a sad attempt at gentility in the room where neighbours and the minister sometimes visited, an outdoor privy, weeds in the yard, no art except for two photographs of grandparents, no books except a Bible and his mother's treasured copy of *A Christmas Carol* and her *Blue Ribbon Cookbook* and the handful of magazines passed around by her equally hard pressed handful of friends. The family had had to heat up bath water and share it, for God's sake, taking turns from the cleanest to the dirtiest. He had been flooded with relief when he heard the place had been torn down. He never talked about his faraway past with anyone—a life suppressed, obliterated like the old house.

He looked at the oak cabinet off to his side and thought it was late enough in the afternoon for a treat of his single-malt scotch. First a sniff and then the peaty burning in his throat, and then the oblivious warmth radiating inside him. He poured two fingers' worth into a plain crystal glass and was surprised to see his hand shaking slightly as he carefully tilted the bottle.

He thought about what could happen if the wrong photographs became public: "All these years of building and protecting how we are perceived in the world. All the effort unappreciated. All the anguish endured at the thought people might misunderstand. It won't be wrecked. I will not let it be wrecked."

He felt the whisky burning in his throat, almost bringing tears to his eyes, and warmth rising in his chest. Visceral refinement. A promise to himself that he had the skill and the determination not to let meaningless indiscretions ruin his life's work, not to let them ruin his life really. There was no one else who might understand. And he had little time left before they would force him to retire. Whatever help his current minister needed was of no significance in comparison. He thought of one of his favourite images from literature—a reference to "the kings and the unhomed angels." It was the only image in which he could see his own face. The political masters were the kings; he was an unhomed angel, a lonely guardian, sword in hand, aging, yet enduring and implacable. No, the needs of his current minister were not significant, not when compared to his moral duty, which was to say his road home.

John Becker rarely thought of himself as needing help. He coped with situations. He had been coping with situations ever since finding easy ways to stay away from Vietnam. His skill in navigating life was a big reason that he had got into cabinet at a young age under Manchester and was still in cabinet with Morehead in charge. But he did have to do some managing here. He called Waschuk and arranged a time to meet. This wasn't something to trust to a telephone conversation. Then he called in Ginny Radescu. She came into the office wearing her professional cheerfulness. The face of a loyal, willing worker, and a discreet one.

"Ginny, there's a task coming up that I'd like you to be involved with. It may take a few weeks. Someone will be doing a review of a big collection that eventually needs to be sorted out. I want someone I can trust working side by side with that person."

"Okay," she said. This was more flattering than a big dinner out.

"You remember the Ostroski photo collection that was bought about a year ago."

"Yes?"

"We're going to start cataloguing it. There are tens of thousands of prints. There are thousands of negatives to go with them. And there may be some negatives that haven't been printed. There's no point in having the collection if we don't know what's in it. It's time we had someone go through everything and make a preliminary arrangement of the work—sort it out by subject matter, by time period, by suitability for public display, that sort of thing. We also need to attach information to photos. I'm going to have someone do a preliminary review, then let Ostroski go through it. You'll go through it with him."

She kept up her co-operative expression despite the letdown. Hours and hours of looking at old pictures and chasing down meaningless information! He noted her ability to keep looking eager to please despite being promised weeks of tedium—another point in her favour—and went on to the main issue.

"That's the job. I need someone from this office involved, someone trustworthy and with wits."

She nodded. He saw strands of dyed-blond hair sift over her delicate ears.

"I'll have someone else looking through the collection first but there may not be enough time for a full review like the one you will do with Ostroski. I will need daily reports on what's turning up in the photos. I will also give you information before you start about particular types of photos to look for. You think you can do that for me?"

"Yes, Minister. I'd be happy to."

"Good. It will take a little time to get this project started. I'll let you know when we're ready to begin."

She looked him straight in the eyes and said, "I'll be ready when you are."

He said, "I'm happy to hear that."

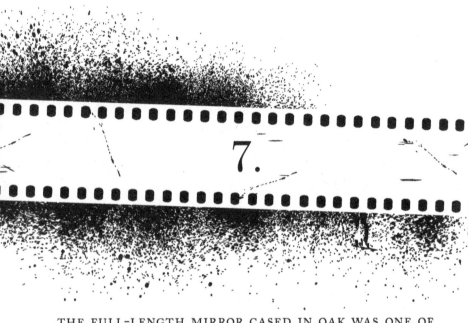

7.

THE FULL-LENGTH MIRROR CASED IN OAK WAS ONE OF Arlene Becker's reliable enjoyments. It spoke of tradition and quality.

Arlene checked herself in it. Everything was in place. The middle was thicker than twenty years ago, but not unacceptably so. The legs were still good. The navy suit breathed respectability and suggested a certain experience with wielding authority. Ready for the world to view. If only the world made itself as presentable to me, she thought as she picked up her purse and headed down the stairs.

She locked the back door, walked across the concrete patio and the gravel pad to the garage and told the dogs to stay. The dachshunds were only half interested in an excursion. Ricky the Doberman was always ready to get into the car. She felt a twinge again, sorry to leave them behind. They were John's dogs but she had long felt an attachment to them anyway. She would have bought one of her own if she had wanted to risk upsetting the social balance among them. She sometimes had idle thoughts of an Airedale or a Wheaten terrier. Whenever she did, she wondered if she really liked dogs that much or if she was just missing Scott and Linda, both off to college now at too young an age. Twins about to become separated by the world. So eager, so vulnerable.

One of her compensations for a real relationship was her sport model Nissan. She had picked it because she liked the idea of the Japanese rebelling against the primacy of the American, British, and German manufacturers who had dominated the sport market for decades. She drove it carefully out the driveway and hit the accelerator when she reached the main road. She was wary of police, but they never patrolled the five-minute stretch of local road that led to the highway.

It was a shopping day. She drove to the west end of downtown and found a meter in front of Ariadne's. It was time to look for a dress that would be a standout at the Christmas parties that were part of the duties of a cabinet minister's wife.

"Something for the Christmas parties, Ariadne."

"Ah, we have a number of choices. Black or red, depending on how formal you'd would like to be, and two that are black with red accents."

"The cut and finish are more important, I think. Eye-catching but not assertive."

"Something to signify personality and respect for the occasion, but not to dominate? No claim of superiority?"

"That's it."

"I think you'll find some suitable choices over here."

She spent a little over half an hour going through the collection and talking with Ariadne. The selection process, the careful search for balance, was second nature to her now.

After the nicely timed visit to the dress shop, part business and part recreation, she drove to the golf club where the symphony foundation was holding its annual meeting. This was the dull group. The art gallery board matched her interests more and was made up of what she thought were brighter people. Most of the symphony board members had been produced by the same cookie cutter—grey hair, tired and wary faces, practised politeness, no interest in going for a drink after the meeting.

Frances Dahl was closest to her when she walked in. "Hello, Arlene. You're looking well. Oh, what a lovely suit."

"Hello, Frances. Thank you. Ready for the budget wrangle?"

"I'm hoping it will go simply this year."

But it won't, Arlene thought. Because Frances and too many of the other board members needed an hour and a half of useless talk about minor details to give their lives some meaning. If they needed someone to talk to, why didn't they find minor physical issues to take to their doctors? They probably did, she had decided. But the doctors were probably too busy to spend a lot of time with them so they needed these meetings as well.

Once the greetings were finished and the meeting was underway she spent the first five minutes thinking about Frances Dahl's hope that things would "go simply this year." She wondered if she should find an excuse to throw in a coarse phrase along the lines of "just like shit through a goose." That would get them commenting about the girl from the country. She backed off mentally, as she had done last year. She needed to be solid and respectable to get her way during the search for the new music director.

They ran the meeting fifteen minutes longer than planned. She had to drive back out of the city in bunched-up traffic. Just as well, she thought. Avoid the temptation to make full use of the car. She let the engine out an extra twenty kilometres an hour on the side road to the acreage. She pulled into the garage, took the garment bag with the dress, closed the garage door, and stopped. A dirty white compact pickup was coming up the drive. It came to a halt a respectable distance from the garage. A young man climbed out and looked at her.

He seemed to be in his early twenties, probably Latin American. A slim body, nearly thin. A wispy pencil moustache and serious eyes. She decided not to act intimidated.

"Can I help you?"

"Good afternoon. I hope so. You are the lady of the house?"

"Yes."

The dogs ran up and circled the young man, the dachshunds growling. She said, "Quiet." They stopped the growling but kept up the circling and kept their distance from the stranger. She saw he was being careful but not showing any fear.

"My name is Roberto. I have been employed in construction but there are not many jobs underway this year. Now I am going through the acreages here to ask if anyone needs any work done. I can do small construction or repair. I can also arrange machinery for snow clearing, do yard cleanup, or book gardening services for next spring."

He looked around the property. He noted the orientation of the house and the garage and the location of the kennel. He saw the wide line of trees and thick hedges. There were big houses on each side of the property but neither was visible. Across the road he had seen a mix of pasture and woods. The colour and design of the house—a two-storey with cedar siding and accents of flat metallic blue paint—was not essential; half an hour later he would have trouble describing it, except for the location of its windows and doors.

"We have all the regular maintenance taken care of," she said.

"Is there any job to be done here? I am willing to work cheap. There is not much construction work now and I don't want to depend on my sister to support me."

She knew she should not be affected by the reference to a sister but she was. She also liked the way he carried himself—self-sufficient, but not arrogant. And he was someone to talk to.

"Have you been in this country long?"

"A few years. I like it here. It was a little better when work was easier to find."

"My great-grandfathers might have said the same thing. They eventually got settled. One found a job that lasted a long time. The others started businesses."

"Maybe things will improve once oil prices go back up. They cannot stay down forever. I should probably take training in a trade, or maybe look into something like accounting. But that would take money. Now I need to earn money."

He thought she looked interesting. She was older, of course. But she had a finished look about her, like wood that had been polished. Her medium-brown hair looked well tended. Her clothes beneath her open coat were good quality without being showy. She looked like she was used to running things, but was still able to see the person she was talking to. He had a feeling that if he stood closer to her he might smell a perfume. She created an effect of something both solid and unnecessary, familiar yet exotic.

"Maybe the work shed could use some repair. There's a bad window for one thing. And there are spots where the ditch along the driveway could probably stand to be cleared out."

"I could do that sort of work."

"What's your name?"

"Roberto Morales."

"May I have your telephone number."

"Yes. Do you wish to write it down?"

She did not want to open her purse with him there and said, "I'll remember it. I've never been afraid that I'll forget numbers."

He told her the number and she said, "I'll call you in a few days once I decide what might need to be done around here. Will that be all right?"

"Yes, I would be glad to do anything for you."

"There wouldn't be more than a couple of days work."

"That is better than nothing. A little work here and there—better than nothing. Thank you. I will wait for your call."

He got back into his truck, turned it around, and headed slowly down the driveway to the road. She watched him until he reached the road and drove off before she walked to the door and unlocked it.

Something wasn't right about that, she decided. She decided not to care, and not to worry about the fact that she did not care.

Roberto got back to the main highway. He would come back to the acreage if Mrs. Becker asked him to, although that hadn't been the idea. The trip was meant to be reconnaissance. He knew Jack had run into a problem with the Mr. Becker, the one in the government. He would have been happy to see the property without anyone there, although in that case he would not have set foot outside the truck with the aggressive and unpredictable dogs roaming about.

He had no plan in mind. Seeing the acreage was simply a matter of being prepared. The more you knew about a situation, the easier to develop a plan fast if necessary. When he got back to the city he went to visit those who passed for his friends. He knew they acted like friends and that he acted like their friend. He could almost make himself believe at times that the comradeship was genuine. He more than half trusted them but did not trust them fully, which he knew was the same as saying he did not trust them. But they let him do small jobs for money. The small jobs were the kind that exposed him to only a little bit of risk from the police. And the friends could be useful in other ways.

But his real friend—as far he had had any real friend in this cold country—was Jack. Jack not only gave Adela work, he took an interest in Roberto and was always ready to help without acting like a domineering father. Looking after your friends was the main thing Roberto had learned in the jungle. That and the usefulness of force.

8.

BECKER LOOKED OUT THE WINDOW OF HIS OFFICE. IT WAS a low-rank office, figuratively and literally. His demotion to the Culture ministry had taken him to the ground floor, which was actually sunk well into the ground. He had a good view of the paved area in front of the legislature building. The flower bed between the window and the broad walkway was depleted now. The trees on the other side were all evergreens; no bright yellow aspens in sight.

The approaching winter made him think again about the two years he had spent getting his master's in agricultural economics in North Carolina. For a kid who had grown up in Wisconsin, living in a place where the first signs of spring could be felt in late February was a revelation. He remembered the magnolia tree underneath his window and the mockingbirds that sang in it. He remembered the bend in the highway where a local farmer had a stand to sell apples and apple cider. That memory stood out because of the Winesap apples, a variety he had not seen back in Wisconsin. Then there were the stranger things like the "Impeach Earl Warren" signs still dotting the countryside years after Warren had left the Supreme Court. The aging signs were forcibly present, just like the university choir singing "Dixie" during the local television station's nightly sign-off, and like the prisoners in striped shirts and pants he had once seen clearing brush alongside a highway. It was a land of tobacco factories and old wooden houses and barbecue shacks. The factories were built of dull brick and the wooden structures were painted in flat colours. It had all seemed simple yet arcane. Strangely, the dreamlike appearance was somehow linked to the reality of anti-Communism and Vietnam, a war immensely far away yet brutally present. Simple beliefs had somehow inflicted a bloody physical and moral tearing apart. The capacity of the irrational to endure and even prevail was a lesson he had drawn too late from that time. He had thought he could go into politics and set things on a better course. If he had understood what he had seen back then—fleeting glimpses of stubborn, earthbound traditions standing up against a flood of passing words and television reports, all as imperturbable as the scent of hay and manure in Wisconsin dairies—he would have realized that some change took a day and some took longer than a lifetime. Some things required not merely changing what people did or thought, but changing who they and even their ancestors were.

He blinked and turned back to the briefing note on his desk. Daydreaming was a bad habit. Yet he thought it helped him apply perspective. Time was never as long as it seemed or distance as far, once you began thinking about how far you had travelled in both. He had learned patience. He was starting to hope he had not learned too much patience.

He suspected that Jeffries was stalling. That didn't bother him particularly. When things had to be moved along he would order action. Jeffries was stubborn and resisted change, seemed at times to fear change. But he was too attached to his career to risk open defiance. The implied threat from Ostroski was another matter entirely. Becker did not want to take that to the premier but he couldn't risk not giving a warning.

The essential problem was how to keep Ostroski's hands off the photo collection while not pushing him into doing something stupid that would embarrass the government. Paying him off would help. But he had to be kept waiting while the collection was surveyed. How long was he willing to wait? How fast could the preliminary survey be done? Becker guessed the answers were: not long and not fast enough.

The phone rang. He picked up the receiver and heard Ginny say, "Mr. Rabani is here." He thanked her and heard the click as the door opened and Ostroski's lawyer was shown in. Neither of them said anything until the door closed again.

"George, how are you today?"

"Fine and hoping to be better after we talk, Minister."

"Please, it's John. I'd be happy if we could keep this business on a relatively friendly basis. Have a seat."

Rabani felt the signals tumbling into place. First name, but no standing up to shake hands.

"I don't know that my client is interested in friendship. He would certainly settle for mutual respect."

"I would too. Though the offer was made to you, not directly to him. It's hard to think with either friendship or respect of someone who would threaten to throw one of my dogs off a bridge—any dog. I knew a fella once who shot his dog because it wouldn't listen to him. Never trusted him after that."

"I realize a strain has been created. Therefore let's try to conclude an arrangement efficiently. My client has certain items to offer you in exchange for satisfactory handling of his photo collection. I will tell you frankly I don't know exactly what he's offering, but he seems to think that you do. I also don't know exactly what his objections are to leaving his entire photo collection indiscriminately in the hands of the government for eventual public display, but I take it some of the images are personal."

"You're referring to the government's photo collection, which happens to consist of pictures that he took and later sold?"

"We're ready to concede ownership, although Mr. Ostroski still feels the government acted in a high-handed and unfair manner when it bought the collection. He thinks coercion would be an apt description."

"That's not really the issue, though, huh? He's happy to concede ownership. What he wants is to be granted certain owner-like rights of review and editing."

"Substantially correct. He feels that is his right. But he is also willing to offer certain other items in exchange for the review rights and for a sum of money he feels more accurately reflects the value of his collection than the token sum he originally received. He suggests the extra items may be worth that amount on their own."

"You're serious about trying to convince me you don't know what they are?"

"I am telling you seriously that I don't know."

Becker studied Rabani's face. He wasn't prepared to make a final judgment. His preliminary estimate: he was looking at a reasonably smart lawyer, possibly a tough negotiator, but an innocent. Here is someone, he thought, who knows that people can be stupid or deceitful or cruel; but does not know how they can hurt one another through carelessness, does not know the bottomless capacity for any given individual to act selfishly, either out of greed or out of the instinct for self-preservation.

"George, are you willing to be a party to blackmail?"

"That's a word that needs to be justified. I have no information that would lead me to think it's appropriate."

Becker paused again, mentally filing Rabani's ability to stay calm.

"Let's forget that then. Let's say simply that Jack Ostroski thinks we can be pushed into a decision without regard for consequences. And let me tell you what some of the consequences are, the ones that we can see at the moment.

"First, he is offering some items but we have no idea whether he may be holding more items in reserve and will try to squeeze more money out of us at a later date.

"Second, anything we pay him will go on the public record along with other spending. We would have to justify a large sum of money going to buy art, presumably more photos. That's a dangerous area for us now. The budget is tight. We're cutting spending on important services and can't be seen indulging in frills. And most important, the government endured a truckload of abuse a few years ago when it spent six hundred and fifty thousand dollars on the Anthony Briller photo collection. I'm sure you remember that. It was supposed to be an important documentation of world leaders, popular celebrities, and exotic locations. None of them had anything to do with this province. As far as I could see they reflected Briller's relief at getting out of the place where he was born and into a lifestyle that fit his tastes. And no one looks at those pictures now. We can't afford to repeat that experience. That was a disaster. Repeating it would be a fiasco.

"Finally, we have no idea what he wants to take out of the collection, or at minimum set aside in a vault somewhere. We don't want to risk reducing the value of the collection. And we don't want to set a precedent of allowing people what amounts to ownership rights after they have sold us something."

Rabani took it in. He was ready for the first and third items but hadn't thought about the Briller angle. He had still been in law school when that controversy broke out. It didn't seem worth remembering but he allowed that politicians might have their own gauge of political value.

"Well, you've put things in understandable form. I still need to clarify one point. Are you saying no? Or are you saying you might reconsider if the price came down considerably?"

"There isn't much happens here based solely on what I want. The operative word is we. I have to consult."

"May I ask: consult your colleagues or consult the premier?"

"All cabinet discussions are confidential."

"When do you think we may have an answer?"

"Days rather than weeks."

"That's a step forward. I will advise my client that we wait until Friday. After that, all bets are off. I can only advise him. He's rather headstrong."

"Setting headstrong clients on the right course is part of a lawyer's job. At least that's my understanding."

Becker paused and studied the face in front of him again. "It's also my understanding that you attended some party conventions when you were part of the university club. There was even some talk of you as a candidate prospect someday. I expect you to do your best for your client. But I wonder if you, aah, keep in mind the, aah, utility of balancing private interests with the public interest."

"Serving private interests is a way of serving the public interest. I would have thought anyone in this government would believe that." Rabani looked aside at the small bust on the mantel over the office's marble-framed fireplace. He had dredged his memory after first noticing it and been reasonably sure it was a likeness of Adam Smith. More than likely, given Becker's background in economics, he thought. "Anyway, that's what I believe," he went on after a few seconds' silence.

"You can't run a dairy farm without putting up with some manure," Becker said. "You can't have politics without compromise. Compromise is just another word for balancing interests. The point is to end up with some milk. But okay. I'll count on you to do the best you can making your client see reason. Please let me know as soon as you can, preferably by tomorrow. Can we agree on that?"

"I'll have to talk with my client but I think we can likely proceed on that basis."

"Good then." Becker rose from his chair, wished Rabani a good day and saw him to the door. He returned to the desk and read recommendations for routine appointments and renewals of regulations until the top of the hour. Then he cleared the desktop, locked papers in a drawer, and left to see Waschuk on the third floor.

He had already arranged the time and walked in without having to wait. Before he began outlining the situation he said he thought the premier would want to hear at least some of it directly. "Are you sure?" Waschuk said.

He was. Waschuk made a call to ask if Morehead's current meeting could be cut short and hung up looking placid. He was using his silence tactic. Normally talkative, he could wait with either a hard or amused stare rather than jump in with an obvious question. Becker was just as happy with that. He didn't like the flat, dry sound of Waschuk's voice. It always reminded him of wasps and their nests—layers of dry paper with a potential nasty surprise inside. He used the next few minutes to talk about a sensitive upcoming board appointment while waiting for Morehead. The premier arrived quickly and Becker picked up where he had left off, with a warning that Ostroski now wanted more.

"He has damaging material that he's willing to trade. He's passing messages in code but I'm sure about what they mean. He's willing to trade items—almost certainly photos—involving a poodle and a German shepherd."

Morehead wasn't in a mood to play the same waiting game as Waschuk. "What the hell does that mean? Are we wasting time here?"

"It means a Frenchman and German. And for all I know maybe others. Japanese would be worse because they would take it more seriously. Do you know about Roussel's house?"

"What house? Roussel who had the Industry job before you?"

"Yes, him. By the look on Henry's face I'd say he knows something about it."

"Just a rumour," Waschuk said.

"Spill it."

Waschuk took a second to arrange the story into brief form. Then he said, "Roussel had the department buy a house about half a dozen blocks from here. It was meant for the entertainment of visiting investors and occasional foreign politicians looking for a little rest and relaxation. With women. There weren't many what you'd call high-class hookers available here. But there were just enough hookers with ambition, a clean bill of health, and some sense of style to keep the place running. Besides the upkeep for the house there were payments made to them. There were also bills for caviar and cognac, smoked salmon, wine and other kinds of booze, you name it as long as it cost a lot. Roussel believed if the government was going to entertain, it should entertain in style. He managed to hide the costs in a combination of hosting expenses, infrastructure spending, and export development budgets."

"Yeah, so?" Morehead said. "That export agency has always been a rat's nest. I know that Billington has a couple of whiz kids in there who line up women and booze for him when he's away on official trips. The agency isn't even in his department. He thinks there's no point in being a minister if you can't enjoy the perks. I haven't stepped on him because I need him. Plus, if it ever gets out, I can cut him loose without losing too many of his constituency people."

"This is different, Premier. You've got major foreign figures. Most of them are still important to us and would be extremely angry about being embarrassed in public. You've got government money in essence funding a brothel. You've got the fact that the house ran for four years before I heard about it and had it shut down, which is not only a long time but raises questions about how well the government controls itself. You've got the fact that it started in Manchester's time and Roussel managed to keep him in the dark. I don't know what he'd be more angry about—the fact that it happened or the fact that one of his ministers was able to keep an operation like that secret from him. Worst of all, you probably have photographic evidence. Maybe worse."

"What the hell does that mean?"

"Ostroski was the official government photographer when all this was going on. He could have taken pictures of the house without anyone's knowledge. He was just enough of a rogue operator that he could have taken pictures of visitors and women going in. A worse case is that he was inside it himself."

"What? Why would he be in there? He was a nothing staffer."

Waschuk decided to spill the whole story: "Just before I had the place shut down a Hollywood producer came up here to check locations and try to wangle some money and production help out of us. I remember that he was tickled to see Ostroski. The two of them had been pals when Ostroski was hanging around the studios in the late Forties and the producer was starting out as some kind of script assistant. They spent time together after the meetings about the movie deal. And the producer was a real Hollywood specimen, a guy who thought women were recreation."

"Then what we're looking at is some pictures from the outside with important foreigners going in. And possibly some pictures from inside showing who knows what people, and maybe a first-hand witness account."

"That's it. We could take the hit some other time. But right now, with all the flak over the spending cuts...."

"What do you propose to do about it, John? I don't see what's wrong with letting this idiot go through the photo collection as long as he does it fast. We can always find a way to hide a payoff in some budget or other."

"That's one possibility," Becker said. "It may also be wise to lean on him instead. He's a blackmailer now. You know that if he gets away with this he may hold some material back and come after us again. He's crazy enough that he may send something to the papers anyway."

"What do you think, Henry?"

"Don't let it fester. Make the guy happy. Don't interfere with him. If he comes back at us some other time we'll probably be in a better position to tell him to shove it."

The conversation played out largely as Becker had expected. He kept a suitably co-operative expression on his face. Morehead and Waschuk were satisfied with seeing that. It was about the most they had learned to expect from him. They looked at Becker's pallid cheeks and the dark, flat circles around his eyes and the shock of black hair perpetually hanging over his forehead. There were only a few touches of grey showing at the temples. Morehead wondered if this was a minister who used a little help to keep a relatively youthful hair colour, which would indicate ambition. He was happy that he and Becker merely had to do business together, and never socialized except for about thirty seconds at the annual Christmas party. Talking with him over a drink would have been a chore.

Becker wished them a good evening and walked out of the executive suite.

Morehead asked Waschuk, "What do you think? I mean about Becker."

"He'll get the job done. He wants back in."

"Yeah? You know, most of the trouble I have with ministers—and the backbenchers for that matter—starts with them thinking they're geniuses because five thousand people voted for them. And then they get to rub shoulders with business executives and NGO directors who really are smart. They start thinking they're in the same league. I'm lucky to have three I can trust to do their jobs efficiently. Becker's always seemed more modest, and smart. But he worries me. That's the real reason I put him in the Culture job. With the others, I can guess what they don't tell me. They don't have enough imagination to have real secrets. With him I have to be more careful."

Becker walked down the hallway and down to his office happy to have received firm direction on how to handle the situation. He had no intention of following it.

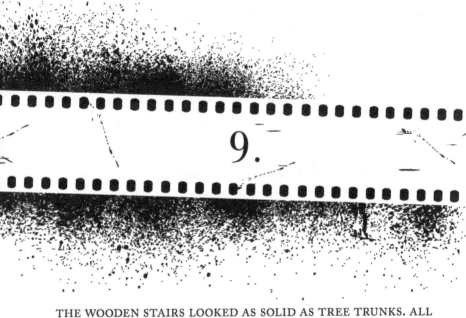

y

9.

THE WOODEN STAIRS LOOKED AS SOLID AS TREE TRUNKS. ALL
the dimensions of the steps and the railings were big. The faint
green tinge left by the preservative added to the impression they
could stand up to both weather and a constant pounding of training
shoes. Even a pounding from guys carrying a little extra weight,
like Rabani.

He was moving slowly on his second trip back up from the road
on the river valley bottom to the top of the steep bank. His breath
came in sharp bursts that raked his throat. The coolness of the air
kept off fatigue but added to the hoarseness of his breathing. He
was feeling good despite the scraping sensation in his windpipe
and lungs. Other things were going well, too. The flow of work
in the office was manageable and predictable for a change. And
he'd been able to tell Ostroski that the government was amenable
to a settlement. They would let him cull the photo collection and
they would pay him fifteen thousand for what they termed the
adjunct collection.

Rabani arranged to let the two parties carry out that trans-
action by themselves, on their own terms. He did not know what

was involved and wanted no part of it. He knew only that Ostroski now had a way out of a sticky situation and could calm down. No more threats involving dogs. Now he could get out of his own sticky situation, too, no longer have to be an agent for implied threats. Best of all, he had a dinner date with Adela Morales.

He did not bother deciding whether she was the reason for another renewal of his off-and-on exercise campaign. The question was hypothetical. He had talked himself into doing the stair runs—partly walks in the early stages—on other occasions. He might have talked himself into it again without the extra motivation. The only certainty was that he had nearly left resuming the workouts too long. Getting started again was tough. He could feel the phlegm in his chest, collected in his lungs the way that dust collected in furnace vents. His leg muscles were halfway between sore and numb.

The violent effort of the fast climb contrasted with the tranquility of the brush-strewn hillside and the river below. He knew the impression of surrounding peace was deceptive. The river was fast-flowing and dangerous. Its bottom was betrayed by potholes and channels deep enough to drown the careless. The tan-coloured grass and dry shrubs on the steep banks covered the trails of foxes, rodents, coyotes, and other small animals condemned to a never-ending bloody struggle for survival.

He breathed the cool air more steadily now, no longer gasping. The nearly still air would yield to an arctic blast sometime in several weeks. The cold would thicken it. Soon afterward, snow would bury the shelters of the handful of homeless people living hidden in the underbrush; they would have to either move or, if they were stubborn, clear their patch of ground like the small birds that toughed out the winter here. It isn't just the animals, Rabani thought. Everyone is in a struggle for survival. The miracle is that most people last as long as they do.

He dragged his legs up the last of the stairs and began plodding down again to the club and its warm shower room. The climb back down took less overall effort but was more awkward and involved more danger of a fall. When he was showered and dressed he got into his car and drove to the pawnshop.

His brother was walking around the lot trying to find little bits of cleanup or straightening to do but was doing so mostly to keep the chill off. They talked for several minutes. Alex promised to dress warmly as the weather grew colder. He said he had gathered a few quotes for his literary arcades project. George said he was glad to hear that and encouraged him to keep working.

He said goodbye and drove to his condo to put on fresh clothes. Then he drove to the restaurant. Adela had said she would meet him there instead of getting a ride with him.

The restaurant was filled with ferns. The differing shades of green complemented the white tablecloths. George wondered how often the staff had to spray the leaves as the air grew steadily drier through the fall and into the winter. Their problem, he decided. He was happy with the illusion of living in a warmer climate.

A hostess wearing black and a smile showed him to a table. He studied the menu for several minutes. He looked up as he saw Adela approaching. Her dress was plain enough to be inexpensive but had enough style to say it was meant for going out. She smiled with a look more of quizzical amusement than of pleasure but that was good enough for Rabani. When she ordered the sole he did the same. He usually ate something more substantial for dinner but he thought having fish with her would make ordering wine easier. She warned him that she could not promise to drink half the bottle. That was fine with him. He might want more than half, depending on how the evening went. He wasn't sure what would make him likely to drink more—a good time or a bad time. He wasn't sure about the wine but was wise enough to ask her preference. Anything but a heavy chardonnay, she said. He filed that in his memory.

They spent two hours in the restaurant. He was happy that they managed not to fall into awkward silences. She asked him about his name: "I can't tell if it's Italian or Arabic."

"Maybe both," he said. "My family's from Sicily. We've been Italian for a little over a hundred years and Sicilian for hundreds before that. But the island was overrun with waves of invaders over the centuries and Arabs were among them. I've wondered whether the name comes from them. Not enough to try to find out."

"No? Why not? The past is the past?"

"Something like that." He looked at the way her hair brushed her cheeks and thought he would be smart not to drink more than half the wine. "It isn't so much wanting to bury the past as wondering how much it matters."

"The past always matters. We have to know it. Otherwise we are babies in the world, not knowing how to talk or what things mean."

"Sure. The issue is how significant any particular past is. Maybe my family was in Sicily for eight hundred years. Maybe they were there for three thousand. In the end we were immigrants, just the way most of the people living here are immigrants. It's all a story of people moving to someplace new. They remember some things, forget others, build new lives."

"I can understand thinking that way," she said. "My own family has Spanish roots on both sides. But I think it is almost impossible for any Spanish family to have lived in Central America for more than three hundred years and not have had some Mestizo blood introduced into it. In that case, what to remember? And now, why remember it? We were a family with more than three centuries of history and ownership. Now we have moved and become immigrants. We should accept that time has passed but we should not forget."

They talked about what they liked to read. Most of his reading was non-fiction. Adela said, "You might like something in the Latin American literary tradition. It is called magic realism. All fiction is magic in its way. This style takes what could be supernatural and makes it seem like the everyday. It is almost like taking fiction and transforming it into non-fiction."

"A funny concept to present to a lawyer," he said. "We're trained to keep the two strictly apart."

"Maybe life is more complicated than that. If you are interested, you could start with Gabriel García Márquez."

"I've heard the name but I've never read anything written by him." He did not add that his taste in fiction ran to Frederick Manfred Westerns and Agatha Christie mysteries, and she suspected there was something he was not saying. They retreated into the common ground of Shakespeare. George told himself he should memorize lines from at least two of the plays, perhaps even a sonnet, so that he would be able to recite more than "to be or not to be." The tour of literature—a revelation of how little their reading had in common—ended with a mention that a local theatre would be performing *Twelfth Night* next month. Neither felt ready to invite the other to see it.

She brought up Ostroski and the pictures abruptly, without any lead-in: "Do you really think matters are settled? Jack has been worried. He seems less so now, but I won't believe they will do what he wants until he actually sees the pictures again."

"I'm reasonably confident. Not one hundred per cent. They have a lot of incentives to follow through, though. I don't know how much he's told you about the agreement."

"And you don't want to talk about it unless I already know. A point in your favour. Jack has told me he will have the right to review the photographs and remove any he does not want published before they are recorded into a computer. He will also receive fifteen thousand dollars to compensate him for what he should have received when he sold the collection."

"And that's it?"

"Why, is there more?"

"Yes and no, nothing material." Meaning nothing he wanted to tell her about. "The main point is he gets to set aside photos he does not want the whole world to see. He will have to leave the prints in the archives but he's satisfied that no one will bother going through the physical prints. Nor will there be much reason for anyone to see the images when they eventually become available by computer. Likely no one will see them until long after he's dead. He's decided it won't matter so much then."

"I'm a little surprised. For Jack, if something matters today it will probably matter fifty or a hundred years from now. He seems to think most things in life come and go, but a handful of things are too important for him to view that way."

George wondered how far he could pry. He had already told her enough to have built up some trade credits. He suspected that she would not agree there was any bargaining going on. He went ahead hoping that she would feel free to talk.

"He seems determined not to let some of his pictures be seen by the public but he hasn't told me what they are."

"No?"

"Do you have any idea what they are?"

She considered during a long, shallow sip of the French wine she had recommended, and relented.

"He has told me twice about a woman named Norma Minton. You know he lived a little time in Hollywood in the late 1940s?"

"He's told me that. He said he managed to find work as an assistant to a cinematographer in a small studio."

"The inevitable happened. He started going out with a young actress named Norma Minton. He said she was not a starlet, although she looked attractive enough that she could have been one. He said she was often the girl in a nightclub or a crowd scene just behind the two stars. I saw one of the movies he mentioned. She was not named in the credits. But if she was the one at a table behind the two stars, she was as attractive as he said. She had to be if she was often chosen to be that visible. Perhaps she was not as strikingly attractive as many of the big stars. Or perhaps she simply was not as good at acting."

"Going out. There's a world of difference between that and a love affair. And another world of difference between a love affair and something so strong that he would do anything to keep his pictures of her private. I assume he did take pictures of her."

"Yes, he said he did."

"Did he say what kind?"

"Nothing salacious. Some on the beach at Santa Monica and Malibu. Some studio-style portraits."

"He simply wants to keep private things private."

"That's right. Jack has very strong views on such matters."

Rabani was informed but not satisfied. He didn't press her further on the photographs. She didn't signal obvious reluctance to talk about them further, yet he had a sense that she could suddenly shut down if he miscalculated.

The talk shifted to family. She told him she lived with "the man in my life." He accepted that without showing surprise. She quickly explained, "My brother Roberto lives with me in a rented duplex. He works in construction when jobs are available."

"I have a brother too, an older brother. His name is Alex. He lives a simple life. You could say he mixes handyman work with literary pursuits.... Tell me about New York and your time at Columbia."

She brightened. "Ah, New York. A city of much energy. I was excited to learn about architectural preservation, its possibilities and techniques. I loved both Central Park and Gramercy Park. One is so huge and public. The other is intimate. It is set into the city like an inlay on a wooden table."

As he listened, he felt she had brought her own energy to the school and the city. Adela did not burst with a frantic need to talk or establish her personality in a kind of competition with whomever she was with. Nor did she radiate a warm sympathetic glow. It took some time for George to realize what impression she was making on him. He dealt with many people. Some put up fronts to hide their chicaneries and weaknesses. Some seemed barely to exist, functioning as little more than faces and an ability to repeat verbal conventions. Adela was part of the world with him. She was present as he was. She was real. That did not mean that he would get to see more of her.

"It's funny to talk about the importance of the past in this city," she said. "I told you that I could not find work in historical preservation here. The people who build here seem to believe in tearing down the past. Everything must be renewed as quickly as possible. But the new construction hardly matters because it is as subject as the old buildings to being replaced someday not too far in the future. It's as if architecture here means no more than keeping up with the latest fashion in hairstyles or hemlines. I spent two weeks in Chicago before coming here. They are starting to restore their historic buildings. Here, history is something to be wiped out, as if one is ashamed of it. Nothing is built to last, which suggests nothing has any real meaning apart from temporary usefulness. Yet society and politics here are oddly based on the opposite impulse. Nothing changes in political and social life here. No, perhaps that is too categorical. Sometimes things change. But that is usually ten or twenty years after the advisability of change has become apparent."

He agreed about the contradictory mindsets: "They probably apply across the entire province. I suppose that creates an atmosphere of drabness. Rather funny when you think how bright and clear the air is here, especially in winter. But I don't know how much it matters in the long run. I know a guy who lost most of his past. He was in an accident and had a brain injury. He still has an active mind and tries to create things. But he can't remember his interest in them for more than a few weeks. Then he's off trying to write something else. That seems a little bit like the constant building and demolition and fresh building that goes on here. Maybe it means he will never finish creating anything. I don't know what it means about the importance of his ideas. To me, as long as he is grappling with the world and trying to establish his own understanding of it, he is alive."

"Does he talk to you about his ideas?"

"Yes, as far as I know, all of them."

"Do you ever try to follow up on them yourself?"

"No. He knows more about them than I do. But I don't worry about that. If he could finish one of his books, that would be a real achievement. I don't think it's necessary, though. As long as he talks about them—even if he never writes a word and tells me for only a few minutes what he is thinking about—he has created something simply by communicating. He doesn't have to finish his books or see them published. How many books survive in the public's mind anyway?"

"You sound like you feel close to this person."

"Yes, I do."

The way I already feel close to you, he thought, even if we never see each other again.

10.

THE TREE TRUNKS WERE SHINING BRIGHTLY. THEY HAD taken on the radiance and sharp definition that had struck Ostroski during his first winter in the city. He had been gazing at lines of trees during the colder months every year since. He could not remember when he realized it was a trick of light. The old studio cinematographers could have come up with the same effect; they probably had more times than he remembered.

The sun travelled an arc low on the horizon as winter approached and then again as it receded. If you faced the sun when you were walking or driving you always had to shield your eyes. But with the sun behind you on a bright day, the low angle of light changed how trees and buildings looked. The surface reflections made everything more vivid. Everything seemed floodlit. When the sun was at its brightest, trees and hedges shone with a glow that seemed to emanate from inside them. At the same time, the light effect produced more clearly defined shadows around the bright forms. The combined effect made the sunlit areas explode into a person's field of vision. Objects seemed more true than in summer.

They claimed attention. Their brightness was on the borderline of being painful.

Why do truth and pain always seem to go together, Ostroski wondered. He let the thought go. He was not given to worrying about questions that he suspected he would not be able to answer.

His shop window looked different in the mid-autumn light, too. He could see the dust and the streaks left by the last washing. He opened the door, walked in and closed it, and flipped the small hanging sign to read "Open" on the outside. He hung his faded tan jacket on a hook in the inner room and started a pot of coffee. He looked at the Ansel Adams calendar and reminded himself to order more Ilford film. He wondered if he should order a red filter as well, or if he was likely to have one come in with an old camera. He took the broom and swept the front of the shop. Then he poured his first coffee of the day, picked up a magazine, and sat on the stool behind the counter, waiting for Adela to show up for her shift.

She arrived half an hour later with her usual sunny "Good morning, Jack." She quickly followed that by telling him something far less sunny. He appreciated her matter-of-fact attitude. He could not have abided a show of concern or pointless anxiety.

"You're sure?" he asked. "I know you're sure or you wouldn't be telling me, but is the person who gave you this reliable?"

"It's second-hand but it came from someone who is reliable. The person it came from originally is in a position to know. Please don't tell that to anyone."

He thanked her and forced himself to keep his temper down. Late in the afternoon, after Adela had left, he sat in the shop with Rabani.

"The son of a bitch is reneging," he said. "He's getting his staff to go looking through the collection before they let me get to it. I don't know what he has in mind but he's playing some kind of game. It has to end by tomorrow morning, or I'll make my move."

"Let's see what we can do to keep things on track first, Jack. From what you've told me it would take a long time to go through all the pictures anyway."

"That's right, it would. But they could stumble on something the first day just as easily as not seeing anything important for a couple of weeks. Or they could just keep a few days ahead of me through the whole collection."

Rabani weighed his options and decided he had to take a risk: "I have to know more about what's going on, Jack. You know I had dinner with Adela the other night?"

"She told me. Said you were interesting. Congratulations."

"She mentioned something about a Norma Minton. Are there pictures of her that you don't want made public?"

Ostroski leaned back in his chair and pursed out his lips while considering his lawyer. He delayed answering for only a few seconds.

"Norma was a fun-loving girl. We had some good times. Having fun in L.A. was easier back when the city was smaller. I don't know whether it would have led to anything. Probably not. I got drafted for Korea. She ended up marrying a sound engineer at Paramount. I haven't heard anything about her in nearly forty years. She wouldn't be all that old so I assume the both of them are still alive. She doesn't deserve to have private pictures of her put on display in some sort of public art collection. They aren't art. They're just old pictures. They got taken along with the rest of the collection because I had them stored away with the others. Haven't tried to look for them in years, decades now."

"Just ordinary snapshots?"

"You mean: was she dressed in all of them? In most of them. There were a couple of tit shots. She wanted to see what she looked like. Like I said, she was fun-loving."

"That doesn't sound like something they'd be eager to put on display here."

"Not in a gallery. This Internet thing, whatever it is, sounds like something else. For all I know they'd make all the pictures available without even someone choosing what should be public and what shouldn't."

"I take it that's what Becker has ordered to be done. Someone will be looking through the entire collection and making notes on what's there, trying to bring some order to what's currently a random collection packed in boxes."

"That's government for you. Spend a lot of money making lists."

Rabani didn't like that answer. He thought it was too indirect.

"Jack, if those pictures were so important to you, why did you keep them in with all the others? Why didn't you take them out?"

"I never expected them to haul away the whole collection as fast as they did. Anyway it would have taken me just as long to go through them all as it will whoever gets stuck with the job now. Sorting out the prints will be bad enough. Trying to check all the negatives would be a lot worse."

"You just dumped what was really important to you in with the other material and never marked it in any way?"

"That's what I did.... Yeah. I can see you're going to be like a dog gnawing on a bone with this. The truth is I didn't want to give up those pictures but I didn't want to see them again either. I don't know. Maybe I thought keeping a record somewhere would help me keep straight what happened. If I got rid of the pictures, all that would have been left would have been the memories. Then I would never have known for sure what was real and what I imagined. Throwing out recorded images won't wipe out what you remember. It's all still there but then your mind starts playing tricks. Maybe I just did what felt right. Maybe I just didn't want to make a decision."

Rabani watched Ostroski carefully throughout the explanation. He thought he saw the right amount of frustration and puzzlement. There was just enough lift at the corners of Ostroski's mouth, just enough crinkling of the eyes, to say his client saw the situation as part of the world's ongoing joke on poor individual humans. That satisfied Rabani. He wanted to see that his client remained the same person and was not putting on an act.

There remained the question of what to do about Becker's apparent determination not to give up full control of the collection.

Ostroski said, "I have a few pictures that are specials. I keep them around here. I'm counting on them. They're nice pictures of hounds—valuable, not as money but as influence."

Rabani was exasperated at the sudden turn into obscure references: "Why would old photographs of dogs be important to anyone, even to a dog enthusiast like Becker?"

"They aren't just any dogs," Ostroski told him. "Becker knows his dogs, I'll give him that. He wouldn't want these put on public view. If they don't play ball, the papers will get hold of them. Not right away but sooner or later. Tell Becker the pictures are all going public if I haven't heard in twenty-four hours that he's going to live up to the deal. I want to start going through the collection immediately."

"You know, Jack, there's still time to work things out more amicably. Let me see what I can do without raising the tension by setting a harsh deadline backed by some kind of threat."

Ostroski leaned back and looked at him. "Maybe you didn't catch why I said I left Hollywood. I got sent to Korea. I don't ever play that veteran card. It was just something that happened. But it taught me there are moments in life that are serious, life and death. They happen fast and you can't play around when they do. Too much depends on how you react. You don't think. You react. If you don't, you regret it. Make sure Becker knows that."

He stood up. Rabani understood that was the end of the talking and did the same. On his way to the door, he asked how Ostroski had found out the collection was going to be catalogued in a rush.

"If I don't say, then Becker can't ask you. As a matter of fact, you don't have to tell him you've heard that. Just say that I'm getting antsy because I haven't heard from them and I look worried enough that you may not be able to control me."

11.

SOME OF THE OLD WAREHOUSES HAD BEEN CONVERTED INTO tire shops or restaurants. Others looked like shells that might still be serving as warehouses but never showed any activity. Rabani walked east past them. He saw the buildings were the same as the last time he'd gone through here except that one restaurant had closed. He turned south, going back to the office the long way, using the time to think.

Teenagers with knapsacks sagging with schoolbooks waited at the downtown bus stops. These were the kids going to a second-chance high school and Rabani recognized the look. They all had hair hanging over their foreheads and ears. They had a tentative air of kids who had absorbed beatings but were still standing.

At a windy main corner he passed an old man pushing a bicycle. The old man had a sturdy upright body and face that looked as if it, too, had absorbed beatings. It was a long rectangle of a face, weathered and ruddy, lumpy like potatoes. The old man was stopped at an intersection but his patter was still in full flow. He was telling people in a loud Eastern European accent that their souls were in extreme danger. Their pride was a sin. All sorts of things they did were sins. Rabani's favourite was, "Your hairstyle is a sin."

He reached the office and asked if Morley Jackson was in. Jackson was a senior partner but that description covered only half of what he actually did at the firm. He was known to the junior lawyers as a resource of knowledge about the law, local society, the arts, and many of the sciences. Better yet he was willing to share his knowledge when asked but did not push it on anyone without being asked. Rabani liked him for other reasons: Jackson praised his work enough to make him think he was rising fast in the firm but had the discretion not to show signs of favouring him over the other young associates, and Jackson was the only person he knew who would suggest going out and talking through an issue over a hot fudge sundae.

This time he wanted only a quick consultation. He went to his own office to check messages and put his feet up on the desk, staring out at the grey concrete and dark glass of the two neighbouring buildings. Two minutes later the phone rang and he was told that Jackson was free. He walked along the thick, dark green carpet in the hallway, knocked and opened the door after Jackson's "Come in."

Jackson was sprawled in his chair in his usual attitude, a book in hand. He was just taller than average and carrying just a little too much weight for his substantial frame. A place behind a desk suited him. He looked up at Rabani with his characteristic inquisitive and weary twinkle—always ready to laugh, but knowing that he might at any moment have to offer consolation instead.

"I think I'm getting dragged into something and I don't know what it is," Rabani said.

Jackson looked at him. "Sounds like you'd better have a seat," he said, closing the book and laying it on his desk. He never used a bookmark.

Rabani briefly outlined the course of the Ostroski and Becker business, leaving out Ostroski's tacit threat. He finished with what had brought him to seek advice.

"Now here's what's bothering me. Ostroski wants money for his photo collection, much more than he got. That part of his demands is clear enough and reasonable. It looks like he wasn't fairly dealt with. But he also wants to keep some pictures of an old girlfriend he had in Hollywood back in the late Forties out of view. He never looked at those photos, he says. He lost track of them in his files. But they apparently still mean a lot to him. Or the woman still does, although he's not forthright about that. Are memories really worth the kind of fight he's apparently ready to get into?"

"Are you sure it's about the memories?" Jackson said.

"That's all I have to go on. The only connection with the present is that the woman may still be alive in Hollywood and he doesn't want old photos that could embarrass her being made public."

"I don't expect that would be much of an issue. The government isn't going to be eager to become known as the purveyor of skin shots."

Rabani took heart from that, knowing Jackson's reputation for quiet connections with senior people in the government.

"That's my assumption," he said. "Ostroski seems to think that any collection of old pictures would be embarrassing, even innocent ones. He says making them public would be an invasion of privacy."

"The old girlfriend's privacy? Or his?"

Rabani leaned on an armrest, his fingers moving up to his lower lip and brushing back and forth and he considered the choice.

"Do you believe that memories are what make a person, George?"

"I've heard the theory," Rabani said. "My own experience is that people have a lot of conscious or unconscious choice about what they remember."

"It's a good question," Jackson said. "Does the past have a grip on people? Or do they create a past to fit who they think they are or who they want to be? The great myths and the epics of literature usually filter a kernel of truth through a layer of imagination. Witnesses are apt to do the same, even under oath in court. You could say that people partly shape themselves by what they choose to remember. But they usually carry things with them that they can't forget."

Rabani thought that over. Jackson asked, "Have you run across a Polish writer named Marek Hlasko?"

"Doesn't ring a bell."

"He was the bad boy of Polish literature during the post-war era. No real surprise in that. First he lived under the Nazis, then under the Communists. A character in one of his novels says, 'Memories are garbage.' He apparently believes that, although it isn't clear whether he wants to. Maybe he is only trying to convince himself it's so. The same character says it's too cruel to force a man to remember the most sacred moments of his life. He obviously thinks calling memories garbage is not the same as being able to dispose of them."

"Maybe it's like that with a lot of people," Rabani said.

"Unfortunately," Jackson said, "you won't know what's driving them unless they tell you."

Rabani nodded at that and sat staring at the carpet for a moment. He got up to leave. Jackson smiled and told him, "Next time you drop in I'll try to have some coffee on hand, so you'll at least have got that much out of it."

I got something out of this, Rabani thought: a pain in the gut—remembering what I want to forget and knowing it will never go away.

He walked back to his office for his coat. He had intended to wait until he got home before making the call but decided he should get things rolling. He half expected to be told the deal was off or would be reshaped. Instead he heard Becker saying that if the pictures meant that much to Ostroski, a joint review of them could be worked out. But that couldn't start until next Monday. It would take time to move the collection to a secure place with room to work and to line up staff.

It was down to haggling over days and Rabani was relieved. He didn't trust a politician, let alone one who had already tried to go back on a deal. A lot of his business came down to compromise and trading. The rule of thumb was that most people were sensible enough not to get into a damaging fight if they didn't have to. But some took leave of their senses. Life wasn't perfect. He hoped he could get Ostroski to agree.

He drove to his apartment, looking at the doughnut shop three blocks from his home but not stopping in for a chocolate dipped or a sour cream. He had dinner planned with Adela Morales on Sunday night. He was pretty sure that he wanted her company. She had become more than a mere incentive to keep him away from another helping of calories.

When Sunday came around Rabani drove over to pick up his brother and take him for their semi-regular visit to the downtown Smitty's for pancakes and ham. After the meal they drove to one of the ravines running through the city and down to the river. The excursions were Alex's rare outings to a landscape that did not consist of asphalt, concrete and stucco.

Once they had been lucky and spotted a coyote slipping into the underbrush after it had watched them for a few seconds. Mostly they saw squirrels and different kinds of birds. Identifying some of them was tough. Rabani was particularly pleased whenever he saw a nuthatch and definitely tell it was not a chickadee. Chickadees were easier to spot. In winter, Alex liked to hold sunflower seeds in an outstretched hand. He would wait for the chickadees to land on his palm and dart their beaks down for a treat.

As they walked and looked for wildlife through the dwindling screen of leaves, Rabani noted the different kinds of bark on trees as well. The trunks stood out more clearly as fall progressed and the days shortened. He had not paid much attention before his regular walks with Alex. Now he recognized the deep furrows on the sprawling laurel willows, the smooth skin on the aspens, the irregular patterns on the spruces and the thicker patchiness on an occasional pine. The poplars had dark spots looking strangely like drawings of eyes. The pines and laurel willows were fewer in number. They mostly grew toward the top of the ravine, where they had likely been introduced by the city or by house owners.

Alex told him about a new book project. He had put the quotations project aside after taking into account that Walter Benjamin had already in effect created a verbal arcades project many years earlier through his lifelong collection of quotations.

"I'm going to write a book called *The Human Instrument*," he told George.

"Oh, what will that be about?"

"Hand clapping," Alex said, "in popular music. The subtitle will be *Hand Clapping from 'Hound Dog' to 'Cinnamon Girl.'* Have you ever noticed how many popular songs have hand clapping in the background? My theory is that human beings respond to sounds made by other human beings even more than they respond to sounds made by instruments. It's a deep music. It probably goes back to the earliest days of humanity."

"That's an interesting thought, Alex. I think I'd like to read that."

"Of course, the big problem will be how to write about music. I'd have to rely on people's knowledge or expect them to buy recordings. Not everyone can go to the library to do research like I can. And then there's the question of boundaries. I think 'Hound Dog' is a good place to start because it represents the breaking out of a revolution in popular music. But the study could just as easily go back to something like 'Deep in the Heart of Texas.' And then I wondered whether I shouldn't go a little past 'Cinnamon Girl' and include Aretha Franklin's *Amazing Grace* album. It was recorded live and a lot of the clapping was done by the audience as well as by the choir behind her. It's possible to make a case that the sounds from the audience are part of the music in that album. The people listening to the record are the ultimate audience. Maybe the audience in the church where it was recorded were actually musicians in a way. All these questions. Isn't life thrilling?"

George looked at his brother, who was scanning the path for interesting leaves and alternately looking up into the trees for squirrels and birds. Alex was still close to athletically strong and lean six years after his accident. Idleness in the library and in the yard of the pawnshop was threatening that look. But help with decent food supplies and regular outings were keeping him in reasonably good shape. There was only a bit of sag around his middle. His dark brown hair was thick enough to make up for a perpetual lack of combing. With better clothes he could probably pass as normal for a few minutes in a conversation with someone who didn't know him. His forgetfulness would eventually betray him—that and his wandering attention, and a proclivity for talking about obscure subjects that he brought up out of the blue and had nothing to do with the preceding part of the conversation.

George was unprepared when Alex began talking again.

"I like it when you walk with me, George."

"I like it too, Alex."

"I missed you."

"We went out a week ago. I'm sorry. I didn't realize that it seemed so long to you."

"No, not that. I think there was a long time when we didn't see each other. It seems long ago to me. I can't remember much from that time. I feel like I really missed you. I don't think I always remember things clearly. Did you really go away? Where were you?"

George stared at the path in front of him. The first fallen aspen leaves were dingy yellow. The leaves from the other trees and bushes were a soiled green or a dusty brown. He remembered parties and a girl, both leading to hangovers in their way. There were three months of dabbling with marijuana; he would be forever grateful that he quit before blundering into a possession charge that would have put a tawdry end to his hope of a law career. He remembered long nights reading texts and old cases, telling himself he had to be prepared for classes and exams while knowing he was glad for the excuse to be absorbed in study. The long hours had led to a high standing in his class and a silver medal. The medal had been useful when he was searching for a firm where he could article, but now he was too ashamed to display it. The medal felt almost like an award for cowardice. He still could not bring himself to drive past the house where he and his brother had grown up.

He finally said, "There was a time when I couldn't come to see you, Alex. I wanted to, but I couldn't. I've been sorry about that ever since. If I could change what happened, I would. But I will never be away from you again."

Alex was quiet for a few moments thinking about this and said, "Thank you."

He was quiet again and then went on: "Sometimes it feels like things are spinning around me. I feel dizzy and don't know what's happening. When I see you, everything falls into place again. Things feel right. And you listen to me when I tell you about my book or other things. Jerry listens to me when he's not busy in his pawnshop. Mr. Sandro listens, too. But it feels like you really understand."

"I think your ideas are always really interesting. I enjoy hearing about them. They make me think."

"George?"

"Yes?"

"I know something happened to me. I had a different life once. I think I used to be able to remember things better. I didn't have to get food from Mr. Sandro."

George hesitated again. This time he felt moisture gathering in his eyes.

"Something did happen to you, Alex. You had an accident. A car hit you and your head banged on another car that was parked nearby."

"I remember being told I was hit by a car. Sometimes I see a picture in my head of a street that's sideways. I'm feeling surprised and looking up at buildings and treetops. I think some people told me that something happened to me. They said I would be different than before."

"We all change. We're all a little different than we used to be. Sometimes after a few years and sometimes after a few weeks. That's what makes people interesting."

"But I'm different from myself, too. I can't remember what I used to be like, but I think I did different things. I don't think I used to write books and build smokers."

"No, you spent a lot of time in school learning how to design buildings so that they would work properly. Then you were going to law school. That was going to help you design the agreements that people make when they put up large buildings. But a car hit you and you do different things now."

"Were people sad when the car hit me? Were you sad?"

"Yes, I was very sad. So was Mother."

"I wish you weren't. I hope you're not still. I don't feel sad. I know it takes me time to finish books but I can finish making smokers. And I can read books in the library. And people are good to me. You're good to me. Jerry and Mr. Sandro are good to me. Losing something doesn't mean you have to be sad all the time."

They walked on and George said, "I'm glad I didn't lose you, Alex. I almost lost you when you had the accident. Then I almost lost you when I didn't see you for awhile. I'm glad we can still be together. You make the world slow down for me, too."

They walked through the leaves and the trees with the different kinds of bark and the scattered chirping of birds and furtive rustling of watchful squirrels. George took Alex to his rented room, asked whether he had enough food on hand for dinner, and left him to his own world.

He had enough time to go home and rest and have something to eat before picking up Adela but he wanted to be among other people. It didn't matter whether they were strangers. He went to a doughnut shop on a busy avenue on the south side, ordered a coffee and sat by himself at a table for two. He sipped his coffee slowly and looked out the plate glass window at unremarkable cars and pickup trucks with extra lights on their grilles and on the tops of their cabs. He watched university students walk by and half listened to the conversations nearest him. Three older men in cheap versions of loose-fitting dress slacks worried about whether the economy or the local hockey team was in worse shape. A middle-aged couple—the man in a baseball cap and thick fall jacket with matching trucking company logos, the woman in mud-coloured slacks and matching sweater—talked about getting their regular lot ready for selling Christmas trees.

He had arranged to go with Adela to a movie. She said she had not been to see one for months. He picked her up from in front of her apartment building and they went to see a Shakespeare adaptation. Afterward they went for coffee, which both of them liked more than alcohol. They talked about their jobs and about Shakespeare's plays and the film they had just seen.

"I liked the naturalness of the speech," she said. "People forget that Shakespeare does not have to be presented reverently, as if it is on a higher plane than the audience. I still remember the time I went with a few friends to a repertory theatre in New York and saw the 1935 version of *A Midsummer Night's Dream*. Watching those Hollywood stars treating a comedy like it really was a comedy was eye-opening."

"I've never seen that one," he said.

"No? It's been around all your lifetime and more."

"I've spent too much of my life reading law books, I guess. But your description makes it sound like it's worth catching. I'll watch for it on television. Did you see many movies when you were growing up?"

"Not so many, and mostly in Spanish. Sometimes English with subtitles. That was a good way to help learn the language."

They were at a quiet table where no one could overhear them if they kept their voices down. He decided the setting would allow questions that had been on his mind.

"It must be a lonely experience moving to a different country where you don't really know anybody," he said.

"You mean, how lonely am I? Do I have a boyfriend?"

"That too." He was learning to take her directness and perceptive leaps in stride.

"No, I don't. Nor is there anyone back home or in New York, although I did have a boyfriend in each place."

"Do you ever want to go back? To either?"

"The boyfriends or the places?"

"The places."

"No. Life in Nicaragua became difficult. New York is exciting but too big for me. As for the other, one learns to live looking forward. You have no woman in your life?"

"No. There was one in university. She wanted to be a marine biologist. She is now, which means she will always live near an ocean. I'm a prairie boy. I like to see the green fields in summer and the geese migrating every spring and fall. I even like the brilliant sunshine on the snow and the quietness of winter here."

"Poetic," she said. "I did not expect that from a lawyer."

"I don't read much poetry. Nature provides enough that I don't have to get it in words. You didn't leave the two men behind with any bitterness."

"No," she said. "There was no occasion for bitterness. When you have to leave your home you begin to accept that life will bring more changes than you thought it would."

"It took me a few months to get over the biologist," he said. "Well, maybe a couple of years. Some things are harder to get over than others."

"Yes," she said. "One remembers many things in life. Some are consequential. Others are silly. I remember a mahogany table in my grandmother's dining room, my mother's mother. I have a clearer mental image of it than of anything else in her house. It's probably because we had family dinners there and I always felt it was the warm centre of the world."

"Love can make you feel that way."

"Love between two people is less stable than love in a big family. It depends on only one other person. It is there or not."

"Is that why you were able to leave the two men behind?"

"It is a matter of expectations."

"You would never expect love to last?"

"It's not that," she said. "It may or may not last. Other things may affect you more. Excuse me, I did not word that the right way. Love may affect you to the same degree as other emotions, but you will remember love and other emotions differently."

"In what way?"

She needed a moment to invent a description that he might understand. She looked at him while she considered the words and then spoke to him.

"Love leaves a song. Injustice leaves a scar."

He had a sensation of coming to the edge of a cliff or a high balcony and looking down a long way. They talked some more about other things. He came back from thinking about high places to absorbing the warmth of her colours and the quickness of the smile in her rounded face.

They put on their jackets and walked out onto the deserted sidewalk, where the light from the café and the street lamps barely held up against the darkness. It isn't so much the weakness of the light that makes the night look dark, Rabani thought. It's the silence of a litter-strewn street nearly empty of people. He looked at Adela and wondered how she measured loneliness.

12.

THE NEXT DAY PASSED LIKE A NORMAL MONDAY. RABANI worked nine hours in the office, went around the corner for dinner at a Vietnamese place a few blocks away, came back to work at his desk until eight, and then drove to his apartment with a few more papers in his briefcase.

Tuesday morning brought confusion and anger. Julia told him a Mr. Ostroski was on the telephone demanding to speak about an urgent matter. He put aside the contract he was working on and picked up his phone.

"They broke into my shop last night."

"They?"

"It sure wasn't thieves. Nothing was stolen that I can see. But the drawers were all opened in front and in back. Things were left reasonably neat but I can see the difference. Someone was in here looking for something. You and I both know there's only one person who would do that, and there's only one thing he would have had people looking for. The son of a bitch is going to pay for this."

"Have you called the police?"

"No. What am I going to tell them? Somebody hired by someone in the government broke in here and moved around some paper and chemical stock? It's got nothing to do with the police. I'll handle this myself. I'm letting you know because you should know all the negotiations are off."

"That makes no sense, Jack. The deal was coming together in a way that should have made everyone reasonably happy. Everyone was going to get what they wanted."

"You're talking about what reasonable people would want," Ostroski said. "Becker is as far from reasonable as a snake. He's doing this because he can't help it."

"Can you just hold on? Let me come to the shop and see for myself. Please, just wait the fifteen minutes it will take for me to get there before you do anything."

Rabani hurried down to his car and drove the several blocks to 108th Street swearing at the new frustration. He arrived at the shop breathing fast because he had almost run from the parking spot he'd found down the street. As he recovered, he worked at keeping the situation under control, speaking slowly and in an ordinary tone of voice.

When Ostroski spoke in the same unconcerned manner he began to worry even more. He would have preferred to see some of the emotion he had heard on the phone—anger, outrage, incredulity—anything but the wearily amused expression that told him Ostroski had already decided what to do and was not in a mood to be dissuaded. He played for time by asking to see what had been disturbed. There was nothing to tell any outsider that the shop had been quietly ransacked. Ostroski had to explain what he had noticed out of place.

A man in a navy overcoat came in and asked for two rolls of Kodachrome. Ostroski served him patiently and turned back to Rabani as the wave of cold air from the door dissipated.

"This is about some pictures of dogs?" Rabani said. "They're important enough for someone to arrange a break-in? It's time to tell me what's going on."

It took only a couple of seconds to start getting what he wanted. He listened to the story of Roussel's house and the well-dressed visitors who came and went on irregular occasions.

"Hell, I never took that many shots of the place," Ostroski said. "I can't even tell you for sure why I did. Probably it was just to study their faces, see how casual they could look. And because it was about the only interesting thing to shoot that I could find at the time. All those years I spent taking pictures of handshakes and ribbon cuttings and meetings.

"I thought from time to time about throwing all that stuff away. I guess I didn't because I took those pictures on my own time. They weren't something the government paid for. I never planned to use them as some kind of lever for anything."

"You never planned to use them but they were special enough that you didn't keep them with all the rest of your photos."

"I said I never planned to use them. Never said I didn't know they could be useful someday."

"And whoever came in here didn't find them?"

"Nope."

"I suppose it's too much to hope that you keep them somewhere sensible and safe."

"Safe enough that they weren't found. Sensible enough for me. The negatives are all in an envelope underneath the linoleum in back. I don't have any prints."

Rabani spared himself the effort of complaining that his client had in effect made him party to blackmail. He knew that would get him only a couple of raised eyebrows and a small smile. Instead he asked, "What now? Are you looking for revenge? Or are you willing to settle for immediate access to your collection and the right to take out anything you want from it?"

"That's all I wanted—a few pictures from the collection."

"Let's see the ones you're willing to sell."

Ostroski walked to the door and turned the "Open" sign around so that it read "Closed." He led Rabani into the back and moved a small filing cabinet. Using a metal ruler, he lifted the aged and dingy linoleum from a corner of the floor. Then he lifted a short section of old wooden board that had been part of the original floor, and pulled up a small envelope. It held negatives, images of a far different and far less dangerous subject than the ones he had hidden in the border of the Ansel landscape—Roussel's party house for visiting foreign officials.

He took the envelope to a work table, switched on a light, pulled out the negatives and gave Rabani a loupe for viewing the images in magnified form. There were eight short strips of film, one with three frames and seven with four each. Rabani looked into the lens and at the negatives. He saw an old house from a neighbourhood he recognized as having been the upscale part of the city several decades earlier. There were also images of men entering the building. One short strip of negatives showed an interior room. In one of those images the room was empty. The other showed a smiling woman with a partially open robe sitting on a chair with one knee drawn up.

"That pose looks like something I've seen before," Rabani said. "Maybe back in university. Like in some book on art history."

"I told the hooker I wanted to recreate a famous painting. She went along out of vanity."

"No prints? For sure?" Rabani asked.

"The hooker got one of her in the chair. I cropped it so that there would be nothing more than an unrecognizable blank wall behind her. I never made prints of the others. Figured they'd be too much trouble to look after."

Rabani looked at him questioningly.

"I don't have money to spend on safe deposit boxes," Ostroski said. "Keeping just the negatives means I don't have to worry about protecting anything else. These are enough as long as the place doesn't burn down. If that happens I'll probably have bigger things to worry about. I don't carry insurance."

Rabani was long past being surprised by anything Ostroski said. He was also past feeling there was any point in offering advice he hadn't been asked for.

"Becker was willing to trade the negatives for access to the photo collection. I don't see why a double-cross would have looked like a better option to him.... Let me try to arrange a meeting to settle things."

Ostroski thought a few seconds but eventually said, "The original deal was all I wanted."

Setting up the meeting was easy in one way, difficult in another. Rabani got through to Waschuk by phone that afternoon. He was told that a meeting with the premier was out of the question. But Waschuk could see him the next morning. He settled for that, reasoning that he would be close enough to the centre of authority.

They met in Waschuk's office over a breakfast brought up from the cafeteria.

"There's a trust issue now," Rabani said. "He thought he had a deal. Then Becker stalled. My client is willing to turn over half the negatives in advance. The rest he wants to keep until the review of the collection is finished."

"We don't have a lot of reason to trust him either," Waschuk said.

He put more ketchup on his fried eggs and said, "His behaviour has been unpredictable and we have no way of knowing whether he'll give us everything he has."

"It's been unpredictable but not erratic," Rabani countered. "He's had a single focus and he's pursued it. As for whether he'll give you everything, what reason would he have for holding out once he has what he wants? He's a realist. He knows better than to escalate the situation into something he can't control. And there's nothing else he would want from you."

Rabani was enjoying his fried eggs and bacon. More than that, he felt he was on solid ground talking to Waschuk. He thought of words like direct and decisive. Rabani had seen Waschuk at party conventions and had heard him described as solid. He was confident that a deal could be reached and relied upon. The forced quality in Waschuk's voice didn't count; people couldn't help how they sounded, only how they chose their words.

"Half the negatives in advance, then. And we give him a room where he can start looking through the pictures. But he can't do it alone. It's public property."

"He won't like someone standing over his shoulder. I don't think that will work."

"It doesn't have to be someone standing over his shoulder. But someone has to be in the same room, looking at all the prints and negatives at the same time he does. That way we have some assurance that he's not pulling out huge numbers of pictures at random, or high-grading the most historically important pictures for sale later."

"He's made it plain there are only about fifty or a little more that he wants. A hundred at most. Out of more than thirty thousand.'

Waschuk bit into a slice of toast thickly spread with grape jelly and answered matter of factly while asking himself what Becker had been up to: "In that case I don't see the problem. Whoever is with him will probably be some secretary. We can't have a manager sitting there just watching for two weeks or however long it takes. Whoever we get won't have a clue who most of the people in the pictures are. Most of the newer staff probably wouldn't even recognize Manchester or any of the old cabinet ministers."

"I can see what he says. But the review has to start tomorrow. He's sure that Becker already has someone combing through the collection. He's not happy. And the whole collection has to be in the room so that he knows there isn't a review going on one step ahead of him."

"That's reasonable," Waschuk said. "If we have a deal I'll make it clear to Becker that any work going on has to stop and the whole collection has to be moved into a locked room with no one in it until we let your client in. We can't write him a cheque for fifteen thousand for a few weeks but we can write a purchase order for an initial five thousand, no problem."

An hour and a half later, Rabani telephoned him from the camera shop to say Ostroski had accepted the deal. Rabani would deliver half the negatives of photos at the Roussel house that afternoon. Ostroski would be ready to start reviewing the other collection the next morning. After he made the phone call, Rabani turned to Ostroski and asked whether the shop would have to be shut down for several days.

"I don't like doing that," Ostroski said. "I haven't taken a vacation in years. People are used to the shop being open. I can probably get Adela to work longer hours. I guess that way she gets a cut of the fifteen thousand. She may as well have it. She needs the money more than I do. I don't have needy relatives waiting for an inheritance anyway."

Rabani looked at his client's neutral expression. The pale blue eyes looked steadily back at him. But the usual amused crinkle around them was missing. There was also none of the relief or elation that would normally light up the face of a client who had won. But he was sure something important had just happened.

He stared a little longer, got no response, and finally said, "What was all this about, Jack?"

"What you heard: keeping someone's image private."

"Since when does a Hollywood starlet, or potential starlet, worry about keeping pictures of herself out of public circulation? Even the skin shots probably wouldn't bother her, unless she's taken up religion in a serious way. And the government wouldn't likely be making any of those public."

"No, they probably wouldn't. All the shots were fairly tame anyway. Most were standard portraits. Maybe three or four had a bit more showing."

"Then what's going on? Why was protecting her worth threatening to throw a dog off the bridge? Was there something else?"

"Yeah, there was something else. Someone else."

Rabani waited.

"You can't repeat any of this to anyone. Not Adela, not anyone in your office, not your diary if you have one, not in any memoirs you may write if you get rich and famous, not any girlfriend you're trying to entertain."

"If it's that important, why tell me at all?"

"I guess you earned it. I can't pay you enough money to cover what it's worth to me. Or maybe because I never told anyone about it but sometimes it feels like I have to tell someone sometime, or it will all be like it never happened. Like a moment that passed in front of a camera without someone tripping the shutter."

"All right, you have my word."

Ostroski waited. He looked as if he were still making up his mind. But they both knew he would begin to talk once he started finding the words.

13.

"YOU HAVE TO GO ALL THE WAY BACK TO UNDERSTAND," Ostroski said.

"All the way back to Rochester. That's where I grew up. My grandfather moved there from Worcester, Massachusetts. He didn't want to work in a shoe factory all his life after growing up on a farm. Bad enough to be born a peasant feeding pigs, he's supposed to have said, worse to be a peasant making shoes in a factory and owning nothing.

"He heard there were jobs at Kodak in Rochester so he moved his family there. It worked out for him. The plant was expanding, there were different kinds of jobs to try, and he ended up being a foreman. It wasn't a bad place to live, either. He said the housing was better. There was open country close by. And there was the lake to swim in on hot summer days.

"My father followed him into the plant. The old man worked in shipping but my father had some high school and learned some of the technical side. He worked in film production. Who knows how many weddings and kids' birthday parties and babies and picnics ended up on film that he made?

"It was a decent life. I could have followed them both into the plant. Kodak was a good place to work. The pay was steady. Bonuses every year. But I got stars in my eyes. My father was a little too old to be drafted into the war, I was a little too young. Not too young to go to the movies, though. That was back in the days before television. Only a few years before but it was a different world. We wouldn't have been able to imagine what was coming. We had radio, but anyone with ten cents to spare would go to the movies, often once a week.

"It was the movies that got me. The stories came and went. A lot of them weren't that good. But the photography pulled me in. I'd already been taking pictures. It was natural with Kodak in town. I went into it bigger than my friends, though. I guess there were a lot of people getting famous taking stills for magazines or for art. The pictures in *Life* magazine impressed me. What really got to me was the way the best cinematographers handled the camera in the movies. Some of them captured images as good as the best still photographers could do. Some of them were great at action. The best were inventive and flexible, without being obvious about it.

"I liked Joe LaShelle, the way he made small spaces look big in *Laura* and *Fallen Angel*. And the way he framed the actors. He also did a swell job a lot later with *The Apartment*. Should have won an Oscar for that one. But it was his early pictures that got me to thinking I'd like to go to Hollywood and give the movies a try.

"So I got on a bus with a bit of money I'd saved from a part-time job. My mother wasn't happy. My dad, I'm pretty sure he thought I might be back before too long but he thought it was time one of the family saw the world outside Rochester. I started hanging around the studios and eventually got a job as a camera assistant at RKO. It was simple work but it let me get on the sets and watch the way the cinematographers worked. The basic rule there was to get the film made fast and cheap. You could still learn a lot watching how they did it. Every now and then they'd throw in a neat trick, too, if it didn't take too much set-up time or look too arty. I even got to meet Joe LaShelle once. He was working at Fox. He told me how he'd started in a print department and worked his way up to camera operator before they let him direct photography. That was all the extra encouragement I needed and I figured the movies would be my life.

"About that time I met Norma Minton. She was an extra who worked part-time as a secretary on the side. She was from Connecticut. She'd decided she wanted a little more excitement in life than working for an insurance company. That was Norma, always willing to have a little fun. She was better looking than a lot of the extras, had this gorgeous dark brown hair and a cute little nose. I was never sure how serious she was about acting. She took voice lessons, but she made remarks sometimes about it being a fairly silly way of making a living. She also thought it was hard on young women. She saw a lot of them come and go. Most of them didn't last long even if they'd looked good in a film or two.

"Norma was always ready to go out for a drink and a dance at one of the nightclubs we could afford. We spent a lot of time on the beach at Santa Monica. That didn't cost anything aside from an occasional hot dog. I took some pictures of her, too. Those are some of the ones I want back, or at least kept private. But they're not the ones I really want kept private.

"We were having a good time together. I even thought I could get serious about her, although I was too young to be sure. Wasn't sure about anything then. All I knew was that maybe she liked me enough to get serious or maybe she didn't. Maybe I could get somewhere in the movie business. Or maybe the first signs of trouble showing up for the studios in the late Forties were only going to get worse.

"Turned out I didn't have to worry about planning for the future. Uncle Sam took care of that for me. I was drafted late in '50. We wrote to each other a couple of times while I was taking basic training. It was always a surprise to get a letter from her. It always made me feel good, too. I couldn't make up my mind whether she was just being friendly and I shouldn't get my hopes up. But the hopes were always sneaking around. I halfway fooled myself into thinking she wouldn't meet anyone else and I could go back to her in a couple of years.

"The writing stopped when I got shipped out to Korea. I was lucky in a way. Didn't get there until the situation had got stabilized. It was still bad but at least units weren't getting overrun the way they were in the first couple of months of the war. Some of the older guys, the sergeants and some of the officers, they'd been in the big war. They said as bad as things were in Korea, they could have been worse. The Germans were better soldiers than the Chinese and North Koreans, and the Japanese were more fanatical. All I knew was my guts cramped up whenever they opened up with a lot of mortars. A couple of times we saw a whole battalion coming at us, trying to wipe us out through sheer numbers. Thank God for the artillery and the Air Force.

"The fighting was bad enough. The war was worse in other ways. You saw civilians getting shot to pieces or burned up or just forced out of their homes and down the road to nowhere. And then there was the whole business of sitting there trying to hold a line. You didn't go forward and didn't go back. You sat there accomplishing nothing while your buddies were getting killed. It was a real mess. You know, they made that movie called *Pork Chop Hill* in the Fifties. It was about a real battle, one of the handful we clearly won. But it was still as phony as most of what you see in the movies. The part about a brave American unit staking a claim on an important hilltop was true. But the movie made it look like the battle made the Chinese accept that we were willing to fight and decide to agree on an armistice. What really happened was they took the hill back from us a few months later, before the armistice was signed. That was Korea, nothing ever really got done and a lot of good guys got killed not doing it.

"I was pretty fed up by the time I came back. It always makes me laugh to think how much of a fuss was made over Vietnam vets throwing away their medals. In Korea they gave away medals like candy. They thought it was a cheap way of keeping up morale. I threw mine off the troopship coming back across the Pacific. A lot of the guys I was with did the same.

"We were supposed to be going home. I found out a couple of years away meant home wasn't the same. The movie business was shrinking. The time I spent in Korea was when TV really took over. Norma was going out with the sound engineer from Paramount by then. No medals, no girlfriend, no job."

Rabani didn't want to interrupt but couldn't let the casualness pass. He raised his eyebrows a touch and kept his voice neutral but commented, "Doesn't sound like losing Norma Minton left you badly broken up. Why is it so important to keep her photos out of public circulation?"

"You don't believe in privacy?" Ostroski replied. Rabani thought he looked almost like he was winking.

"She was a good kid. Why should her pictures be available to a bunch of gawkers just because I wanted to keep a few to remember her by? But no. She wasn't the centre of my life. I wanted to have more time with her. She was a lot of fun to be with and a good person in a lot of ways. But if it was just her, I'm not sure I'd be willing to get into all this trouble. Maybe I would. I don't mind making trouble for guys who think they've got the world by the tail. Maybe I wouldn't. You don't know whether you'll cross a bridge till you come to it. There are other pictures. Of someone else."

Rabani leaned against the back of his chair. He looked at Ostroski and decided he wasn't seeing the usual flicker of amusement. He wasn't even sure that Ostroski would go on. His client was on the brink of telling the real story. It was going to hurt. Rabani saw Ostroski look down at the floor. That had never happened before. Ostroski looked people in the eye. He kept looking down, apparently deciding whether to finish the story.

Rabani waited until he thought he had a better chance of hearing what had happened if he gave a little nudge. He said, "It's up to you, Jack. I'm a lawyer but I need to know only what affects my ability to represent you. You don't have to tell me about your life if you don't want to. I think, though, I can represent you better if I know what's going on."

When Ostroski looked back up, Rabani saw a different gaze. Ostroski was looking at him but also seemed to be looking through him. He seemed ready to talk. But would he really be talking to Rabani? Or to himself? It didn't matter to Rabani. Listener or eavesdropper, he wanted to know why his client was willing to hold a dog hostage on a bridge and probably conduct a form of blackmail against the government, which meant he was capable of doing other unpredictable things as well. He wanted to know more about why he had begun to feel like he was standing on a high ledge himself, unsure what winds were blowing or what strangers with malevolent intent might be near.

Ostroski said, "I could use a beer. You want one?"

"No thanks, Jack."

The small fridge that held rolls of film also held a few cans of beer at the back. But Rabani had never seen Ostroski drinking or smelled beer on his breath.

Ostroski walked into the back room, took a can out of the fridge, walked back to his chair, popped the can open, and regarded the tab as he slowly bent it back. He looked again at Rabani with an expression half engaged and half focused on something far away. Then he plunged into his memories.

"I was at loose ends. I got lucky. The movie studios were laying people off but the TV studios and local stations needed people who knew their way around cameras. A friend of mine got me a job as an assistant operator on a Western series that looked like it was on its way out but was going to be in production for another couple of months. Then I got luckier still and ended up working on a news program for a station down in San Diego. After that I was employable. I could handle both film and live production.

"I stayed there long enough to learn the ropes. Then I went back east. I'd thought about going to see my folks after coming back from Korea but I wasn't ready then. After a year, I was. I spent a few weeks visiting them and other family. Working at Kodak still wasn't my idea of a career and I had what I'd learned about film and TV in my back pocket. I started looking around. Then a job came up in Buffalo. It was close enough to my family but just far enough away. And really far from California. I admit I was still thinking about Norma from time to time and wondering if I'd made a mistake letting her get away, not that I had much choice what with the draft.

"People sometimes laugh at Buffalo. For a guy from Rochester it was a down-to-earth place. Factories, a lake port, one end of the New York Thruway just getting built. Bowling alleys, taverns, and cheap restaurants where they knew how to fill you up. Parks all over the place, too. And TV stations. Mostly they were a way for the owners to get rich feeding off the carcass of the movies. Now and then they pretended to deliver culture. And WKJ was the pick of the bunch. Not because it was the best. It was the most original. That was because of the owner, Kirby Jenner.

"He made his money in insurance. He thought he could make a lot more by getting in on the ground floor of television. But he had an entertainer side to him. He was a Shriner and he liked to drive the cars in the parades. He was nuts about Jack Benny, too. Sometimes I thought the chance he might find another comedian he liked as much as Benny was almost as important to him as the money.

"He ran an operation that was about as close to family as a TV station could get. It was mostly a great bunch of people except for the finance manager, who was a real prick. We used to go out to Miller's Tavern at the end of a week and have a good time together. Some of us started going bowling before we went to the tavern. The two guys who ran the orchestra for the Polish polka show on Sundays started that. Jenner didn't go to those get-togethers. He was downtown with the crowd that went to charity dinners and concerts at the auditorium. If he wasn't in those places, he was invited to some private home where they could afford caterers.

"He was pretty approachable at the station, though. We had a lot of laughs watching him fume at the advertising one of the other stations ran. Their promo material featured a couple of little elf-like characters. The elves were supposed to be like the eyes and ears of the station. They called them Iris and Earis. Old Jenner, he'd get so worked up about them you'd think he was dealing with the imps of hell. Some of it was jealousy. Every now and then he'd say if he could have a couple of leprechauns shilling for WKJ he'd clean up. Course, that could also have been part of his poverty act. He paid us decently enough, but he always made out that he was stretching the budget thin. He paid us decently. He didn't want to pay us well.

"Those were the days when you could still do crazy things on air. I remember once Bill Gracey, who did the weather, tried to do a spot on water skis out on the Niagara River. There weren't live remotes back then. There weren't even satellites. We had one truck that took a film camera out to fires and accident sites. Gracey arranged for it to do his water skiing. Every trip cost a lot of money. That one also cost us coverage of a big warehouse fire. Old Jenner blew his top at that one and he didn't show his temper very often. Everyone was laughing about a week later, though. I always thought Jenner did too, although he never admitted it.

"Some of what was going on was more serious, if you thought about it. One of the things was the border with Canada was being blurred. A lot of Canadians used to come over to Buffalo in those days. It was their idea of an exciting getaway. Kind of like a northern version of Tijuana, I guess, except tamer. Well, they couldn't go every day but they could watch TV every day. I didn't have a good notion of it then, but later on I'd talk to people from the other side and find out they were learning about everything from breakfast cereal they couldn't get in Canada to the names of senators and congressmen. Some of them said they started knowing more about American politics than about Canadian. Eventually, we could catch some Canadian stations in Buffalo but we didn't watch as much of their stuff as they did of ours. Only the hockey fans tuned in to their stations regularly.

"The bigger thing was the way that television was eating up the past. I told you Jenner was nuts about Jack Benny. Well, think about that. Benny and a bunch of other stars of that era came out of vaudeville. Then they got into movies and radio. Then they moved into television. TV was so hungry for material in the early days that it kept raiding the past. First some of the big stars, then every movie made since the silent days. Not all the movies were available at first. It started out with old serials and B Westerns. But gradually, more and more movies got released to television. By the Sixties, they were all used up. Most of the ideas for TV shows were getting tired by then, too. Even *Star Trek* didn't last long. There was a kind of tombstone for the whole business sometime around '70 or '71. The Schlitz beer company put together a film made up of short clips from old shows going right back to the early days. It had just about everything. Ran for several hours. They distributed I don't know how many copies around college campuses. It was an advertising thing for them. But what it really meant was that television had got used up. First it used up vaudeville and movies and radio, and in the end it used up itself. Then the movie producers started making films with language you couldn't put on television for another thirty years. And the TV shows started recycling old stars and old story ideas. TV had used up everything that came before it. Then all it could do was to keep bringing stuff around a second or third time and chewing on what it had already swallowed. Like a cow. There wasn't anything left. Why do you think there's nothing on TV anymore even though they keep starting more channels?"

Rabani didn't answer. He wasn't sure what a more or less correct answer would be. Nor was he sure that all the theorizing would stand up to careful scrutiny. But he knew the question was just a sidetrack. He stared at Ostroski until the monologue started again.

"Yeah, okay, I'm beating around the bush. That's beside the point as far as Becker's concerned.

"The point is Gloria. That was her performing name. The only one she needed. She did call herself Gloria Sandring, but she was just Gloria as far as everyone at the station and anyone around Buffalo was concerned.

"The first time I saw her was on television. You could have knocked me over. I'd just got to Buffalo and wanted to have a look at this station I was going to work for. The apartment I'd rented had a set in it. I turned it on the afternoon I got there and the kids' storytime show was on. Only they weren't showing the story just then. They were showing the fairy princess who introduced the stories. That was Gloria. She was in a flouncy white dress. It had sequins that sparkled so much they played hell with the cameras. She had a tiara on her head, full of zircons that glittered like diamonds. She had one of those wands with a star at the end in her right hand. And you probably won't believe it, but she had magic. It helped that the picture even on the best sets was a little fuzzy in those days, lent a blurry kind of half reality to everything.

"It would have been better if I'd seen her in the studio. I saw the illusion instead. I'd been around long enough to know the difference. But she was all the magic that was television in those days. You saw her on the screen and you just knew that something make-believe could become true. And the worst part, the worst part—after I'd been around her awhile she made the same magic in real life.

"Looking back, I never figured out whether it was her I fell for, or someone I dreamed up. Maybe she was in a television show playing in my head. Maybe I'd been in the business too long. At the time I probably would have said only that she confused the hell out of me. I guess that's one definition of love.

"It wasn't supposed to work out that way. We started going out for a drink once every couple of weeks. Then it was more like once a week, between the visits to Miller's with the rest of the crew. I'd look at her when we were with the others and try not to look at her too much. That was easy in one way. She seemed more real than the other people at the station. It was like looking at her filled my eyes. Other people I could see, but somehow they weren't completely there.

"Then we started fooling around. We never did have sex although we got close a couple of times. She worried about getting pregnant, even with a rubber. Said she had risked that with her first boyfriend back home and got worried sick. Once she literally had been sick for a couple of days with the flu and got into a panic because she thought it might be morning sickness.

"After a few months I didn't know what I wanted more—get her into bed or hope that whatever was between us would turn into something more than just a good time. It's funny. When I look back, the most intense physical thing that ever happened between us was one night on the way to the tavern we held hands. There were four of us in Randy Eberhart's car, he was a floor director. We were in the back seat together and she took my hand in the dark. We started squeezing our hands together and somehow that was about as close as I ever felt to anyone. But even that didn't prepare me for the topper.

"A couple of weeks after we took that car ride, she asked me out to have some lunch in a park near the station. It was a nice day. It was warm enough but a little cloudy and we were sitting in shade. She started talking about life across the river. We went there a couple of times. A place called Crystal Beach. It had nice warm water and good sand but people like it just as much for the amusement park.

"She told me she grew up on the Canadian side, over in a town called St. Catharines. Her real name was Sedlak. Her mother looked after the house. Her father worked in a GM axle plant and one of her brothers had followed the old man into the plant. Her other brother had just gone up to work in a nickel mine in Sudbury. She was talking about them, and about her American uncle who worked at the Nabisco plant in Niagara Falls, on the American side. They made shredded wheat there. She used to spend a couple of weeks each summer with her uncle and aunt. She had another uncle who worked in a paper mill in a little town on the

Canadian side called Thorold. The U.S. was more exciting. That's how she ended up crossing the border. I was listening to the way she talked about her family and feeling she was more than someone fun to be with. She was really likable. Special and down to earth at the same time.

"And then I saw light shimmering around her face. At first I wasn't sure what it was. It was just some brightness like the sun had come out more. Then it got bigger and turned blue. It was blue and moving, not really sparkling but shimmering with points like electric spikes at the outside edges. And around that a narrower gold border suddenly appeared.

"I was staring at this and saw she was starting to look at me funny. She must have been wondering why I was just staring. It was the damnedest thing I'd ever seen. I didn't want to say or do anything that would make it go away. It lasted about a minute and then it faded.

"I never told her. I was too dazed to tell her then and there never seemed to be a right time after. We didn't have much time. I never did figure out what the hell happened. You hear people talk about auras. But they seem to have in mind a kind of glow about a person. This was more like the northern lights, something you could clearly see, and in full colour. Naturally I hoped that it meant something about how she felt about me. Then years later I read somewhere that people can talk themselves into seeing things like that. Hell, you can even see things like that if you get a migraine, I guess. In the end I decided to believe that I just had a kind of tuner open up in my mind and saw a kind of life force radiating out of her. She had that.

"She wasn't alive much longer, though. A little later that summer she went out onto the river with Jenner's son, Chad. He had a nice motorboat. They went out at night and had a few drinks out on the water. Buffalo could be awful hot and muggy in the summer. It was cooler out on the river.

"The way he told it after, she decided to walk along the side of the boat, which had an edge about as wide as a foot. He got scared and told her she should get down. He said he even started moving toward her to take one of her hands and help her down. She started laughing. It was laughing that caused her to lose balance. She fell into the Niagara. Even offshore from Buffalo it has a pretty strong current. He lost her quickly in the darkness. Didn't even hear her shouting. He tried to look for her but the more he looked the closer he got to the falls. He was shaken up but didn't want to go over and eventually gave up and turned back.

"She probably drowned before she went over. She'd had a few drinks and cold water shocks you. Plus there was the current. One big one and lots of little ones running this way and that. She could even have hit some rocks on the way to the edge. Canadian police found her in an eddy downstream from the falls the next morning.

"I'd said goodbye to her on her way out of the station. Didn't know she was planning to go out in the boat. Didn't even know she was spending time with Chad. Not that there was any reason she wouldn't. He was good looking and had money. I don't think she was one to be after money, although in some ways I didn't really know her all that well. Anyway, he wouldn't have wanted to get serious about her. He wouldn't have wanted to lose one of the station's stars by marrying her. For that matter, he was small fry in the business. If she wanted money, he had it, but if she wanted to marry up in class, she'd have taken her chances in New York rather than Buffalo.

"I'd taken a few pictures of her. Just for fun to see how she'd look, not to remember her by. She wanted to see how close a portrait would make her to looking like a movie star, too. Most of them were black and white. A handful were in colour. She had these starburst eyes—mostly green with an orange flash in the middle. You couldn't see that on the black and white TV screen but it was the first thing you noticed about her in real life. Smacked you in the face. Never seen any eyes like them before or since.

"After she died I never wanted to look at the pictures again. Didn't want to throw them away either. They ended up in my collection. That's why I want to go through it all. She's not going to get dragged into public view. Not if I can help it. She's gone. She's been gone for years. Just like all that live television she did. No one's turning her into a zombie. I don't want to be responsible for bringing her image back into life. It doesn't matter so much for me. The photos I can live with. I could even stand to look at them again now, I guess. They'll use up my memory and help me forget. I should look at them again and hope they do that. It's the pictures of her in my mind, the ones that I never put on film, that haunt me."

He stopped. Rabani let out a breath.

14.

SHE LOOKED AROUND THE ROOM AS SHE HUNG HER COAT IN the open rack and lifted her purse onto the shelf across its top. At least the room didn't have cubicles. There were times the rough grey fabric lining of the cubicle dividers bored her into a frenzy, made her think of loud music and vodka. This room had two tables. There were even splashes of colour if you counted beige as a colour.

People tended to think of Ginny Radescu as beige—too lively to be grey, not dominating enough in a group of more than three to be anything more than beige. That was fine with her. She had learned long ago that she could not stand out in a crowd, and that there was no reason to. What mattered was making a difference to one or two people. She learned that at about the same time that she learned something else: having a face that people usually thought of as plain rather than pretty did not matter if you had the right body underneath it. She exercised and ate lettuce. She drank vodka but avoided orange juice because she'd heard that it contained fructose, which she'd heard was bad for the waistline. Anyone given an advantage in life should be smart enough to keep it.

Ostroski came in half a minute later and took off his coat and hat. They were supposed to go into the room at the same time and leave at the same time. They had already said hello in the building's main foyer. He had reminded her of her father and uncle: working class, but with eyes that said smart. That didn't bother her. She wasn't there to spar with him, just to watch what pictures he was looking at. She figured she had just as good a chance of staying awake as he did.

"Let's start with that one," Ostroski said. He pointed to a cardboard box at the side, intending to start at the top of the stack in the middle and work his way to the corner.

He lifted the box onto the table but didn't sit down. Instead, he turned to her and said, "Just so I can keep track, who are you spying for?"

"Whoever asks me what I've seen and has some say in whether I keep my job."

"How many is that?"

"Probably could be about five."

"But not that many will be interested."

"I hope not. I don't want to spend as much time answering questions as looking at thousands of pictures that mean nothing to me."

She saw the wrinkles around his eyes stretch just enough to suggest he thought her answers were entertaining. He looked at her eyes and saw a light almond colour, a hue he didn't recall having seen before. She gazed back at him steadily. He didn't see hostility; he wasn't sure whether he saw boredom.

"Good," he said. "The less time I have to spend explaining to you what any of these is about, the faster we'll get through them."

They settled in for a long grind of staring at images. After the first half-hour he was surprised at how many he'd forgotten. Pictures of natural gas processing plants, pictures of an alfalfa pellet plant, pictures of politicians standing around with some of them holding spades sunk partway into the ground, pictures of politicians surrounded by kids, pictures of highway overpasses, pictures of visiting politicians and business leaders from outside the province. Had he really earned a living for years taking pictures of things no one cared about?

It was a lucky start, though. He could measure how well she would stand up to the strain of paying attention for hours on end. He decided to take a break after every fifty minutes, getting up to stretch, getting a coffee at the start of one hour, going to the bathroom the next. He thought about locking the door each time he left and asking her to walk down the hallway with him. He decided that was pointless because he could not be there night and day. In the afternoon, he cut down the drinks and switched from coffee to cola. After that many hours of dull flipping through paper, a good fizzy cola would at least give him the gassy satisfaction of a full stomach.

It went like that for two days before he got to boxes from Hollywood. On the morning of the third day, he opened a file and saw Sunset Boulevard, taken at sunset. He wondered if he had thought that was funny, or if he had just liked the light. Or maybe he'd just happened to have free time then. Photos from the RKO lot followed quickly. He'd talked to his watcher a few times, mostly about the weather and the best places to buy a good hamburger. He had discovered he didn't really mind her looking at the pictures with him. Now that he had something exotic to tell her about he began a desultory commentary.

"That was the New York street. They used it for a street in any big city. You've probably seen it a number of times."

"Probably not. I like pictures with a lot of colour and scenery. I don't usually watch anything with old city streets in black and white. I remember I wanted to see *Gidget* when it showed up on TV when I was about eleven but my mom said I was too young."

"That was in colour and set in California."

"Like I said."

"Some of these shots were taken near the beach where they made *Gidget*. Some right on it."

"Why did you take them in black and white?"

"Better definition. And never trusted colour not to fade." He paused. "Also it was cheaper."

He saw the first photo of Norma Minton. It was the first one he'd taken of her. A sound stage was in the background. He remembered she had looked a little more than ordinarily pretty by Hollywood standards, but also unusually self-possessed. That was one of the things that kept her in the bit parts. The producers didn't want women looking as capable as the male leads.

He talked about Malibu as he set aside the first photo of Norma, surprised at how little effort it took to keep his voice steady. About forty years now, he thought. Radescu didn't ask him who the woman in the photo was or why he was removing that one from the files. Either she's been told what to expect or she's been told to take a good look and keep her mouth shut, he thought. He stopped explaining about the studio and the beaches as he continued to flip through the photos with the government woman watching beside his shoulder. He found more of Norma in the studio, some of her on the beach, and two of her on the beach with her breasts showing. He didn't like it that someone else saw these. She did not comment on them. He quickly found himself thinking instead about how he'd managed to take them: it must have been a quiet time with the nearest people a good hundred yards away.

After they knocked off for the day she found a telephone and called Becker. He had asked her to report whenever Ostroski removed any photographs. She told him about the pictures of some starlet she did not recognize.

"And that's all?" Becker asked.

"It's all for now. We'll be back at it tomorrow. There are still a lot of boxes to go. Keeping awake is the big problem."

"Hang in there. This is very important." He let the implied promise of a reward glimmer through the words. "And you're watching for the kind of picture I told you about, even if he doesn't take it?"

"Yes, there's been nothing like that so far."

He thanked her and they hung up. Half a minute later she walked down the hallway, and took an elevator up nine floors to the deputy minister's office. Jeffries wanted to know when Ostroski found something worth taking, too. He also wanted to know if a certain type of picture showed up, and whether Ostroski took it out or not, but the kind that interested him was different than what Becker had described.

She looked at his bland face and wire-rimmed glasses above the barely pink, round cheeks; she thought again how much he resembled her old high-school principal. Something about him seemed more dangerous, though. He even sounded dangerous when he told her, "You can report by phone from now on. I wanted to see you once."

When he smiled he always seemed to have something else on his mind. That was all right with her. She never dreamed about outsmarting anyone she depended on, only about keeping him happy. In this case, all it cost her was a little boredom, which she thought was what people were paid for in most jobs.

Still, she was glad to get out of his office and head downtown for one of her regular dinners with her friend Rosa. It was a weeknight. She kept herself to one glass of white wine. On a Friday night she would have drunk more. She made up the difference by talking with Rosa about the silliness of spending days looking at old pictures, and trying to spot certain pictures for two different bosses.

Next morning she was back in the beige room with the mottled grey carpet that was getting worn in the middle and didn't match the walls. She started talking to Ostroski without planning to. Talking came naturally to her. It was something people did, like drinking water on a hot day. It relieved the mind-numbing flip-flip-flip of the photographs being turned. He didn't seem eager but didn't seem to mind either. To her surprise, she found his stories about the early days of television were moderately interesting.

"Television came late to this part of the country," she said. "My mom and dad told me there wasn't any until 1954, and then it was just the CBC. They watched the hockey and the late-night news. There was a show about an RCMP guy somewhere in the north but nothing much exciting ever happened in it, they said. My dad said he sometimes watched a show about a couple of truckers, called *Cannonball*. It wasn't on very long."

"I think I remember that one," Ostroski told her. "It had a couple of American actors in the lead roles but it was made across the river, somewhere around Toronto. Didn't have much excitement in that one either. Don't know about the series about the RCMP guy but I'll bet it was the same. We noticed that shows coming out of Canada were usually more about ordinary people doing ordinary kinds of things. That's why it was easier to get people in Canada to watch our shows being broadcast from Buffalo. Most of what we were showing came from Hollywood. I heard that even some of the ads seemed pretty exotic if you were watching from across the river. I remember someone telling me that there were ads for breakfast cereals like Trix and Chex, things people in Canada hadn't heard of. It made them curious."

They finished a box and Radescu got up to get the next one. She liked the way that Ostroski was willing to let her do some of the physical work. She waited through the first dozen or so photos from the new box before she took up the conversation again. She didn't want to exhaust it right away and have to spend hours in silence.

"Didn't you ever get bored just taking pictures?" she asked.

"Nope."

She stopped an urge to ask if he ever got bored looking at pictures. Half an hour later she suppressed it again. Then she began daydreaming about clubs and dancing. Then a photograph caught her eye and she said, "I think she looks sort of familiar, like I should know who that is."

Ostroski looked at the print he had been about to flip quickly. He had already turned over two much like it. "Don't know if you'd have any reason to know what she looked like. This is Hesperia Tindall. She was the lieutenant-governor. Not all that long ago but long enough to be ancient history for you. You were probably in high school."

"Oh," Radescu said. "I think I've heard of her. She looks like she wasn't used to smiling."

"She wasn't. That was back in the day when lieutenant-governors had a choice. They could be smiley and read stories to kids or they could be in more serious pictures that people saw occasionally in newspapers. Tindall didn't smile much. She probably thought it would clash with the old-fashioned military-style uniforms she liked wearing. Why do you ask?"

"She just looked familiar."

He didn't look at her and didn't hear any more questions. It was the first time she had asked him about anyone in any of the thousands of photographs they had seen so far.

The rest of the day passed without that kind of excitement. His right arm was tired and he had started alternating, turning the prints for about ten or fifteen minutes at a time with one arm and then using the other. After they left the clutter for the night she walked back to her office and filled in time looking at papers from her desk drawer. She said goodnight to Helen, who worked at the desk opposite her own, and looked around. No one was within earshot. She punched the number buttons for Frank Jeffries. It was his direct line.

"Mr. Jeffries? It's Ginny Radescu."

"Oh, Ginny, how are you holding up? It must be a boring routine by now."

"Fine. I guess I'll last until it's over. I called because I saw some pictures of Hesperia Tindall today. You said that was one of the things to watch for."

"Yes. And how were they?"

"There was nothing special about them. There were a couple of portraits with her by herself, and a few more of her in crowds. Some like what you said to look for."

"She was alone or with a formal group in all of them?"

"Mostly it was the usual type of occasion. There were two photos where she was with another woman, holding hands in one of them and with her arm around the woman's waist in another."

"The same woman in both?"

"Yes. But on different occasions."

"All right. Did you make a note of which box these were in?"

"Number forty-nine."

"Thank you, Ginny. I have confidence in you. Please keep watching and pay attention to everything you see."

"I will. I'll call again when there's anything to report."

"That will be fine. Have a pleasant evening."

"You too, Mr. Jeffries."

She hung up and stared at papers in the in box on the right-hand corner of her desk. She looked at her watch and realized she was hungry. She decided to have a quick salad on the way to her Jazzercize class and heat up something from the freezer when she got home. The rest of the evening went routinely. She felt herself smiling during her workout. Moving around was a treat after a day spent mostly sitting. She knew she fidgeted in her chair and wondered if Ostroski noticed. She did the dishes and watched the late-night news, mostly to see if there was anything she should be aware of happening at the legislature.

It had been a quiet day. Nothing much beyond the petition against wearing turbans in the RCMP. She didn't see why people had to insist on dressing like foreigners when they moved to a different country. She moved into her bedroom, hung her dress in the closet, put on her pink and mauve pyjamas and went into the bathroom to brush her teeth. The telephone rang. She sighed, wondering who would call after eleven, and walked back into the living room, flipping on a light on the way.

She said hello and heard the deputy minister's molasses-like voice: "Hello, Ginny. Sorry to bother you at this time of night. Hope I didn't wake you up."

"No, Mr. Jeffries, it's fine."

"Good. I wanted to check with you on the number of the box containing the photos of Hesperia Tindall. You said it was forty-nine. Are you sure?"

"Yes. I remember it clearly because my youngest uncle is forty-nine and has his birthday next week. He's saying turning forty was no problem but fifty has him looking for grey hairs."

"I see. Absolutely no question then."

"No. It was forty-nine."

"Ah. You see, I was curious about those photographs and thought I'd have a look at them myself. Hesperia and I were friends, you know. I went downstairs and had security open the door for me and looked through box forty-nine. There were no pictures of Hesperia Tindall in it."

She paused and said, "I don't know how that could be."

"You left at the same time as Mr. Ostroski?"

"Yes, we locked the door and the security man was down the hallway. He would have seen if one of us had gone back."

"Was there ever a time after you saw the pictures that you left Mr. Ostroski alone with them, or turned your back on him for some time?"

"Yes," she said hesitantly. "I made a quick trip to the washroom late in the afternoon."

"Ah, and that was the only time?"

"Yes. Should I not do that?"

"It's all right, Ginny. I'm just keeping track of what's happening. Those photographs form an important record, you know, and we've paid a lot of money for them. We agreed to let Mr. Ostroski remove some, but we want to know which ones. You saw him remove a few of that starlet?"

"Yes, the starlet, and he wrote down what he was taking."

"But nothing else?"

"No."

"Thank you, Ginny. Please don't mention anything about this to Mr. Ostroski. I'm sure we can straighten everything out. You're being a big help with this project. I'll remember it."

"Thank you. Good night, Mr. Jeffries."

"You won't let me down, will you? I would hate to be let down."

She felt suddenly queasy and said, "No, Mr. Jeffries." He hung up.

She walked into her bedroom, slipped beneath the covers and turned off the table light. This was one of the times she was happy to be at a pay grade low enough that she didn't have to worry about why anyone was strangely interested in meaningless old pictures. But now she was worried, after hearing what she interpreted as menace in the deputy's closing words. She fell asleep thinking about the vodka and dancing that would reward her for getting through another work week and hopefully getting clear of this task. She dreamed that she was walking along a Mexican beach with John Becker. It was hot. The surf made murmuring sounds. She felt like she was smiling. Then she turned her head toward him and saw he had grown a drooping black moustache and was wearing a sombrero.

Jeffries was still awake, staring out the living-room window of his penthouse apartment at the amber dots of sodium-vapour street lights and the occasional cars moving up the road with pools of light sliding across the pavement in front of them like floating ghosts. His eyes gleamed and his jaw clenched tight. He was certain now that he would have to go further than he'd originally planned. But he was comfortable in the knowledge that he had always been willing and able to go as far as necessary to impose his will.

15.

THE CROWD WAS WELL DRESSED, IN A SECOND-BEST WAY. Enough glossy finish to show money, not enough to suggest that this event was the highest rung on the social ladder where they thought they belonged. Not enough to suggest they didn't have a better suit or dress in the closet.

Arlene's gaze swept around the room. She smiled as she remembered the last time she had seen a truly high social event. That one had more prestige attached to the invitation—a speech by British Prime Minister Gladys Harcourt. Officially, she had been on a state visit to a thriving and dynamic corner of the Commonwealth. Unofficially, the tour had been a thinly veiled political insurance effort, an exercise in solidifying local support for testing of cruise missiles over the northern part of the province. Harcourt had been well briefed. She lavished flattery. Her speech had praised the local boldness and entrepreneurial spirit and forward-looking attitudes. The crowd had lapped it up. Arlene remembered not being surprised. What made her smile was remembering the scene in front of the hotel with Harcourt's three-car motorcade and accompanying police escort on motorcycles. One of the police riders had squeezed the brakes a touch too late and crunched his front tire through a tail light on one of the cars. Arlene had savoured the lack of reaction—the feeling from the uniforms on the bikes and the plainclothes in the cars of "Oh, that egg dropped on the floor, good thing there's another in the carton."

She looked at her husband's profile. His chin and jawline were still good. No wattles or jowls yet, although she could see where they would start. She wondered what she would think of him then. She wondered whether he was already seeing her that way—a fading, middle-aged reminiscence of someone he had met and once fallen in love with, a woman with a prominent aquiline nose and hair that had started to need help staying a medium brown.

Beads of condensation stood on the water jug near the centre of the table. A buzz of conversation hung in the air. She had never before met the man on her right who had introduced himself as Gerald Furyk. He looked confused and a little intimidated by the setting. She decided she should turn to him and add to the buzz of conversation but he excused himself, saying he should visit the little boys' room before dinner.

She saw Kendall Stratton approaching. He was wearing a spotted tie in this year's colours and a blue ultrasuede jacket. His face blared with the certainty of a man who owned a motel and two fried-chicken franchises and had parlayed that into a seat in cabinet.

Stratton nodded to her as he stepped up. "Mrs. Becker. Looking lovely as usual." He turned to John and said, "Looking forward to the chicken tonight? Don't drop a piece on the floor or it might bounce back up on your lap. I should have brought a basket of my own. All these brown faces on the serving staff, they probably don't know the difference between a juicy piece of fried chicken and the stuff they feed the crowds here."

Becker said, "Jealousy doesn't become you, Ken."

"Hell, I don't care if this hotel does more business than my little operations. I've got enough to get by with. And I can afford to be more picky about who I hire. More picky than the RCMP, anyway."

"Someday you'll be happy to see those folks coming into your stores. A customer is a customer."

"Maybe. But I hope I've sold out by then. Want to make enough on the deal to set myself up in a sunny place in Mexico. I hear there's a little colony of retirees from this part of the world starting to form down there."

"Amazing the Mexicans will let in all those white faces."

"They don't care about the colour of the faces. Only about the colour of the money we bring with us."

Arlene considered the colour of his perfectly symmetrical false teeth, tinted off-white just enough to avoid a dazzling brightness. She caught herself staring and looked away.

Stratton pulled a chair over from a nearby table, leaned closer and spoke in a lower voice: "You hear about cabinet in the morning?"

"No. A meeting? On a Thursday morning?"

"I've been asked to spread the word but Waschuk will be in touch with you to make sure. Just half a dozen of us. Notice a peculiar smell in the air before you came into the hotel?"

"Not to speak of. The usual downtown mix of exhaust fumes and a bit of garbage."

"You will by the time dinner's over. A faint aroma of rotten eggs. A sour gas well blew out near Broken Pines. It's an old railway whistle stop a couple of hours' drive west. Sounds pretty bad. The well's a big producer. The gas caught fire. Between one thing and another it could be burning a week or two before it's capped. That's two weeks of news stories about people gagging on the smell and everyone asking why we aren't regulating better so that these things don't happen. The boss wants to get on top of it first thing in the morning. We'll have to control the news flow and set up communication channels so that we're first to know of any developments."

Becker said that sounded like the right response.

"Anyway," Stratton said, "a morning meeting is a good reason to get out of here early. Between the chicken and the boring crowd this is one of those times you wonder why cabinet salaries aren't higher."

Arlene fought back an urge to ask why he'd need a higher salary when he already had enough to plan an escape to Mexico. She studied her bread plate and water glass as Stratton went on.

"That's just today's crisis. We gotta do something about the way this country's getting taken over. I mean, turbans on RCMP officers? Next it'll be forcing the Queen to record her Christmas message in French as well as in English. I know you're kind of on the fence about it but me and a couple of others have an idea for a court case. I'd like to talk to you about it. Not here. Want to step over to the Palm Court as soon as dinner is finished? They've got some American trumpeter playing there tonight. I know you like jazz, and a trumpet will be loud enough that no one will be able to overhear us."

Becker thought for a second and then said he'd walk over ten minutes after dessert was finished. That was staying long enough to count as a respectable attendance at a charity event.

"See you a little later, then," Stratton said as he stood up. "Nice to see you Mrs. Becker."

She nodded to him as he turned to leave. Then she said to her husband, "You didn't ask me if I wanted to stay here instead. Or does he expect me to stay anyway and leave you boys to your private talk?"

"I don't think Kendall cares one way or another. I'd be happy if you'd come along. In fact, I'd be interested to hear what you think about whatever idea he and the others are cooking up."

Arlene smiled at a couple walking two tables away as she said, "Even the jazz would probably be more interesting. I might walk over for that. The blowout sounds serious. Oil just makes a mess. Sour gas is dangerous."

"The politics are probably more serious," he said. "Billy wants things to quiet down for a few months. This won't help his plans."

"Will a court challenge about RCMP uniforms help his plans?"

"We'll see about whether to go ahead with that. But it ought to be entertaining to hear what the boys have in mind. Maybe they ought to have uniforms of their own—lumberjack jackets, and baseball caps with oil company logos on them."

He looked over to the table holding the paintings and wine that would be going up for auction after dinner. The town was getting sophisticated.

Furyk stepped quietly into view and sat down. He still looked tentative. Arlene turned to him and said, "Tell me, Mr. Furyk, have you lived here long? I haven't seen you at events like this before."

"Oh, I've been running a small auto glass business for years. Finally got far enough ahead that I thought I could start supporting some of the people who do good work around the community."

"You're here by yourself?"

"That's right. Mrs. Furyk died two years ago. I didn't like to go out by myself at first but I'm starting to get used to it. You can't shut yourself up from the world."

She said, "Oh, I'm sorry to hear that."

"Don't worry. Can't be helped."

"Still, it must be a trial, and a shock. I hope you've recovered well."

Becker heard their words droning on and began registering what they were saying. He looked at his wife. From the side and little behind he could see her concentrating on Furyk with her head inclined slightly forward, the way she looked when she took something seriously. He remembered that he had fallen in love with her because somewhere in the depth of her countryside aristocratic bearing he had seen a glow of empathy. He saw it again now, almost a visible warm light behind the glitter of her diamond earrings.

They sat through the event responding automatically to a well-established routine—politely warm applause for the university president, careful handling of plates and bowls by the wait staff to avoid splashing sauce on their clothes, friendly nods to familiar faces, neutral conversation with the strangers at their table, discreet glances at watches after dessert to determine when leaving would not be rude.

"Would you rather walk over Palm Court or drive?" Becker asked.

"Drive if you think there will be parking spaces," Arlene replied. "These aren't really walking shoes."

They drove to the lot half a block from the club and walked to the door. Arlene said, "You won't need me to talk to Stratton. It looked as if he wants to discuss business anyway. I think I'll take a stroll to the outlook and take in the night view of the river."

"All right. It will probably be dull. I see Santa in there with Stratton. They may feel more comfortable talking at that if we're not there together. You'll be missing Phil Woods, though. You won't be cold?"

"The wrap will be sufficient. If I get chilly I'll come back to the club but take a seat away from your table if it looks like you're still dealing with weighty and secret affairs."

She turned and strolled away, glancing up occasionally to see how many stars were visible despite the glow from the city lights.

Becker pulled the door open and felt the gust of warmer air and the almost physical force of the trumpet notes carried on thick waves of drum and bass vibrations. He skirted past two tables to one on the far side, occupied so far by Stratton and by Santa, known more formally as Claus Ellerman. He didn't look at the crowd because he was absorbed once again by the contrast of the strangest pair of friends in cabinet. Stratton was broad and shiny like a 1956 Oldsmobile, right down to the row of false teeth that looked like a chrome grille. Ellerman was a stringy, tall farmer from the dry lands in the southeast. His constituents and fellow legislators in the party called him Santa because of his skill in wresting money out of the capital budget for community halls, roads, rinks, hospital improvements, water infrastructure and anything else that might satisfy voters that they were listened to and respected. But the nickname was a standing joke as well, and not just because he was tight-fisted with any spending beyond the borders of his constituency. Ellerman was not just thin, he was skinny. His round eyes perched over sunken cheeks that stretched down to a small mouth gathered in what looked like a perpetual pout. The funereal effect made his frequent jokes endlessly surprising, even to those used to hearing them.

"Hello, John," he said, turning but not getting up. "Ken is just educating me about jazz. He knows a lot about it. I understand he has the best collection of Glenn Miller records in cabinet."

That sort of remark often had people feeling off balance with Ellerman. Becker decided not to ask if he was joking. Instead, he said, "I understand you've had a rough week. Getting Fincher's car towed out of the parking lot must have taken some effort."

"Just a phone call. When you're minister of infrastructure help is just a phone call away. Fincher wasn't happy but he had no business parking up on the surface. He has an underground spot with all the free car washes he wants. If he wants a surface spot right outside the door too he can ask me. But he won't. He knows I know he lent his car to his kid for a trip up to Yellowknife. He got the government to pay for the damage when the kid hit a deer and skidded into a ditch. He owes the public about eight thousand dollars."

Becker smiled. "I hadn't heard about that."

"It happened. Early this summer. Just because he's provincial treasurer doesn't give him the right to decide his ministerial vehicle is covered for whatever damage he inflicts on it."

"Has he done anything else?"

"You mean aside from being a general run-off-at-the-mouth smart boy? I wouldn't be surprised. But he had no business parking in that surface lot. Those who transgress must accept having to do penance."

Becker remembered the fuss during the previous election when Ellerman had decided to put up his own signs rather than the ones printed by the party. The Ellerman signs read: "Waste not, want not." The other side of Santa Claus.

The music stopped and Shaw introduced the next tune. Becker asked himself how long it had been since he'd seen a live jazz performance, how long it had been since he had moved from the electrically charged atmosphere of the States to this oil and cattle country where even the cities felt rural, how long it had been since he had experienced a moment of peace or pleasure without feeling a wash of ache and anger in the background. He glanced out the front window to see if Arlene was still in sight.

She was not. She had walked away from the club past the old McPherson church and along the line of poplars leading to the small widening of the sidewalk that served as a viewing point over the river. She pressed against the black iron railing and gazed across the valley. The lights of the taller new apartment buildings and condominiums hung silently in the air on the other side. They reminded her of people going about their business, oblivious to anyone who might be watching them. A cluster of old houses and brick buildings that once held small businesses lay scattered on the flat bank on the near side of the river. The old iron bridge crossed the valley nearly a kilometre off toward the right. She recalled reading a description of how it had been built. She could not remember when she read it but knew it was the first time she had come across the words "boxed girder." The river itself wound through the deep valley, a dark path hidden from the surround-ing prairie land. The lights from the new buildings high on the upper banks cast faint reflected lines on the water's surface. They weren't strong enough to illuminate the flowing water. Whenever she looked at the river, Arlene sometimes thought about its source up in the mountains. Some of the water came from rain but some originated in a glacier. It was the melted legacy of unimaginable cold and pressure from ten or eleven thousand years in the past. She could not see the current and eddies in the night darkness but she could picture the relentless flow in her mind's eye.

Footsteps tapped softly on the sidewalk toward her right. She did not turn to look. They kept sounding closer and stopped. She still did not look, wondering now but not worried because whoever it was had stopped off to one side and not directly behind her. Then she heard a familiar voice.

"Arlene. Taking the night air? Or taking in the view?"

Now she turned halfway. "Hello, Frank. A little of both. You?"

"I suppose you could say a little of both for me as well. I look at the university over there and think about how much it has changed over the years. All those new buildings. All the old houses taken down to make room for them. So many new students, more all the time. Yet the spirit remains the same, or should as long as the people responsible take care to preserve it."

Arlene looked toward the lights of the university buildings, dim fluorescent glows behind the silhouette of the old railway bridge.

"The past always has something worth saving," she said. "The question is always what part of it is worth saving. I remember some of your colleagues saying there was no real Canadian literature worth studying. They even fought against the establishment of a Canadian literature course. No one would try to make that case now. We're all better for the change. I wonder still which side you were on."

"The sides in a quarrel can be ephemeral. The continuity of the institution is what's important."

"And when you give advice to ministers, is that how you put it? Do you say any decision is right as long as it supports survival of the government?"

"The cabinet ministers usually have that thought uppermost in their minds before a discussion even starts. But it's true I'd be foolish to urge them to take many risks. Or to turn a blind eye if I saw any of them pursuing a risky path."

She turned away from the river to look at him squarely again. "You didn't stop here for idle reminiscing, did you? Are you even here by accident? Or did you see me coming here? Were you watching from someplace in the club?"

"I was there. Not conspicuously. Keeping up with the latest cultural advances in the city. I did see you and John at the window and thought about how long it's been since you and I had a talk, just the two of us."

"Have you missed that?"

"You were always stimulating, a breath of fresh air."

"Congratulations. Another question dodged. How many thousand are you at now?"

They stared at each other. Clicks of stiletto heels broke the silence. Two women with dark eyeshadow, hair piled high and skirts hemmed higher walked by. They headed toward the hooker stroll four blocks west. Jeffries looked around and sighed. The corners of his mouth slid down.

"So much for culture," Arlene said. "Building it up must be a struggle here."

"Ah well," he said, "Boswell was consorting with prostitutes when he wasn't recording nearly every word that Samuel Johnson uttered. That hasn't dimmed his reputation much. Being careless about reputation is never a good idea, though. Some things are winked at, others cause damage."

"Not if they never come to light," she said.

He hesitated and went on, "John seems to take a perfunctory attitude toward the province's reputation. He does his job but no more. Something may be developing that could be significant. I have to attend to it. I don't think he would actively frustrate my taking care of the situation. But he seems to have his own priorities. They may inadvertently get in the way of higher priorities."

"Not your own personal ones. You mean, of course, the priorities that should be followed for the good of the province."

"Exactly."

"You didn't follow me here for old times' sake." She half-smiled as she said it, more to herself than to him.

"A small project is going on," he said. "It's in the nature of a review of artistic material. I think something potentially dangerous may be in the material. But I also have reason to believe it's now in the hands of a man who is not to be trusted. John has the man under observation but I think John is looking for something else, something I don't know about. It would be best if John were kept apart from the review until it is finished. Ideally, it would be best if I knew what has attracted his interest. But I should at least have a clear field to concentrate on finding what is really important in the material."

"You want me to spy on my husband, and to steer him in a direction that suits your interests."

"The best interests of the province."

"And just how am I to go about getting him to volunteer information about this secret project? And then to divulge whatever private interest he has in it?"

Jeffries smiled with a regretful small tilt of his head to the right. "It's only a matter of possibilities, of course. But if he should express annoyance at anything in the next few days, perhaps you might lend him a sympathetic ear, be a willing support to him. He may even begin to tell you more if he thinks you are the one person he can count on to be on his side. He may be lonely."

She let that pass. With Frank Jeffries it was best to let every little provocation, every probing needle pass. "And then?" she said.

"It would be a natural event for the deputy minister of Culture to have lunch or tea sometime with one of the city's leading supporters of cultural organizations."

The corners of her mouth drew up, making her look amused again. "And if I politely declined?"

"That would not necessarily be disastrous but neither would it be a help to the province."

"And if I told you to go jump in the river?"

"That would not help either. Nor would it be a way to remember old friendship."

Her face remained unchanged but her voice hardened: "Friendship? Is that your story now? I remember what you did to me. You didn't call it friendship then. You exploited a young co-ed and you called it more than friendship then."

"You were hardly innocent and defenceless. And it was hardly the only relationship ever struck between a professor and a student."

"No, it wasn't. I got over it. Maybe I knew all along it was a passing thing and your attention would wander when the next year's class walked into your lecture room. No, what made it different was what I figured out several years later. There was no shortage of pretty, eager sophomores willing to accept a lot of attention and more from a professor who'd published two books and had spent a year at Oxford. Why me? Out of five or possibly even ten other possibilities? I admit I was flattered and it took years to realize it wasn't any personal quality that attracted you. It was my name. My father's standing in the province. Oil and cattle meant prestige. And prestige was what attracted you. Your own family was never grand enough to suit your image of yourself. If you couldn't have your own oil wells and own cattle ranch you could have them vicariously. Was the idea of being associated with them enough? Or did you actually think of creating a formal link like one of those diplomatic marriages that old royalty used to arrange? Did you actually dream of marrying into a family with a name as well as money? And probably getting out with a divorce a few years later?"

He had gone from the hint of a wry smile, to letting his mouth sag open with a look of pain from an unfair attack, to a neutral expression, head tilted back ever so slightly in a pose of gravitas and self-possession in the face of gathering hysteria.

"Arlene." He paused. "I won't try to convince you of anything. The essential point is this. I need to have something done to protect the reputation of the province. God knows there are few enough people now in the government with a firm grasp of we mean to the life of this country. Of how important it is to preserve our example and leadership. You of all people, with your background, should understand that. Your husband may or may not get in the way but it's best to keep him as far removed as possible. If he does get in the way and a disaster results, the consequences for him would be unpleasant."

"You're forgetting something," she said. "I haven't spent all these years helping build his political career only to watch it go up in smoke. And I've been building ties to the community. They aren't as numerous as yours. They could well be more relevant. You've been wielding authority in your little corner of the world long enough to lose track of who's where on the scale of importance. Don't threaten John. That will threaten me too and you'll be surprised at what will happen. I'm not a young undergrad now."

Jeffries listened without changing expression. "I've told you how things stand," he said.

She was not finished. "Just how good is your memory of old times, Frank?"

"Good enough," he smiled.

"Do you remember Walter Melnychuk?"

Now he hesitated before answering. "That poor boy who hanged himself partway through his final year?"

"That poor boy who told one of his friends he was confused about his sexual identity. He used to have tea with you. I would have thought you would remember him better. Was it just the co-eds you used to flatter with your attention, and then offer them more?"

He pursed his lips while keeping his gaze steadily on her for two seconds, five seconds, ten seconds as she stared back. Finally he said, "You're in deep water, Arlene. Sharks swim there."

He looked her up and down as if considering her for the first time. Then he turned and walked back toward the parking lot beside the club. She watched him for a few seconds, listening to the steady tap of his leather shoes, and turned back to the river. After a few minutes, long enough that she thought he would have reached his car, she walked back to the club. She felt a flatness inside her as if she could not get her lungs properly inflated with each breath.

Along the way she passed the old United Church again. It had been named after one of the early missionaries in the territory. She thought about the audacity of early arrivals—deliberately seeking a place in a far and winter-hardened land for the purpose of trading for furs, or starting a small farm, or converting strangers to a foreign religion. The red bricks of the church wall were developing a smooth, glazed surface after seven decades of exposure to weather and vehicle exhaust. Yet they had stood up well. She thought she had shown more audacity with Jeffries than she had ever tried with anyone. And that she could learn to use it, cautiously, just as well as her great-grandparents had done when they also had come out to this place of glorious summers and killing winter cold.

She opened the door of the club and found John and his two colleagues. They were talking casually while looking at the quartet on stage, so she assumed that whatever business had taken place had been completed. She joined them and talked long enough to be polite. John knew she would be wanting to leave and had no reason to stay longer himself. They said their goodbyes and walked to the car.

About forty minutes later they were approaching the acreage. Through openings in the stands of poplar and birch and spruce, sloughs reflected the moonlight and the lights of acreage homes. Most of them were ranch-style bungalows but occasionally there were two-storey statements of new wealth. John had said little during the drive and she had not tried to talk with him. Near their driveway, he spoke.

"It looks like I'm going to Broken Pines the day after tomorrow. I'll have to meet the premier first but apparently they think I'm just the smooth talker to be out there for the government. I'm supposed to monitor the well capping and talk to the media every day. The drilling company is bringing in a bunch of Texans to put out the fire and stop the gas. I suppose I ought to be flattered but I don't see why it's a job for the culture minister. Industry or Energy would have been more logical, I would have thought."

Arlene said, "Are you going to ask why they're giving the job to you?"

"I will, but I already have a good idea from Santa. The priorities committee met this evening and decided I was the best fit because I get along with the media and I used to be in Industry. Not a job for rookies, it seems. Santa did say it sounded as if someone had already put the notion into Billy's head before the meeting."

She watched the trees, the sloughs, and the fields surrounded by horse fences slide by. She asked whether he would be gone more than three or four days. He said it could be closer to a week because the capping job was going to be complicated. That was why an experienced crew was being brought in from outside. But he would make sure it was no longer than a week and would start trying to spring himself after three days.

"You'll be all right on your own?" he asked.

"Yes, I'm used to it. I'll take good care of the dogs."

"I guess you may have some meetings in town, and there's June to come over for coffee."

"I'll get by."

"And there's that young Nicaraguan to keep you company. It seems like there's no shortage of work for him to do around the place."

"Yes," she said, looking out the window. He worked his lower lip under his front teeth, wondering why he had not been able to bite it before blurting out something he knew he should not say.

"I suppose you'll have enough to do and enough other people around to keep you company," she said.

"I suppose," he said. "It doesn't matter. I'm used to being on my own, too."

16.

IN THE BRIGHT EARLY SUN THE SPRUCE TREES LINING THE highway reminded Becker of green marble. Their needles had a hard sheen. He listened to the hum of the tires as he looked out the window, bored because one of the security staff was driving.

He would rather have been in a small plane anyway. He regretted that the well site was not far enough away to justify a flight. Night flying was best. He liked the glow from the dials on the cockpit panel. In a twin-engine, there was usually a radar screen too. All the onboard lights were reassuring. However dark the sky, however much cloud was obscuring yard lights from the farms below and the islands of light from scattered towns, the lights on the panel, the numbers and lines on the gauges, said everything was fine. He knew others did not trust small air-craft. He did. The steady buzz of the engine was like a recurring promise. The thin sheets of metal and acrylic windows making up the plane's body enclosed a safe platform from which to view the unpredictable world.

"We should be there in ten minutes," the pilot said.

"All right, thanks." Becker did not start any further conversation. Underneath the boredom he felt a nagging—what? Not worry. Not curiosity. A feeling of something not quite right, something not squared up.

A security man picked him up at the bare-bones airstrip. They drove into Broken Pines past dull Quonsets with backhoes and BobCats parked outside, past a Shell station, then past a small, light blue box of a building with a "Sears Agency" sign in one window and a "Greyhound" sign in the other, and a café with a few pickups angle-parked out front. They stopped outside the Elks Hall where Stratton had arranged to set up a communication headquarters. Becker got out of the car, stretched his back and legs, and saw only two people on the sidewalk further along the block. The media would be here soon filling up space like a flock of geese, he thought.

Stratton was already inside. He had established a private space in a small room. Coffee was ready. They began laying out the agenda for the first day.

"The Texans won't be talking to the media," Stratton said. "That guy Winton who runs their show is a sour old bastard. He says he won't waste time with reporters. Doesn't want us interfering by hanging around the operation either. Doesn't want a bunch of cameras out there. And doesn't want any local help because his men are the best and he wants only the best. All he wants is another notch in his reputation and more money."

"Best to let him stay out of sight then," Becker said. "Sounds like we don't have to pump up his ego. Is he even going to keep us up to date on how his team's progressing?"

"He'll brief my constituency president about mid-afternoon each day. That's Gary Hofstra. Gary runs a well servicing company. Winton liked that. He said that way he'll have at least some hope that someone will understand what he's saying and he's going to say it only once."

"Not ideal timing. We'll probably miss the evening newscasts. We could end up being nearly twenty-four hours late with any updates as far as the evening newscasts."

"Can't be helped. But the way this is going to go, there won't be much rapid change from day to day. Just gradually getting closer to securing the cap and putting out the flames."

Becker sipped his coffee and looked out the doorway at the drab greenish walls of the hall.

"I've already had the marching orders," he said. "Report steady progress. Be reassuring. Tell the frightened public that the fumes and whatever unburnt gas is still escaping won't kill their pet cats or give their kids lifelong asthma. I hope they don't notice it's all a piss-poor excuse for actually getting the capping done."

"Heck of a thing, isn't it? We think we're getting into politics to take care of taxes and schools, build a few hospitals and roads. Then we find out we spend half our time being psychologists for a bunch of scared sheep."

"Why Kendall, you usually show respect for the voters. I probably hear you talk about the grassroots more than anyone in caucus."

"It isn't like running a business," Stratton said. "Customers are always right. Voters? Sometimes they have to be shown what's right. Gary will be here in half an hour to tell you what you need to know for today's press show. Don't look at his left hand. He's missing a finger. Not unusual around here but he's been moaning about it since he got it crushed in one of his machines three years ago. He's lucky he didn't lose them all but he carries on like no one else has ever had that happen. Hate to think what he'd be like if he lost a leg. You may as well stay here for now. The motel was full this morning and won't be able to let you check in until later."

Becker sipped more of his watery coffee and was happy he'd brought along two long briefings he'd wanted to read, and the latest Larry McMurtry novel. He saw Stratton eyeing him speculatively and cocked his head to indicate a question.

Stratton seemed to want to think over whatever he had in mind. He let out a breath through his nostrils, and said, "Do you know how you ended up with this job?" Becker didn't see any need to reply. His answer was apparently going to be wrong.

"Waschuk recommended you. That isn't strange. What's strange is I heard the boss mention that Frank Jeffries initially came up with the idea and planted it with Waschuk. Now why do you suppose he would want to do that?"

Becker pursed his lips, pulled them apart with a smack and kept his tongue between his front teeth as he stared through a window at the uncertain sky. He thought about laughing it off by saying "Frank always appreciates talent." He didn't have to as Hofstra walked in.

Stratton introduced them. The talk veered off toward the stuck-up nature of the firefighting crew, then toward how much good effect the government could achieve by enhancing its tax credits for well drilling. They agreed the Texans would have to be lived with. Tax credits were more complicated but it was clear Hofstra was not looking for anything like commitment; he was just planting an idea.

The day passed slowly. Becker had a sandwich in the hall later on and was sitting with Stratton when Hofstra came in. Becker avoided looking at the injured hand but found his gaze drifting away from Hofstra's slightly hooded eyes, wary eyes magnified behind thick lenses. The slightly upturned corner of Hofstra's mouth fell one condescension short of a smirk. Hofstra said the briefing for reporters was set up for 3:30 on the road to the well site. He added, "Quite the production. Looks like you're the import TV star brought in to comment on the foreign well crew. I guess the rest of us from 'round here can just sit back and put our feet up and watch the show."

Becker squelched the urge to look at Hofstra's thick waist and comment that sitting back with feet up in front of a TV seemed to be par for the course in Broken Pines. Instead he said, "We'll hope it's a good one for the audience the next few days. This town depends on a lot of steady tourist traffic. It doesn't want to get known as the place with the sour gas well blowout that couldn't be stopped." The two men traded aloof stares until Stratton began talking about how much he depended on Hofstra's fine work with the local organization.

Afterward, Becker had the security man drive him to the motel that would be his home for the next few days. He emptied his suitcase into the dresser and the closet. Then he lay down on the bed, resting his eyes after looking through the windshield glare on the drive out, and testing how much mattress sag he would have to put up with. He was half surprised to find a regular smooth bedspread rather than one made of chenille.

He closed his eyes but did not sleep. He knew Jeffries would go along with keeping photos of the Roussel house out of circulation and preferably destroyed. It was strange that Jeffries seemed to regard that business as little more than a passing irritation, just a tick more annoying than having lettuce stuck in his teeth. But Waschuk was handling it. Not even Jeffries had ever said anything about Waschuk being incompetent. Yet the old snake had wanted him out of the way. To do what? For what private agenda?

And then he drifted, and started thinking about his own private plans. And drifted more, as he knew he would, as he had become used to doing month after month and year after year—to the point where he no longer knew whether he was circling back to the same obsession out of compulsion or out of secret and painful pleasure. Or out of guilt.

He saw her lying on the concrete sidewalk, one leg splayed out onto the asphalt road, blood seeping incredibly quickly and pooling out from under her back. He had imagined it thousands of times now, each detail set in place and refined until everything was in the place he thought it must have been in real life. He had never seen a picture of her lying dead, only dying. The television camera had missed the moment she was hit but recorded her life draining away. Two other students tried to keep her talking. One of them was trying to compress the wound and slow the flow of blood and had largely blocked the camera's view. He knew the scene well enough from the many times the tape had shown up on TV over the years. He had seen it over and over. Then he had reconstructed it more fully in his own mind. He had talked to two of the students who had been there, listening to the way their shock had turned to numbness as they described the National Guardsmen aiming rifles from down the street. And he had listened to their memory, half distrusted by him but insistent on their part, that a nondescript, shortish man with brushy, slightly greying hair had been at the scene with a 35mm camera. And finally, when he studied the tape carefully as he saw it replayed one night, he saw a nondescript, shortish man well back in the crowd carrying what looked like it might be a camera.

He sat up quickly, forcing himself to move and think about what he had to do now. He opened the green curtains, wondering how much dust would puff into the air if he shook them. The sky was still grey. Good, he thought. Less contrast to dramatize the televised images of the plume of smoke rising out of the fire at the well.

Stratton's dark blue Mercury Grand Marquis pulled up in front of the motel room. Becker picked up his jacket and walked out. He turned to close the door and turned back to see the car's passenger door opening. Stratton was at the wheel. Hofstra and the security man were in back. They drove out of town in silence.

Stratton turned south off the highway after a few minutes. Nearly twenty kilometres down a gravel road, they stopped at a roadside clearing where two government Jeeps were parked. An assistant deputy minister from the Renewable Resources ministry introduced himself. He had thinning hair and his lips were compressed by the weight of responsibility when he wasn't talking. He briefed Becker on the situation. Essentially, the story was that the crew was gathering the material and equipment to put out the fire but that step might take two days, depending on the state of the wellhead. After that, it could take another three days to remove twisted and blackened metal, set a new wellhead in place, and turn off the gas flow. Meanwhile, everyone downwind could be assured that toxic fumes were being widely dispersed by the prevailing west wind and no one's health was in danger.

"What about people with asthma or emphysema or unusual allergies?" Becker asked.

"The guys from Health say everyone should be okay. Of course, people with respiratory or other special concerns may want to stay indoors. They should also be urged to call their doctor if they feel any difficulty breathing."

"Then it's not all okay."

"For the general population it is. We haven't heard of any problems so far for people with specific concerns."

Becker let the vagueness slide, knowing it was all he would get for today, even if he was a cabinet minister: "Time to get this show on the road. Where are the camera trucks?"

"Down the road about a kilometre. They're about two kilometres from the well site."

The short convoy rumbled down the road, vehicles spaced far enough apart to avoid most of the gravel spraying up from the tires. A handful of open spaces between the trees showed the foothills rising dark green out toward the west. To the south, dark smoke rushed into the pale sky, a dense column close to the ground, widening into a smear spreading out toward the east with the prevailing wind.

They stopped at a small clearing where a dirt road met the gravel. Becker assumed the smaller road was used service trucks headed to another well site. The junction could also be a turn-around point for snow clearing equipment.

The usual three camera trucks were already there. The reporters, already getting anxious about deadlines, gathered as the government people stepped out of their vehicles. A Resources Department communication director Becker knew as Cindy quickly set out the ground rules. Becker delivered his five sentences of update and the questions began.

He had been at the job long enough to know that the details mattered little as long as he didn't say anything dumb. He noted that Cindy had set up the cameras and positioned him so that people would not see a roiling column of black smoke behind him.

He also had his back to the surrounding bush so that they could not get behind him. The purpose was to look calm and attentive.

The words in the opening statement he'd been given included references to "flow rate" and "particles per million" and "well within guidelines." The point was not the technical information but Becker's serious but easy manner, the visual sense that here was someone who knew what was going on and could be trusted. He was an economist but he still had a lot of Wisconsin dairy farm in him. He had enough experience in politics now to know that being chosen to handle the task was a plausible decision. He also knew that plausibility was often a trap.

He forced his mind to snap back to business. No leeway here for a mistake. But as he answered the last two questions his gaze focused less on the reporters and more on the insistent black pillar looming behind them. It was out of the cameras' view but squarely in his—an intrusion, a thing out of place, inspiring fear with its lazy and uninterrupted flow into the sky, a puffy scar on the green surface of the pine and spruce forest.

One question more. Becker explained the premier would not be coming out to view the blowout because there was no need. The situation was being handled by competent experts; the incident would not measure up to the two fabled oil-well blowouts that occurred right after the modern industry had got underway in the 1940s. The message: we've handled worse situations, and you can't even tell now where they happened. He hadn't looked at Cindy, knowing he was delivering the goods and not needing reassurance.

Yet he found his mind wandering again as he finished. What was he doing out here at the fringe of the boreal forest, talking to television cameras as if he'd made that his life work since he'd been in high school? How had that become part of him? In one way he was not surprised. He had noticed recently that most people, even those chosen randomly by reporters for "average person" comments, seemed comfortable with a lens pointed at them and a microphone held in front of them. Not like the early days. He remembered that well into the early 1960s ordinary people and politicians alike had talked in stilted phrasing when being filmed for the news. They hesitated over words, and spoke more loudly than normal. They acted as if they were talking on a quavering long-distance telephone line. Now he never saw that. When had people changed? How had it happened? Did it mean that television had become another familiar tool, internalized the way that steering a car went from being a conscious task to being a set of almost automatic reflexes?

As the camera operators put their equipment away and the trucks started back to town he told the others he wanted to walk up the gravel road toward the fire crew's barricade. He thought he should get as close to source of the unending smoke as possible. As he walked he thought more about how the electronic web that people lived in had changed.

The images themselves had changed—from film, sometimes second-rate in its picture and sound quality, to smooth videotape. The first shows he could remember seeing had presented ghostly images of the past. He remembered Westerns and adventure serials that had been made in the 1930s and brought back nearly twenty years later to fill screens and the imaginations of young minds. He remembered cookie-cutter comedies, and variety shows featuring what he had later come to realize were recycled vaudeville stars. He had watched game shows, and news and weather programs that followed predictable formulas and featured avuncular men, and movies that gradually came ever closer to the current time. He remembered the original three-part *Davy Crockett* story on the Disney show. Amazing, he thought, how people still regarded it as a cultural phenomenon but missed its real significance. It had taught a generation of young people that heroes rebelled against authority, that the way to decide on a moral choice could be summed up in Crockett's words: "Be sure you're right, then go ahead."

And then it had been as if television had chewed through all the past images and styles and had caught up with the present. That had happened most visibly on the ABC network, which began running shows like *77 Sunset Strip*. But the trend quickly spread to other networks that began running other shows that seemed contemporary, like *Route 66* and *The Twilight Zone.*

And then had come a lurch in time, as if television had used up the present too and was starting to drag people into the future. He remembered watching the *NBC Nightly News* with sober Chet Huntley and impishly wry David Brinkley. He thought that was what sparked his interest in politics. Their show had something of the vibrant modernism and awareness of changing times that people felt from the Kennedy presidency. Such impressions turned out to be only tentative. Both Kennedy and the news show were still entangled with venerable institutions, with the past.

Yet the future was just around the corner. It was uncaring. It was not as ugly as the temporary absence of civilization during the Second World War but it showed things could get that bad again because the future did not care. The break came around 1963 and 1964. He remembered getting a queasy feeling from a report on the Huntley-Brinkley show about unrest with blacks' economic prospects in northern cities; it was clear the heroic struggle for civil rights in the South would be part of a much more complicated and intractable struggle.

He remembered the way he and his friends had reacted to the cancellation of fresh, eye-opening series like *It's a Man's World* and *The Richard Boone Show.* Middle-brow tastes and corporate need for money had said there was no room, not even a small corner, on television for new ideas. If you wanted something that felt like a future built on new ideas you could buy a Bob Dylan album. The future being foreshadowed on television was Richard Nixon.

He remembered the Kennedy assassination and the live-TV shooting of Lee Harvey Oswald—the one a grim reminder of the world's ugliness and the other a harbinger of a time when you might see anything on television, old restraints gone, even the privacy of death gone. The televised Kennedy funeral procession was a decorous hold-over of traditions. Oswald's murder—death on live television—was the future.

And then, Vietnam. On television. Night after night of young men in helmets marching or running through tall grass. Some marching or running to their deaths. Helicopters. Rifles and machine guns firing at targets the camera couldn't see. Medics holding IV bags. Vietnamese peasants watching the grind of war all around them and hoping it would pass them by but knowing it would bring some of them to their deaths. Company and platoon commanders talking about writing letters to the families of young men who had died ugly deaths. One of them was sent to the parents of Grayson, whom he'd known since they pedalled tricycles down the sidewalk together and traded *Donald Duck* comic books. Grayson killed by mortar fire, body shredded—how badly and in how many places never known, because never seen other than by his platoon mates and medics. Only dead. Only remembered with the promise: "Someday, someone will pay." But no one had paid. Not the bankers and politicians who had wanted to stop communism but whose sons had somehow got medical or student deferments.

The only one who had paid was the girl lying in her own blood on the sidewalk. And the man who shot her had not paid either. Another criminal with a face unseen. He had gone into politics to make someone pay for Grayson but had somehow ended up in this place at the edge of the northern forests where Vietnam was only a word. Someone had to pay for something—if not for Grayson then for the girl. If he didn't make someone pay for something, then what was he living for? To hand out cheques and make cliché-filled speeches? To build up one more year of pension service while he put off actually doing something? And now here he was, the momentary TV star for the government of a place he had barely heard of before he moved to it. Was television dissolving him too?

He heard a crow cawing and brought himself back. The faint rumble and hiss of the blowout slid back into his awareness. He saw again the spruce and pine and underbrush growing out of the muddy brown dirt and wondered how he could have been staring at it all without registering what he was seeing. He felt sweat on his back and chest underneath his fleece vest and turned and walked back to the vehicles, listening to the crunch of the gravel and feeling his hiking boots slide a millimetre or two as they pressed loose surface stones down into the road's firmer layer beneath. Tomorrow would be time enough to walk up to the barricade nearer the well.

Back in Stratton's car he didn't talk much. Stratton told him that Cindy thought the session with the cameras had gone well. "Good," he said, and looked out the side window at the treetops flitting by against the unmoving leaden cloud cover. At the edge of town, Stratton said, "You've got three choices for supper here—Greek, Chinese, or burgers." Becker thought a couple of seconds and said, "Let's try Chinese tonight, Greek tomorrow."

He stopped at his motel first to splash cold water on his face, thought about changing his shirt but decided not to, and read for nearly an hour before Stratton returned to pick him up and drive to the restaurant. They took a table against a side wall, cutting down the number of potential eavesdroppers around them. The meal was a touch better than he expected, the sticky and sweet sauce offset by vegetables that still retained some crispness. Stratton told stories about running fast-food operations, lowering his voice when he talked about the difficulties of choosing whose kids to hire.

As they talked, the stations back in the capital ran tape from the roadside on their evening news shows. Morehead and Waschuk watched appreciatively, each in their own homes but both thinking the item had been a good first step. Jeffries saw both the performance he'd expected and confirmation that Becker was away for at least two days, then poured himself a scotch and opened his volume on the paintings of Gustav Klimt. Rabani half paid attention as he hurried through an unappetizing meal, and wondered what legal liabilities might emerge from the blowout. Ginny Radescu didn't watch the evening news; she had a tuna salad before going out to the studio for her Jazzercize class. Jack Ostroski wasn't watching either; he was holding his razor blade between a thick forefinger and thumb, slicing a new pocket for negatives in the matte where he'd stored the other negatives. This time he was not sure why photos of an old politician who had been turned into a figurehead were important. The prints were already reasonably safe under the linoleum in the back room. Roberto Morales did not normally look at the evening news but caught a bit this time as his sister watched while waiting for their dinner to heat up. He noted that the announcer said Becker would be staying at Broken Pines to monitor the blowout.

17.

THE NEXT MORNING DID NOT HAVE A MOMENT THAT COULD be called daybreak. A dull light gradually spread and partially bleached the sky from dark to light grey. The hazy sun looked more like the moon.

Morales listened to the tool box bounce occasionally on the floorboard to his right. The dull metallic clanks of the wrenches and screwdrivers inside kept him company as he drove down the highway east of the capital. He didn't like listening to the radio in the morning. The CBC was full of airy-fairy talk, and the private stations were too breezy and loud for that time of day.

He wondered if she listened to the radio, and whether it would make any difference to how he thought about her. A real woman. Not like the girls he remembered from his childhood. Not like the hard-eyed women who hung around with his friends. Someone with more like the elegance and manners he remembered among his mother's friends. Someone he would have grown up to deserve and have if Nicaragua had stayed the same, the kind of woman he had dreamed about during nights in the jungle. The full woman he deserved now that he was a man, but also the kind and measured one who might dissolve his unfocused anger and answer his questions.

He left the highway and several minutes later turned the white truck into the Beckers' driveway. The gravel crunched under the tires as he pulled up slowly beside the house. Usually he drove fast even in a driveway. Here he liked to be careful, non-intimidating. He noticed Arlene spotting him through the kitchen window. He took his time climbing out of the cab and looked at the screened kennel area where the four dachshunds greeted him with snarling barks, stepping from side to side in agitation. But they were used to seeing him by now and settled down quickly. He saw her open the back door. She came out onto the porch, walking to the edge, placed where she would be looking down at him and he had no reasonable way to get up to the same level.

"Good morning, Mrs. Becker," he said.

"Good morning."

"I will finish scraping the last windows in the shed and repainting the frames today."

"That's good," she said. "I'll get a cheque ready for you. I hope a cheque is okay."

"I'm sure it will be good," he said. He kept looking at her. "I wonder if there is anything else to do here. Work is still not easy to find in construction."

"Sorry, we're in good shape for the winter now. If something else comes up I'll be certain to phone you. You've done a good job. And it's nice to have someone around the house from time to time." She smiled as she spoke. He smiled back.

"I am happy to hear that." He paused but saw her still smiling. "Señora, I am happy to see you sometimes too. I need the money for the work. If I did not, I would still be happy to come here just for your company."

He paused again, waiting for any response, not seeing any but not seeing discouragement either. "Do you think you think perhaps we could talk sometime? For a visit, I mean. Perhaps even after I finish the painting today?"

She tightened the smile and let her eyes open further into a more quizzical, almost amused expression, and said, "Nothing better for you to do? Life can't be that boring for a young man like you."

"Ah, there are things to do, but it is not a question of they are boring, it is a question of are they interesting. You are interesting."

"Surely you know younger women who must be more interesting to you."

"Not so many," he said. "Not so interesting to talk to."

"We haven't talked much aside from arranging what work to do around here."

He kept looking up at her, two steps higher at the edge of the back porch. "You have told me about the plants and trees growing around the yard. You have told me about your interesting plans for the shed. I can tell you would have many more interesting things to say if we talked together."

"It's a little chilly out here today," she said. "And I do have some things to arrange before driving into the city this afternoon."

"I thought only that with Mr. Becker away at that gas well you might feel lonely," he said.

"I'm never really lonely. If I start feeling that way I have friends to talk to on the phone and people to see in the city. Being a cabinet minister's wife is a sort of job, just not a paid one."

He was hearing discouragement now but did not give up. Being discouraged had not been the way to stay alive the times he had knelt behind tree trunks and screens of leaves in the jungle with an AK-47 in his hands, listening for sounds.

"But I do not often see you smiling like you were when I arrived this morning. You have sometimes seemed lonely. Women have told me I am good company. I have many stories to tell. Some are funny, unless you would rather hear the exciting ones. And I could make you coffee as well as I paint the window frames, even better I think. You would be happy with the way I make coffee."

She looked at him, looked at the dirt-streaked white pickup, looked into his eyes again, and said, "Roberto, I think you should just finish the work. I'll bring the cheque out to you."

He smiled again, this time with less crinkle around his eyes. "It is a shame to see you here with no company, and never tasting my coffee."

"You're wrong," she said. "I always have company here."

He looked slowly down the driveway and around the yard. He looked back at her and held out his left hand, palm up, as if to ask who was always here.

"Ricky," she called. The Doberman loped up silently from its shelter outside the kennel area. It glanced at Morales and looked up to the porch. She pointed at Morales. Now the dog turned and set itself lower toward the ground. It didn't growl or bark but its lips pulled apart slightly, showing teeth and watching the man with full attention.

He did not like dogs but knew better than to move suddenly. He smiled again, looking up directly at her, and said, "I see now you have company. I am sorry if I can not match the friendship of your dog. I will finish the painting and go, unless you no longer think it is necessary."

"You can finish," she said. "I'll leave the cheque in your truck."

She waited until he walked into the shed. She told the dog to sit outside the back door as she went back into the house to write the cheque. Half a minute later she came back out, opened the truck door, laid the cheque on the seat and went back inside, locking the door after her. Ricky paced around the porch and sniffed at the grass verge of the driveway, looking up now and then as he heard the occasional sound from the shed.

Morales finished before noon and walked slowly back to his truck, making a show of disinterest as the Doberman followed his movements, fully engaged. He turned the truck around in the space between the house and the shed and drove out faster than he had driven in, bits of gravel arcing up from the back wheels.

"Bitch," he thought. "Anglo bitch."

Arlene kept her gaze on the symphony foundation's draft annual report as she listened to the truck rattling out toward the road. She had not been what she would call afraid but felt relief at hearing the young man's departure. Attention from someone a good twenty years younger had been flattering. His presumption had been distasteful and his overconfident air concerning.

She felt the pull of an easy thought—that his assumptions, or hopes, were just what a person could expect from a stranger, a brash newcomer to the province, someone who knew nothing about how it had been built. She remembered, though, that overconfident and negligent and even dangerous men could be found anywhere. Men like Anne Trimble's husband, who had built a reputation as a leader in the oil industry for decades while leaving his wife at home for endless days and belittling her whenever she ventured an opinion. She had ended up shooting him five times with a .22-calibre pistol as he sat watching a hockey game and drinking straight scotch. He spent a month in hospital but survived because she had not had the sense to use at least a .38 and because a neighbour who'd been walking by had called the police and an ambulance. She had told the police the bloodied satin-finish upholstery on the couch could be replaced but she was sorry that good scotch had been spilled.

Abusive or negligent husbands were one thing. A husband drifting in and out of a marriage like a figure appearing and disappearing at the edge of a heavy fog was quite another. Arlene thought again about what her husband had looked like on the evening news. He was calm, in charge, even handsome in his pallid way. She'd thought in the early years that she could see him running a ranch. Still could. He had the stubbornness. But he would never have settled down to a commitment like that, an attachment fixed to an immovable expanse of grass and earth. She wondered if that was how he saw her—a symbol of attachment to land and to its traditions. Was her fixedness too much to bear? Could someone who had moved here from another country ever fully understand what it meant to inherit a hundred and more years of a family's presence in this one place? And if he could not attach himself to one place, what did that mean about his ability to keep attached to her, or to anyone?

She pictured him again as he'd appeared on the screen last evening. He had probably appeared like a normal politician to others. She knew the half-attentive hollowness in his eyes. He'd been doing his job but also thinking about something else. Months after they had met, he told her what he had often told others during his university years but had increasingly closed up inside himself. She remembered the desperate diffidence in the way he had told her about his best friend's death in Vietnam. He had said, as she was sure he had said many times when he was younger, "Someday, someone will pay."

Now there was no one left to pay. The old men who had insisted there was no alternative but to turn Vietnam into a blood-streaked swamp were already retiring from public view. The younger men who had almost magically come up with student deferments or safe National Guard service or medical excuses were already climbing high up the political ladder. She knew some people had found keys to the escape door. An American oil executive visiting her father during those turbulent times had come to dinner and told them, "None of my friends' sons have been drafted."

She knew John used to have dreams. He saw his friend's body being torn by a mortar shell. Sometimes the friend died right away and sometimes he lived for several minutes screaming or moaning. Once she had suggested he see a therapist to help clear the imagined memory. He had replied that it would do no good, that you could come to terms with a real memory, but an imagined one would always come back in different form. The dreams had faded. She hoped they were not coming back. She didn't think about the possibility that Morales had his own nightmares. Now he had anger, too.

He was driving back to the capital fast, tailgating and cutting close in front of vehicles that he passed. Nothing worked out the way he thought it would. He could picture a different life for himself and he could never find his way to it. When he reached the city he drove past his sister's rented house and to the fortified house where his friends kept their drugs, their cash and their guns.

The house was less than a kilometre away from the store where Alex Rabani built smokers and displayed them for sale. Alex was there a few minutes after noon when George pulled up and got out of his car to go for his weekly midday walk with his brother. Alex looked out the open door of what he considered his workshop and broke into a surprised light smile. He put his red plaid flannel jacket on over his pilled steel-grey work sweater and walked out to join his brother.

They strolled down the avenue and turned left onto the street that would take them past the old churches. Anglican, Methodist, Greek Orthodox and, just off on a side street, a dull yellow clapboard building that served as a Buddhist temple. George knew Alex liked the old buildings; they represented stability to him. George saw them as poorly attended historical survivors, abandoned ships on a beach where the tide was going out. Only the evangelical church in what had been an abandoned office building closer to the city centre was gaining congregants.

Alex looked at the curled brown leaves hanging onto the old elms and Norway maples in the hard autumn air. He saw tradition. He looked at the fallen leaves littering the sidewalk and small yards, some of them flopping listlessly in a small gust, and he saw lines of movement. The thought of lines reminded him to tell George about his new book project.

"It's going to be called either *Lines on the Prairie* or *The Country of Geometry*," Alex said.

"I thought of it when I looked down the avenue in front of the store. The avenue bends a little bit as it goes east. Most of the other streets here go straight. Then I started thinking about curling. That's what it's mostly going to be about. Sort of a history of curling but I think I'll visit some rinks and write about what I see there.

I was already inside the Glenrock Club and watched some games. They have old metal signs on the back walls advertising Macdonald cigarettes. You know? The ads with the blond Scottish lass?

"The signs were part of the overall atmosphere. They were a tradition, just like everything else in the rink. And there were all those regular lines. Everything on the sheets of ice is measured and exact. The boundaries are all straight lines. The targets are all perfect circles, just like the rocks. The rocks are all lined up fitting snugly together until they're played. And then everything about the game is geometry. It's all about angles, and keeping everything inside lines or on top of circles. I wonder if that's why people like curling. Maybe what they really like about it is the order. Everything is where it's supposed to be, even if the rocks sometimes go where no one expects. It's probably not a coincidence that people like curling here on the Prairies. All those straight highways and secondary roads. All those flat horizons and farms divided neatly into sections and quarter-sections."

George said, "That would make an interesting book. You know, I handled the disposition of a will about a year ago for a widow whose husband used to measure their land. She asked me if I knew of a good place to dispose of the equipment that surveyors use to measure angles."

"You mean a theodolite?" Alex asked.

George looked at him with widening eyes. "Yes, that's it," he said. "A theodolite. Anyway, Mr. Jespersen, when he had spare time on summer Sundays, used to go out on his fields and measure lines with his survey equipment. They weren't visible on the ground but he could picture where they existed according to a survey plan."

They walked several minutes more, turned a block west and came back up toward the Italian grocery where George intended to buy a long sandwich to share, and a couple of soft drinks. Maybe two cans of Chinotto. Both he and his brother sometimes liked a touch of bitterness to offset the sweetness of the salami and the red pepper spread.

Alex began talking again. He said, "Everyone knows exactly where they are on a farm or a curling rink. Sometimes I feel like I don't know exactly where I am."

"What do you mean?"

"It feels like everyone I know seems to fit in somewhere. Mr. Sandro, you, the librarians, even my customers. They know how they fit in with other people. They know their work. Sometimes I feel like everyone else arrived here on earth with a map and someone forgot to issue one to me. It's like I'm wandering around in a strange country but everyone else belongs there."

"You fit in with me, Alex."

"I always like walking with you, George."

They entered the grocery and walked past the vegetable displays because George knew Alex always liked to see the produce, especially the more exotic ones that Mr. Sandro did not carry. He also liked to look at the cans of different kinds of beans, and the packages of figs, and the cooler packed with cheeses. The shelves were modern but the displays somehow left an impression of everything being stacked on polished old hardwood. Afterward they took their sandwich and the two drink cans and sat eating lunch in the park across the street. They didn't talk much there. They heard the dry leaves rustling.

18.

OSTROSKI WRAPPED UP THE PHOTO REVIEW IN GROWING boredom. He flipped through the images at a homestretch pace. He had been talking more with Radescu. Spy girl or not, she was more company than he was used to having. Her changed behaviour was noticeable. She had stopped going out for bathroom breaks without him days earlier. She also arrived before he did every day and went out the door after him, locking up as if the room were her own apartment.

He didn't push for an explanation. Mostly they talked about photography and cruises. He could rattle off theories of composition and lighting without thinking about it much. That didn't slow down the review. Her stories about floating around the Caribbean or around the Bahamas with her friend Rosa occupied him a bit more. The free drinks sounded good. Being shepherded into quick walks past expensive shops in tourist towns full of people who needed foreign money as badly as farmers needed rain didn't sound as appealing. Neither did the onboard entertainment. But he had ended up thinking she was not as dumb as he'd originally thought.

Her business wasn't being an office assistant. It was figuring out how to do whatever her bosses wanted and do it well. He became sure that she kept her own goals in mind even while she did her best to please whoever she was working for.

He left the government building and slowly walked back to his store, stretching the trip to fifteen minutes. It was late afternoon. The sun blared dully from the southwest, a smoky orange bruise in the light haze. It slipped lower toward the horizon each day and had reached the point where it intruded into line of sight for anyone looking south. Winter, it said, is coming and there is nothing you can do about that.

He walked through the scuff of dead leaves and paper litter to the shop and opened the door. Adela looked up from a book and smiled a hello.

"Jack, you are back half an hour early."

"We're finally finished looking at those old pictures. Now I can get back to sitting around here waiting for customers to show up. Thank you for holding the fort."

"De nada," she said. "Really, I was able to read most of the time here. I did vacuum the floor today and dust the shelves."

"Good. Dusting never occurs to me. I suppose it would if the dust got thick enough."

"It was good to be here all day and have time to myself. Roberto has been in a bad mood."

"Oh?" Ostroski said as he stepped into the back room to hang up his jacket. He made a detour to his small fridge and came back out to lean on the counter with a beer in his hand.

"He won't say why. I've learned to let such episodes pass."

He considered her reply. "But you still worry about him."

"Of course." She paused and closed her book. "Jack, there is something I think I should tell you."

He looked at her and waited.

"This city likes to think it is big but it is really a small place. I know a woman who knows Ginny Radescu. They go out to bars together and sometimes on vacations. I saw her last night at the

Latin cultural centre. She told me the Radescu woman got a little drunk the last time they were out together and talked a little about reviewing those photographs with you."

She waited for a reaction, saw only his eyes not blinking and went on. "Radescu told her you were funny sometimes and had interesting stories about the old days in Hollywood. She was a little sorry that you probably had hidden some things from her. She thought you probably took some photographs out of the collection while she was out of the room. That bothered her because she did not want to get into trouble. She did not mind you doing things behind her back because it was not her business. But she did not want to get into trouble. She is a little afraid."

Ostroski thought over what he heard. He did not care what Ginny Radescu thought of him. He took a long pull on the beer. "This mutual friend of yours, does she know that you know me?" he asked. "That you work here part-time?"

"I told her some time ago that I work in a shop with old camera equipment. I don't think I told her your name. It was not relevant."

"And she hasn't been asking questions?"

"No." Morales did not elaborate unnecessarily. Nor did she make a habit of prying with questions about things that did not directly concern her. Ostroski pushed air out through his nose to signal an end to the subject and said, "Make any sales this week?"

"Business was as usual."

"Just enough to keep the fridge stocked, buy a pizza now and then and pay the rent so I don't have an excuse to close the place."

"And to pay me," Morales said, wearing her best expression of solemnity.

"Right," he said. "I'll stop at the bank on the way in tomorrow. Unless you'd trust a cheque right now."

"I can wait," she said. "You look tired."

They usually stayed away from personal exchanges. He took another long pull from the bottle and said, "Didn't know days of sitting could be so wearing. Your muscles get sore not being used. And your back gets stiff from leaning over a table."

He stopped, then continued, "I don't know if it's more my back and eyes feeling tired or just being tired of looking at all those moments from the past. Most of them didn't amount to much. It's like seeing your life flash before your eyes and realizing maybe you didn't accomplish anything aside from paying the bills."

"You recorded many things that would have disappeared," she said. "The government would not have paid for the photographs if you had not made a record of many things for history. You know, that's why I am interested in preserving old buildings. People should know about those who went before them. What life was like. They should know what was important to people in the past and how their past helped make the future."

"That's what they tell me," Ostroski said. "The lawyer been around?"

"Not here. We have arranged to go out on Friday. For dinner, and perhaps a movie if we find one we may both like. Or perhaps to the Downstairs Club to see a singer from Montreal. She is intriguing because she paints her face blue and white. I also liked one of her songs that I heard on the radio."

"You arranged to go out? Is that like a date? Or different?"

She gauged the angle of his eyebrows and slight smile and decided he was being humorous rather than inquisitive. "It is company."

He listened to the silence following her short reply and said, "Are you saying I could use more company myself? I've got my hockey on TV and those kids in the photography class over at the college once a week. They're full of ideas and hope. They're about all the company I can cope with. They keep my head buzzing."

"Yes, I know. You keep saying they are pains in the ass. But you keep going back and I have never heard you say you had to fail any of them."

"Why should I do that?" he said. "They'll run into enough failure on their own."

Morales looked at the clock and said it was closing time. He said he would look after the final cleanup and the cash register.

She went in back, picked up her coat and said, "Goodnight, Jack," as she walked out the door.

He said, "Goodnight," drank the last swallow of beer, and looked at her silhouette against the light from the street lamp as she crossed in front of the window. He assumed she was going home but realized he did not know, and that he rarely knew where she was going or why. He decided this would be a good night to treat himself to a restaurant—the Romanian place with the cabbage rolls. He had another beer with dinner there and another when he got to his apartment, but none of them helped bring on more than a so-so sleep. Too much was running through his head. Too many images from the past flashing through his semi-dreaming vision; too many memories about what he had done and not done; too many questions about why a few photographs of a former lieutenant-governor with her arm around the waist of a former premier's wife would be important.

Next day he went to the shop and worked on a balky Leicaflex that he knew could bring a good price if he got the focus working properly again. A few customers stopped in for film and one for a lens brush. Another in a mid-grey topcoat browsed the selection of old equipment on the shelves, as was his habit about once a month. Adela arrived after lunch hour. He did not wait to talk with her but went to the bank for her pay. He brought the cash back and said he would be gone for maybe an hour to talk to the lawyer.

Rabani's office was like a different city than the one through which Ostroski had walked the eight blocks from the shop. Outside there were drab coats and roaring diesel buses punching sooty smoke into the sky as they accelerated. A former movie theatre's empty poster display cases were tombstones marking the end of a life that had begun in the vaudeville era. He saw silent faces intent on their own affairs and sidewalks littered with candy-bar wrappers, empty coffee cups and sugary drink cups, dust, occasional stains that looked like food spills or spit or worse. Inside the law firm was a universe of hushed voices and deep green carpet. The colour made Ostroski think of tables covered in green cloth in a quiet pool room. He wondered when he had last been in a pool room. Probably in the States, he thought.

He was shown down the corridor to an open door. Rabani stood and shook his hand and invited him to sit on one of the solid chairs in front of the desk, not one of the fully stuffed fabric-covered chairs over in a corner, apparently reserved for more intimate or delicate occasions. Good enough, they weren't friends anyway.

"How have you been?" Rabani asked.

"Getting a sore butt and dried-out eyes. Nothing a couple of beers couldn't fix."

"Glad to hear it. Are you set to wrap things up now?"

Ostroski reached into a pocket. "I have the rest of the negatives here." He put them on Rabani's desk, just out of the lawyer's reach.

Rabani leaned forward, picked them up, turned and held them up to the light weakly seeping in through his window.

"Doesn't look like much," he said as he turned back to Ostroski. "All this disturbance for a handful of pictures of an old house."

"Well, there are pictures and there are pictures. Putting up a flag doesn't look like much. If you had the negatives from the flag raising at Iwo Jima you'd have something. It all depends on what pictures mean to someone."

"This should satisfy them," Rabani said. "You should receive your cheque in a couple of weeks."

"Good. I'll be glad to get this over with." Ostroski stood to leave. He sat down again when asked to wait for one more thing.

"The government will be satisfied," Rabani said. "I'm not sure I will be."

"You don't have to be. You're the middleman."

"That doesn't mean I can keep my eyes shut to everything. You told me you were going to be taking out photos of a Norma Minton and a Gloria Sandring. I understand you removed a number of photos of someone described as Norma Minton. But none of any woman named Gloria. How did that happen?"

"I noticed that, too," Ostroski said. "Didn't find any of her."

"I asked how that happened."

"Must have never left any of her in the collection."

"Never left? When would they have been taken out?"

"A long time ago."

Rabani watched for eye movement or shifts in posture. He thought he might be seeing a hint of Ostroski's mocking humour but wasn't sure.

"I'm not playing games with you. I got rid of those pictures years ago."

"You said you wanted to make sure they never saw the light of day or ended up in anyone else's hands. What was this about if you'd already thrown them away?"

"A long time ago I didn't want them in my hands either. That was a mistake. I thought I could tear them into little pieces and throw them out and that would be the end of it, but that backfired. I got rid of the pictures. I couldn't get the way she looked out of my head. I knew there wasn't much chance but I hoped I'd find one or two still in the collection. I didn't. Now I'm stuck with memories of what she looked like, and the memories probably make her a lot closer to perfect than what she would have looked like in a photograph. Pictures don't work the way you think. If you look at them often enough you get your fill of them. Eventually, you don't need to look at them more. You move on to other things. I've never been able to move on from her."

Ostroski didn't give it a dramatic reading. His expression remained impassive. "You happy now?" he said.

Rabani moved his lips out, considering what he'd just heard. He took a long breath in and said, "I could be happy. I believe you. That leaves one other loose end, though. There's some thought you took photos out of the room when the Radescu girl wasn't there. If they weren't of Gloria Sandring, what were they?"

"So the spy's been at work. Her boss didn't tell you what they were?"

"Why would they tell me? Maybe you took more than one kind of picture out of the collection."

"Nope. Just a few, all of the same subject."

"Dammit, Jack, I'm trying to help you and you act like it's fun to play games. This is serious."

"Yeah, I know. Okay, I took some pictures of the old lieutenant-governor, Hesperia Tindall. The girl showed some interest in them. Why would that dried up old prune be of any interest to anyone? And why especially the ones of her with old George Manchester's wife?"

"You jeopardized the whole arrangement to satisfy your curiosity about something inconsequential?"

"What do they care? There are dozens of pictures of Tindall in the collection. For that matter, what proof do they have I took anything? You don't even know if I'm pulling your leg about this. How do they know the Radescu girl didn't take anything?"

"For Christ's sake."

"I thought lawyers were trained to be unemotional, like scientists looking down at mice running around in a box."

"That's enough. I repeat, did you really jeopardize the whole arrangement to satisfy your curiosity about something inconsequential?"

"You just collected the negatives they asked for. A handful of other pictures aren't going to wreck the agreement. I'm not wrecking it either. I'm not holding any more negatives of the Roussel house and there are no prints except for the one I told you I gave the hooker and nothing in it was identifiable. She may not even have it anymore. Hell, I don't know if she's still living around here or even still alive. And if some other pictures are inconsequential, why are they grinding you about them?"

"I thought there was a reasonable person under that crusty joker act. All right, you can probably get away with it. That concludes our business. I'll send you the bill."

Ostroski stood up and headed for the door. When he reached it he turned and said, no wry crinkles around his eyes or his mouth this time, "You still have a lot to learn about people, George. I hope you learn fast before you learn the hard way."

19.

IT HAD TAKEN FOUR DAYS TO CAP THE WELL. BECKER DROVE
out to the same bush site every day for the media. By the time he
did the final show the national networks were carrying the story.
He was amused to think people who had no idea who he was would
see him in Newfoundland. He had been there once for a ministerial
conference. Icebergs off the coast and throat-burning rum. A cold,
damp wind on the hill east of the harbour. But somehow part of a
deep historical network. Not like the end-of-the-world feeling you
got looking out across the Beaufort Sea up in the Arctic. He had
been to ministerial conferences in many places now. Get into politics and see the world. The dells and woods of Wisconsin seemed
far away and ordinary after all the years. He wondered if all the
immigrants who had crossed the Atlantic since the early 1600s
had thought that way about the Old World—whether after seeing
the New World the old one had seemed far away and ordinary.
Yet where you came from was never completely ordinary; it was
indelible and had a pull to it, like gravity.

He went back to the capital immediately after the wrap-up
on the last day. He could have stopped in to see who was around

the executive suite after being dropped off but he walked to his car and drove home instead. Only the dogs were there to greet him. He checked to see they had been fed and had water in their bowls. He closed the gate to their area and walked to the house.

There was leftover stew in the fridge. He was down to his last two forkfuls and had just opened a bottle of ale when the phone rang. He answered and heard Morehead's familiar soft drawl. He used to wonder if the drawl had once been broader and been clipped by years here in the north, or if it had always been understated, the product of a man who had decided at a young age that he would be part of a larger world and should sound like he belonged.

"You did a great job out there," the premier said. "That show could have turned bad on us if we'd sent someone out there who fumbled it. You projected authority and confidence. Exactly what was needed. Made the best of the situation. I think it will fade fast. We just have to make sure we don't replace it with some other disaster."

"Thank you. It helped a lot they got the damn thing capped reasonably fast."

"Helped in more ways than one. We were getting grief about not using a local crew. The in-province guys will have to admit the Texans got the job done pretty efficiently."

"Not that they made any friends out in Broken Pines. But yes, they did their job. Will you need a summary at cabinet?"

"Naw, I think everyone watched the whole thing unfold on TV. I'd like to see you in the office tomorrow, though. Say 9:30?"

"Certainly. I'll be there."

"I've been rethinking the cabinet posts. You showed a lot of strength out there. A lot of poise under pressure. We're not getting that in every portfolio, including some where it's needed. Henry agrees with me. The Culture ministry leaves too much of your talent going to waste. Would you be willing to take on a bigger file?"

Becker calculated the odds and the recent performance of fellow ministers and decided Energy was the mostly likely spot where a new face was needed. The risk was that Morehead was talking about Social Services. Energy was much more likely.

"I'd be happy to serve wherever you think is best," he said.

"That's fine. Just what I was hoping to hear. See you in the morning."

"At 9:30. Thank you, Premier."

He walked back to the table and finished the stew standing up as he carried the plate to the sink to rinse it before putting it into the dishwasher. Then he picked up the bottle and carried it into the den. This was a football night on television. He watched football infrequently but tonight watching a game seemed a good way to wind down after days of tension. Producing a few seconds of authoritative reassurance for the cameras was simple enough in its way. The words flowed easily. He had mastered the look of relaxed intelligence long ago. He hadn't realized until after the fact that grad school had been good training for getting the right look and sound while talking at least as much as for learning about economics. What wore a person down was the knowledge that every second on camera was a walk through a field of bear traps. Any stumble in delivering the words, any choice of words that hinted at confusion, any expression betraying weakness, anything that could be misinterpreted in a damaging way—any of those mistakes would be sure to end up in front of hundreds of thousands or even a million people, some of them tolerant and some not. He watched a Winnipeg running back brought down by a gang of tacklers after struggling for a gain of two yards. Like that, he thought. Everything is a grind and there are many more tackles than touchdowns.

He sipped at the beer occasionally, savouring the taste rather than just drinking. He thought about trying to look up some Pabst Blue Ribbon. He had become used to Canadian brands but remembered that he used to like Blue Ribbon. The announcer and colour man kept up an engaging excitement about the game. The colour man, an old quarterback, was especially good, Becker thought. He marvelled again at how the pros could spot patterns instantly, point out subtle things about how the players moved or how tactics were set up on individual plays. Maybe that's like politics too, he thought.

He had nearly finished the beer when he heard Arlene coming up the driveway and into the garage. He waited on the couch rather than getting up. The back door opened and closed. The sound of hangers being moved along the rack and boots being put into the closet came faintly over the sound of the game. She walked into the den and he looked up with a patient smile and said, "Hi." She strode to the couch, sat beside him, put an arm around his shoulders, gave him a short kiss and said, "Hi." He saw her hair neatly in place and her eyes apparently smiling along with her lips.

"It's good to have you back," she said.

"Good to be back. Good to have a chance to rest and have homemade food."

"I'll bet. I had to put up with so-so chicken with two of the board members tonight at The Ferns. Not up to snuff. Their regular cook must have the night off." She drew back a little and looked at him as if discovering something new. "I watched the evening news every night. You did a great job. No sense of crisis and very understandable explanations."

"Thanks. The premier seemed pleased, too."

"Well he should be."

"Everything okay at the symphony?"

"Oh, the usual. There's never enough money. There are always complaints that the conductor is uninspired. He is, but his contract runs another year. We've started looking for a replacement. A fresh face may help ticket sales and sponsorships."

Becker turned off the television. He looked out the window at the silhouette of the big poplar across the side yard. The moon must be bright tonight, he thought. He looked at his wife and watched for her reaction as he told her that Morehead had called him into the office next morning, probably to offer a bigger cabinet post, probably as energy minister.

She beamed at the news. Unfeigned happiness, he thought. "Oh, John. Really?"

"Just an educated guess, so far. He's going to offer something. The worst case would be Social Services but I'm pretty sure it's Energy."

"That's wonderful." She gave him a quick hug, stood up and almost whirled before sitting down again and taking one of his hands. "I knew they'd have to offer you more. You're too valuable. Especially compared with the others. The way you handled Broken Pines showed that."

"I suppose so."

She turned to look at him. "You don't sound happy about it."

"I'm happy to have something more meaningful to do. A portfolio like that will add weight to what I say in cabinet on other matters, too. I'm worried that I got the job by being an actor. I hope they let me do more than be a reassuring face on the evening news. Being on television these last few days ... I feel like there's a bigger image now but less of me."

"But you will be more. You'll do more. Once you're energy minister you'll be more able to set your own agenda. You won't have final say but you will have real authority. And staff you can direct to draw up plans."

"I wonder," he said. "I wonder how much of it is real. Maybe most of it is show. The department can probably run itself three hundred and fifty days of the year."

"Then make the other fifteen count. John, it won't be like that. Haven't you figured out what's important after all these years here?"

She turned back to the window and gazed at the moonlit trees, imagining the vast land stretching in all directions, to the pastures and dry croplands in the east and south, the dark but life-filled forest in the north, the scrub-filled farms edging up toward the foothills in the west and finally the mountains, the "shining" mountains.

"Sometimes I think it takes an inordinately long time for people like you and Billy Morehead and others who come here to understand. You all grew up in a different world. You think consultants and television images determine everything. They don't. Do you know we didn't have TV on the ranch until I was ten years old?"

"I think you've mentioned that once or twice."

"I suppose I did," she said without smiling, still looking out the window. "My sister and I were lucky. There were hardly any stations to watch in those days. That didn't much matter to us. We knew what counted. The land. The land was the only real thing. The thing everything else came from, depended on. The land and our memories. They aren't ephemeral like an evening news show or another poll result. The land and everything our family experienced with it is part of us. It's what we grew up believing. That knowledge never got encapsulated in an hour-long documentary and then filed away after it was broadcast once or twice. It's always been there and always will be."

He kept himself from asking whether it was the land that counted more or the social position of those who owned the biggest pieces of it. He said instead, "I grew up on a farm. Remember?"

She turned back to her husband. "I know that. This is more. Don't you see what being energy minister means? You'll have a direct relationship with everything here. With the people here. You'll finally be a part of this place. Not part of the passing parade in the legislature or one of the office workers who come and go in downtown buildings that come and go. Really a part of here, really belonging."

He was looking at her not knowing if he felt resigned or flummoxed. He knew he was not angry. And not completely surprised, yet somehow taken unawares.

"I didn't realize I was still here on a visa," he said.

"You're going to be like that? Oh, John. Don't you see what this means to me?"

"I think I do. I'm starting to wonder what it means to me. A year ago I would have been happy to take a promotion. Now I'm wondering what's really important in life."

"Including me, I suppose."

"Don't let's start that. It's late. I'm tired."

"So am I. I'm going to bed. If you can't figure out what's really important in life, go outside and look at the stars in the sky. Pick up some dirt in the garden and feel how it crumbles through your fingers. You'll probably want to say goodnight to the dogs anyway."

She climbed the stairs, moving neither fast nor slowly, moving as if going upstairs were the same as accepting fate.

He sat for a few minutes, got up and rinsed the bottle in the sink, then walked to the back door, put on his red plaid flannel jacket and took the empty bottle to the cardboard case in the shed. The dogs watched him in the glow of the yard light. He walked over to their large run, opened the gate and knelt down to rub their ears and pat their backs as they gathered around him. "Hey, Ricky," he said softly. "Hi Mitzi, Gretchen. Did you all miss me?"

From deep in the trees beside the long driveway he showed up as a large mass in the telescopic sight. The crosshairs centred on the left side of his head. As he turned to the other two dachshunds the crosshairs dropped slightly and centred on the middle of his back. Roberto held the rifle steady. A hunting rifle, not like the AK-47 he had once used but perhaps better for a single, straight shot. He let out a breath and imagined squeezing the trigger and hitting his target squarely. It would be easy. What was to stop him? He held Becker in the crosshairs for nearly half a minute, gauging how well he could keep his aim centred as his target shifted among the animals. Only a slight squeeze away. A movement of a few millimetres with his finger.

He saw Becker straighten up and leave the dog run. It was just as well. He had nothing to gain by killing the man, only much to lose. He watched Becker enter the house and he gently laid the rifle onto the litter of poplar leaves, spruce needles and twigs on the ground to his right. He felt safe, knowing the breeze was coming from the direction of the yard. The dogs would not be picking up his scent. He would lie here motionless, making no sound, seeing if he still had the patience and stamina within him to wait in ambush until the time was right.

It took perhaps an hour. He saw the last of the lights go off in the house. There was still adequate light from the moon. He waited another half-hour to allow time for the man and woman to fall asleep. A sting of emotion ran through him as he wondered if they were really falling asleep. The man had been away for days. No, he decided. If they were making love they would have started sooner. Who cared, anyway? The woman was old, merely an interesting idea. But she had turned him away. People had been turning him away since he had left the jungle.

He checked his watch and saw it was time. The Doberman was lying still outside the little shelter, apparently asleep. None of the other dogs was moving. He picked up the rifle and looked through the scope. Head or heart, he wondered. The head was a little more of a challenge. No, keep it simple. He lined up the upper part of the dog's body, certain the bullet would do enough damage even if he did not hit the heart exactly.

He squeezed the trigger. And stopped as a shadow fell through his line of vision. He froze in confusion for a split second, then realized a leaf had fallen. He looked up at the tree limbs searching for the one that might harbour a malicious spirit. Or was it not a prank but a warning from God?

Not satisfied but finding no answer, he took two deep breaths and aimed again. He squeezed the trigger. And flinched as the thought of another falling leaf flashed through his mind. The bullet cracked into the wood of the shelter behind the Doberman's head. The dog jerked up and barked. The dachshunds came to life and barked a few times. None of them sensed an intruder and they quieted down within a few seconds. Roberto had initially thought he may have grazed the Doberman or clipped one of its ears. When the barking stopped quickly he knew he must have just missed. He asked why. Killing a dog should have been easy. Time enough to answer that later. Now he saw a light turn on in the upper floor of the house. He raised into a crouch and began to make his way back to the truck. He had to move fast enough to get away cleanly but carefully enough in the darkness not to arouse the dogs further. He hoped that Becker would clump down the steps of the back porch and talk to the dogs. That might make enough noise to help cover his escape. The truck was about five hundred metres away.

Both the Beckers had awakened with the noise. They agreed they may have heard a cracking sound before the dogs started barking but they weren't sure. John stepped into his yard boots and pulled his heavier fall jacket over his pyjama top, switched on the yard light and stepped outside, not sure what he might be looking for. He walked slowly to the pen. Ricky greeted him as he opened the gate.

"What's up, boy?" he said, leaning down to give a scratch behind the ears. Ricky had been pacing. The dachshunds had quickly lost interest and settled to go back to sleep. John looked around for about half a minute, saw nothing unusual, bent down slightly and said, "Okay, Ricky. Everything's okay. Did you see an owl or a coyote? Hmmm?" Ricky looked up at him, panting. He said, "Quiet now. Let's get some sleep."

He walked out of the pen and closed the gate slowly behind him. He was in the house, had switched off the yard light and was taking off his boots when a small truck engine started from behind a screen of trees down the road. He did not notice the splintered holes in both sides of Ricky's shelter until he went out again for the morning feeding. If a bullet had made the holes it could have flown some distance into the woods. A small needle in a large haystack.

Over breakfast, he told Arlene what he had found. She had a suspicion about what had happened but chose not to tell him right away. He was still wondering as he drove out onto the road why she had not looked more worried or asked more questions.

20.

THE MEETING WENT ABOUT AS HE HAD EXPECTED. Morehead and Waschuk both complimented him on his performance at Broken Pines. Morehead said he wanted a strong voice in Energy, one capable of representing authority but also able to present complex matters to the public in an understandable way. That was not to say the current minister was doing a bad job. But some big decisions regarding royalties were coming up. A minister with communication skills as well as solid experience with business issues would be the best choice to handle the likely raft of criticisms. Morehead did most of the talking; Waschuk did most of the reading of expressions and listening to nuances in replies. Becker took in the deep carpet, the broad oak desk, the landscape paintings on the wall that he was sure a protocol officer had picked out and that Morehead likely viewed as a concession to the tastes of official visitors.

The closest thing to a negative signal cropped up when Morehead said, "You're a guaranteed star now."

Becker answered, "Stars fade. What I see and appreciate is a chance to be of service in a post where I think I can help."

Waschuk noted that the nicely modest hint of pleasure at taking on higher status was modified by what sounded like fatalism. The cabinet needed controlled ambition, not a penchant for mumbling "Vanity of vanities, all is vanity." However, the rest of the fifteen-minute talk went well. Everyone had streaks of the unknown in them. The known quantities in Becker were experience, skill, and an apparent belief in loyalty, to the party and the province if not to the premier.

Becker left the executive suite and took the three flights of stairs down to his own office to check on what had backed up during his absence. The smooth terrazzo floors and beige plastered walls produced his usual reaction of being trapped in a place built on artificial dreams of solidity and permanence.

He said hello to Ginny and the other admin assistant, who both seemed genuinely happy to see him. Cary, his executive assistant, seemed relieved. Cary filled him in on the department's responses to recent action requests, on the more prominent funding appeals and invitations that had come in, and on the preliminary list of items for next week's cabinet meeting. Becker did not say there was any reason he might not be handling the Culture file there. The routine catch-up and two telephone calls to heads of arts organizations took nearly two hours. He looked up at the clock on the mantel—the body of the clock was a horrible ceramic interpretation of a classic wood timepiece but was too recent a gift from too prominent an artist to dispose of just yet—saw 11:45 and walked to the closet to put on his jacket. He told the admin women he would be back about 1:00 and set off for a walk up the hill and into the ragged, aging edge of downtown.

The camera shop was absurdly close when he thought about it. Just over ten minutes away on foot. Becker breathed the dust of microscopic soil particles and dead vegetation that filled the autumn air. The light breeze rolled an empty coffee cup near him on the sidewalk. He let it pass, thinking he would leave the fun of stamping it flat to someone else, and then asking himself when he had become too grown up for the most elementary fun. The shop had a small, faded sign over the door rather than one hanging out over the sidewalk. He looked up at the sign, took in the chalky paint on the chipped window frame, and opened the door without pausing to think anything over before he went in.

A woman with brown eyes and shoulder-length brown hair looked up from behind the counter. Becker was mildly surprised to see a Latin American face—possibly Mexican, he thought, but possibly from further south. Her direct expression and lack of any greeting other than "good morning" said she might have recognized him. He said he was hoping to talk to the owner. She said he was in back and went through the doorway to see if he was free. Ostroski came out ahead of her. He hesitated in mid-stride for the smallest moment when he saw Becker but strode behind the counter.

"Mr. Becker, is it? What can I do for you?"

"I'd like to have a talk. Preferably in private."

Ostroski considered that and said, "Adela, you can go for lunch now. Bring me a coffee on the way back?"

She said she would. The two men looked at each other while she got her coat and went out the door, not obviously looking at the visitor, not seeming curious or concerned.

"You never explained how you managed to get hold of my dog," Becker said.

"It was easy. I knew you bring them to town one at a time for the groomer and I knew you get your secretary to take them for a walk at lunchtime. I also knew she doesn't walk them the whole time. She leaves them loosely tied to a hydrant in front of the same café every time while she picks up a snack. One loop of the leash. Nothing even to untie."

"Why me?"

"Why not you? You're the culture minister. Culture had my collection. Making the point directly with one person was better than trying to make the point with the whole government. Nothing personal."

"Threatening to throw my dog into the river was personal."

"I was the one who got tackled by a cop. And threatened with criminal charges. Anyway, you got your dog back unharmed. I got the deal I wanted for my photos. The government got the negatives of the house. And I guarantee you personally there aren't any more negatives or prints floating around anywhere. What have we got to talk about?"

Becker didn't see signs of either nervousness or belligerence.

He said, "Let's talk about old pictures. I think you have more that I'd be interested in seeing. Not of old houses or old politicians. I understand you were in Wisconsin in 1972, visiting an old friend. Probably in a little town called Riverton, a college town."

"You pals with some detective?"

"Call it coincidence, followed by diligent checking. You would have been down there just about the time a college girl got shot at an anti-war demonstration. No one ever pinned down who fired the bullet. All they knew was that a number of Guardsmen fired their rifles, but only one bullet hit one person. One of the Guardsmen was responsible. I saw the tapes from the demonstration like a lot of other people did. I saw them a number of times. The manager at one of the local stations was kind enough to run them for me. And once I saw a man in back of a crowd carrying what looked like a 35mm camera. People don't carry cameras in a situation like that if they don't use them. The man looked short and wiry. He had short hair, and from what I could see, a kind of a wild expression on his face. I admit the cameras only caught him from the side and only for about a second. I got to thinking this man looked something like a younger version of you."

"You got to thinking. You saw someone's face from a lot of years ago for maybe a second. You thought you saw a camera but you didn't see him taking any pictures."

"Here's one thing I do know, Mr. Ostroski. I know you took some pictures out of your collection while you were reviewing it and Ginny Radescu didn't see you doing it. I also know you had negatives of the Roussel house hidden away. That tells me you're capable of hiding other photographs, negatives or prints or both."

"You been taking lessons from your dogs in barking up the wrong tree?"

They stared at each other for a moment. Becker went on.

"If someone had photographs from that event I would dearly like to see them, Mr. Ostroski. I think it would almost a public duty for them to be made public."

Ostroski let a corner of his mouth turn up. "Made public. Doesn't sound like you're looking for someone to turn over pictures to the provincial archives. Sounds more personal. Why would that be?"

They looked at each other again. This time Becker gazed down to Ostroskis lightly cleft chin and down to heart-height on his chest, and then back up to his glinting blue eyes.

"All right. I'll give it to you straight. A long time ago I had a friend. He wanted to serve in Vietnam. I told him not to. He could have had a deferment. But he was a southerner whose father fought in Europe. Most of his ancestors fought in the Civil War. He said going was his duty. And I didn't try hard enough to talk him out of it and he never came back. He died for nothing. I said someone would pay for that someday. But no one has. It's hard enough to find anyone responsible for anything, let alone bring them to account. But someone can pay for that girl. I used to live in Wisconsin. Not at Riverton, but I had a friend who taught there. I know what an effect that killing had on the community and on her family. And I know that only a handful of people know or probably know who fired that shot. Even if there can't be a criminal charge, someone can be brought to account for that murder. Someone can in some measure be made to pay. It will be at least one entry on the other side of the ledger."

"And you think I can finger the guy who did it. And I should be happy to help you, and maybe ruin his life in the bargain. If he's still alive and if he cares."

"That's right. I think you're able to do that."

"Find yourself another accomplice, Becker. You know something? I don't think I'll tell you if I was there. And if I was there I wouldn't tell you if I took any pictures or what they showed. It was wartime. A lot of innocent people die in wars. Vietnam wasn't the only place that ever happened. Sometimes the people responsible pay and sometimes they live with what they've done, if they even know what they've done. If they have a decent bone in their body that's payment enough. They pay every day."

Becker thought about making a comment like "very noble" but held it back. He looked around the shop, at the grey day outside the big front window with the chipped and faded paint on the outside sill. He looked back at Ostroski.

"Let's cut the crap, Ostroski. There's another thing I know. Someone fired a rifle into my yard last night. I found a bullet hole in the wall of a shed just above where one of my dogs likes to sleep. I think someone may have been aiming at the dog and missed and lost his nerve after the first shot and left as fast as he could. And as far as I know you're the only person who likes to take out grudges on my dogs. What grudge have you got against me? And what makes you think the police couldn't find some evidence linked to you?"

Ostroski let a loud sniff out through his nostrils, but he avoided flattening his mouth with contempt.

"I don't have any grudge against you. And I don't fire rifles at dogs. If I did I think I wouldn't miss. But I haven't fired a gun since Korea. And I haven't held one in my hands since 1953. They're awful things."

More silence. "The fact remains that someone did fire a rifle at one of my dogs last night. I'm guessing it was a rifle because he would have kept his distance. And I don't know anyone else who has threatened one of my dogs in the past."

"Let's get at least this much straight. I don't have anything to do with guns and if I did I wouldn't be shooting innocent dogs. I don't think I would even have dropped that dachshund of yours in the river. If you think no one else has any reason to do something like that, why don't you think about what you were doing for the last week? A sour gas well blew out and drove a bunch of people out of their homes. Probably made some kids sick even if you guys wouldn't admit it. And you were out there every day looking people in the eye like their friendly insurance salesman and telling them there was nothing to worry about and the government would make sure it wouldn't happen again. Why don't you think about that?"

"Or I could report the incident to the police and suggest where they might start investigating. Would Miss Adela like it if you had to close your shop, even temporarily?"

Ostroski raised his voice at that: "You leave her out of this. She's got nothing to do with it."

Becker looked around the shop walls. Cameras sat on well-dusted shelves. One section held film packages and accessories like lens filters. The equipment and shelves were clean but the walls behind them had faded cream-coloured paint that could stand to be washed and seemed to date from the Fifties or Sixties. He turned back to Ostroski and said, "Maybe you should start thinking about yourself as well as about her."

Becker turned to leave. He turned back to Ostroski and sighed and said, "I'm not going to rush this. I'm not going to forget about it either. By God, someone is going to pay. I think you hold the key to that. Think about giving me that key. If not to do what's right, then to avoid collateral damage." He opened the door with the faded sign hanging against the glass, reading "Closed" when viewed from the inside of the shop, and walked into the brown dust and dull, overcast sky of the day.

Ostroski watched him leave. A tightness constricted his throat. He walked into the back room, took a beer out of the fridge, snapped off the cap with a listless movement of his right hand, drank nearly half of it before he pulled it back down to the top of the work counter, and gazed at the floor, waiting for Adela to come back.

21.

RABANI PUSHED OPEN THE BROWN DOOR FACING THE ALLEY and gazed up the scratched, worn steps. He climbed to the upper landing. His breaths came faster from the effort. This time he did not wonder again about regular exercise and a better diet. His mind was absorbed in pain.

He took his copy of the key out of his pocket, unlocked the door, and walked into Alex's room. The bed was neatly made. That habit had somehow survived along with Alex's ability to find ideas to write about. Books and papers lay in four separate piles on the makeshift rectangular table that served as both desk and dining table. Someone who didn't know Alex might have said they were stacked at random. A typewriter with a sheet of paper in it faced away from the opposite wall, leaving an open space on the near side just large enough for a bowl or dish and some cutlery. A hot plate lay on a shelf attached to the wall on the other side of the room where a small sink denoted a kitchen area. A few cans stood on the shelf above it. A half-size refrigerator filled the rest of the kitchen space. A shirt, some socks and underwear lay strewn at the bottom of an open closet space. More shirts, two pairs of slacks, a pilled brown cardigan, and Alex's heavier winter jacket hung in the space above.

Rabani walked to the table, pulled out the wooden chair and sat down. He looked around the room and out the window, which faced the flaking clapboard wall of the building next door. He felt his stomach clench as he turned to look around the room again, estimating how many boxes or garbage bags he would need to gather Alex's possessions. The jacket and canned goods could go to the nearby community centre. He would take the books and papers to sort out later. The rest could go into the garbage. It wouldn't fill more than two or three boxes or plastic garbage bags.

Footsteps scuffed up the staircase. Rabani had a wild thought of his brother returning and stifled it before he saw Dominic Sandro standing in the open doorway. He looked at Sandro's broad face, a face inherited from farmers and stonemasons, strangely fitting above the grocer's smock, and could not come up with words.

Sandro said, "George, I saw you come in. I wanted to tell you I am very sorry about your brother. It's terrible."

"Yes. Thank you."

"If there is anything I can do."

"No. Thank you. You were very good to Alex. You did more than enough already."

Rabani stood and walked over to Sandro to shake hands.

"I want to thank you for looking after him so well. He was happy here."

"I didn't do much. He was a good tenant. He was a good man. A little different. But always polite and never a problem."

"I know you gave him things, bananas and other food. Those dish towels."

"We have to help each other live. That is the only way."

"I'll have his things cleared out by tomorrow. I may even come back later today to gather everything. Can I put what I won't take away into the large bin out back?"

"Of course. You just ask if there is anything you need. I'll be downstairs until nine."

They looked at each other a moment. Rabani groped for more to say, at a loss for words that he never felt at work, numb with grief but not wanting to spill it onto the man in front of him. Sandro felt torn between being at a loss for words and wanting to say something more of comfort, between sadness at the death of the strange but likable Alex and curiosity about Alex's brother, who had always been friendly but a little distant.

He said, "I will remember him. He often had interesting things to say. I will remember how he hated the sight of cantaloupes. He avoided the aisle where they were stacked. But after the time he told me he didn't like them he never complained about them."

Rabani smiled, partly out of remembering his brother, partly to acknowledge the attempt to ease the sadness.

"You'll have a service? You'll let me know? I would like to come."

"Just an hour's visitation at the funeral home, I think, and then the cemetery. Our mother had a plot arranged next to hers. You know it will be a small gathering, probably most of them people from my office."

"I will be there." Sandro was still not sure whether to ask about what was on his mind but there could be no other time. "The police said he was standing out in the middle of the street, right on the centre line. The driver didn't see him in the dark until it was too late and then Alex seemed to be scared and jumped the wrong way right into his path. George, I keep asking what he was doing out there almost at midnight, standing in the middle of the road just looking."

Rabani drew a long breath and said, "I think he was looking down the centre line. He told me he was planning a book that had to do with geometry, lines and circles. It was going to be about the game of curling but also about the way the country here is surveyed in straight lines. He said it was also going to be about the way things and people could find their places. Everyone had a place to fit in. I think he thought he fit in here. You made him feel at home here. Thank you for that."

Sandro tilted his head with curiosity as he listened to the explanation and nodded when it was finished. "I'll miss him. My thoughts will be with you. My wife's too, and she will add prayers.... I have to get back to the store. Let me know about the funeral and remember, tell me if you need anything."

He turned and walked slowly down the stairs. Rabani looked around the room once more and walked to the other side of the table to look at the paper in the typewriter. He saw Alex had begun an idea there and read the words: "Sundogs are rainbow circles formed in the sky on bright winter days. Unlike the aurora borealis, they do not shimmer and continually change colour. They are stable and follow definite rules of light refraction. Their colours divide prismatically and they describe a precise angle around the sun. That makes them similar to the circles on curling rinks. Can we think of patterns in the winter sky as reflecting patterns on flat ice? What is...." The words stopped there.

Rabani pulled the paper from the typewriter, folded it neatly in three, holding it on the table to ensure the sides of the sheet lined up and the fold lines were straight. He held the paper rather than pushing it into a pocket. He walked out and locked the door behind him without looking back. He thought he would remember the room as he had seen it now. He thought he would use plastic bags to gather the leftovers of his brother's life later in the day. They would be easier to carry to the bin, or to the community centre if anything looked useful and reusable. A large moving box would be better for the papers and books. He would return the books to the library and thought he might burn the other papers rather than reading them. He did not know what was written on them but he knew the way his brother had thought.

He drove across the river. It looked sluggish and dull. The sun was bright enough through the flat cloud haze to create a strobe-light effect as he passed under the iron girders of the old bridge. He turned into the neighbourhood where he and Alex had grown up until their parents had moved to a bigger and newer house the year he finished elementary school. The houses here were small compared with the ones being built now. They had a common general appearance and layout. Yet they seemed more distinct from one another than the ones being built in the new subdivisions. The yards were all individual too. Every house had its own distinctive paintwork and landscaping and, occasionally, its own fence or hedge. All these people had their own ideas. Whenever he drove around the newer areas he had an impression of similarity that he never had here, even though the old neighbourhood had probably started out in the same stamped-from-a-pattern way.

He parked one street over from the old house, wanting to come up on it gradually. He walked down the block to the corner and stopped to look into a yard where he heard odd voices. Then he saw what had drawn his curiosity. One of the voices belonged to a whitish parrot with a pointed lemon-yellow crest sweeping back from the top of its head.

A woman with a round face and glasses held the parrot on her hand. A man who was probably her husband walked over to join her. Rabani guessed they were well into their seventies.

The woman saw him looking over the white picket fence at the fringe of a lilac bush and said hello. "This is Esmeralda," she said, indicating the bird. "Can you say hello, Esmeralda?" The parrot shifted its feet, looked sidelong at Rabani without committing itself to a full gaze and said "Hello" in a cross between a croak and a screech.

The man joined the woman and the bird. He had glasses too, and an indulgent, amused smile. "Esmeralda is enjoying her afternoon walk," he said. "We take her out and trust her not to fly away. She did twice, but she came back in about fifteen minutes. You're used to the good food here, aren't you, Esmeralda?"

The woman said, "Oh, she would come back anyway. She likes us. That's why she stays. But we like to see her enjoying her food and happy."

"Yes," the man said, looking at the woman. "That's how to keep people around. Keep them well fed and they won't stray very far."

"But not so well fed they become fat and just sit around all day," the woman said.

Rabani heard an accent from somewhere in Eastern Europe. He wondered if they had picked it up from their parents in Canada or if they had escaped the destruction of the war and made a new home here. He looked around the yard. A cherry tree stood in the middle, recognizable by the leaves still hanging onto the branches. The fences were lined with the dry autumn remains of what he thought were impatiens, columbines, delphiniums, and an occasional rose.

"You have a beautiful yard," he said.

The woman smiled and replied, "Thank you. That's what you get if you know how to feed the gardener not too much or too little. It's easy when he is happy to have the same things most of the time."

The man smiled and raised his eyebrows. "You never know. Someday he might decide he wants goulash instead of sausage and sauerkraut. Maybe fried potatoes instead of boiled."

"You hear that, Esmeralda?" she said. "Maybe we should write a menu like in a restaurant. Would you like one too?"

The bird cocked its head and shifted its feet. It apparently saw no reason to reply. They talked about the weather and how it had been fine until the last few days and would probably be fine again for a few weeks before the first snow arrived. Rabani liked the way the couple did not ask him what he was doing walking around the neighbourhood. For them, he was company. Maybe they had a lot of other people in their lives or maybe they did not. Maybe they had a normal working life in their background or maybe they had lived through horrors in the war. They seemed happy to have each other and the bird. He wished them a good day and walked up to the next corner. He realized they were company for him as well, but he wasn't sure whether he had taken a few minutes to talk with them because he enjoyed it or more because it was a way to put off seeing the house.

When he approached it, he saw the old Manitoba maple in the front yard had been taken down. He knew the tree had been getting unruly and frail but he still missed it. A small long-needled pine had been planted near the old tree's spot. The frame around the front door and windows had been repainted blue instead of the green that he remembered. He looked down the side of the house and could see a sliver of the backyard. The smell of damp caragana leaves flooded into his senses. The sidewalk was developing cracks. It was still the old concrete laid down during the construction of the neighbourhood. He remembered small happinesses. He thought he could see Alex playing catch with a red and blue sponge rubber ball. Then he could see himself, three or maybe four years old, riding a tricycle up the sidewalk to greet Alex as he walked back from school. Red plastic streamers hung from the ends of the handlebars. Alex was grinning at the sight of his younger brother. His light brown hair stood up in tufts, slightly unruly even then. Rabani felt his chest tighten. He felt like he might cry, but didn't. He looked up past the tops of the old elms growing in the boulevard between the sidewalk and the road and saw medium grey clouds sliding against the background of light haze. Maybe the sky will cry for me, he thought.

He walked to the end of the block and doubled around to his car. He had changed his mind about clearing out Alex's apartment, deciding to put it off until the next day. Back at the office he closed his door and telephoned the funeral home where his and Alex's mother had been taken. He agreed to go there next morning to make the final arrangements. Then he looked up Adela's number in his card file, suddenly not sure he could remember it accurately. It took three tries spaced ten minutes apart before she answered. He said he needed to have dinner with her and hoped she would be free. She did not ask him whether anything was wrong or comment on the short notice, but he told her his brother had died.

She was silent a few seconds and said, "I'm very sorry. It was unexpected?"

"A traffic accident," he said.

They met at a small Vietnamese place a few blocks from Adela's apartment. Rabani chose it rather than his usual places. He did not want to have dinner in a restaurant he associated with happy times or that seemed celebratory. They ate beside a wall one table away from a window that soon became spotted with drops from a light drizzle. Adela occasionally prompted him with questions about his brother but mostly let him talk about whatever came to mind. He left long silences, comforted by her presence more than by her words.

"He felt like he didn't belong here after the accident that left him with a brain injury," Rabani told her. "Not in this city and not in this province. He said he felt like a stranger here. He wondered whether people really accepted him, but he also wondered how much he could really want to belong to a place that did not feel like home. He seemed to have some idea of what home would feel like. His apartment felt a little like home for him but it wasn't enough. When I asked him once to describe it, he couldn't name a place or even say what would make him feel comfortable. All he said was that I would be there."

Over the occasional clack of plates being set down or removed, and through the quiet voices at other tables—much quieter than in bigger mainstream restaurants, Rabani noticed—Adela told him that losing relatives was difficult. "I worried constantly about Roberto when he was taken away. Now I worry about him because in some ways he has never really come back."

"How does he feel about living in Canada?" Rabani asked.

"He gets along well in some ways. Certainly he is as happy as I am not to be caught in a guerrilla war. But he always appears restless. We left Nicaragua and the fighting he was forced into. I'm not sure he completely left it behind. Being a child soldier, a large part of his life involved fighting. Is it possible he can leave that behind? I don't know."

"Are you seeing him do things that worry you?"

"He is my little brother. I am the only person responsible for him. I worry. If anything happened to him I would ask what I could have done differently. Is that what you are thinking? Are you going to blame yourself that your brother was hit by a truck in the middle of a road on a dark night?"

"No. It was an accident. The only way to prevent it would have been to keep him constantly under watch and virtually locked in his room at night. Guilt applies when you could reasonably have done something to prevent a tragedy. For his death I feel only sadness."

They talked desultorily through dinner and over iced coffee afterward. Rabani was comforted less by the conversation than by being with her. When they left the restaurant the light rain had stopped. They walked along a wet sidewalk, dappled with water pooled here and there in slight concave depressions in the concrete. Sometimes you don't fully know the reality of an object until something brings it into relief, creates perspective, Rabani thought. The first accident had done that with Alex, bringing out new ways for him to look at the world. He thought about what the accident and his response to it had revealed about himself too. But he did not say this.

He felt the brush of Adela's arm every few seconds through his jacket. He heard the click of her shoes on the concrete. He realized that he felt at peace walking beside her. He had already realized in the restaurant that she was far more reluctant than to talk about her life than he was to talk about his. She generally told him what she observed, not what she felt.

Two blocks east, another meeting was going on in a small Chinese restaurant. It was more than a café. Vermilion screens and lanterns lent an air of formality. Jade green accents and two ink drawings of boats near a bamboo-laden shore highlighted the off-white walls. Other diners were busy with their meals. Becker and Radescu had chosen the table farthest away from them. They were talking about the strange project with the photos and about how it had got stranger. First Ostroski had apparently taken away some photographs. Then Frank Jeffries had shown unexpected and undue interest in the collection, or rather in a small and unknown part of the collection.

"He wanted to know about pictures of Hesperia Tindall and whether Jack was showing interest in them or even taking some away. He also wanted to know which box numbers held any pictures of her. Here's the weird part. He asked a few times whether any of the pictures showed the old bat touching anyone or with an arm around anyone or even seeming to stare intensely at anyone. But I was not supposed to tell you what he was asking about or doing. Not anything. And here's the really weird part. He asked me whether you and Jack seemed to know each other and get along well. It was almost like he suspected the two of you were somehow in cahoots."

"Yes, well, Frank has a conspiratorial view of the world. I guess you get that way if you're inclined to traffic in constant small conspiracies yourself. It's Jack now, is it? I didn't realize there was some charm under that crusty exterior."

She laughed. "Oh, he's charming all right. Sort of the way the little cactus plant next to my window is. But he tells some interesting stories about Hollywood and the early days of television. He's seen a lot. He talks about those things if you're patient enough and don't press him too hard."

"I'll have to keep that in mind."

"John, there's something else I have to tell you. Mr. Jeffries sounded angry the last time I talked with him on the phone. I got the impression he was sure that I'd see more pictures he was interested in and there weren't any. Then he asked again about the ones Jack may have taken away."

"Ostroski may be too mischievous for his own good. We made an arrangement to get some photographs back from him. By we I mean the government. They could have been a bit embarrassing if they'd got out. He didn't have any reason to keep them from us except maybe as a bargaining chip. He's going to receive a decent quid pro quo for them. I'm still not convinced that was his only motive in keeping them. He strikes me as someone who likes to stir things up."

"A shit disturber."

"That's him to a tee. I'm thinking it's a hard habit to break."

He looked at the tranquil boat scenes on the far wall, and then at the fringed lanterns hanging from the ceiling. Then he squared his gaze on her, first on her full lips, then with an effort on her mascara-shadowed eyes.

"Ginny. I have to tell you we can't meet anymore."

Her head tilted just enough for him to see the slight change in angle. Her lips came open but she said nothing.

"I really care for you. But after this blowout business my face is more recognizable. It's probably going to become more recognizable still. There's no place we'll be able to go and not have people recognize me and start talking. That won't be good for me or for you. You don't want to be the woman with a reputation."

She sat silently, absorbing the shock. Then her eyes narrowed and her mouth flattened into a knowing smile as if he had shown himself to be what she'd half expected all along.

"I get it," she said. "You're a TV star now. Onward and upward. No women on your arm except your ranch aristocracy wife. At least as long as you're in cabinet."

"Please, keep your voice down."

She sighed. "Sure. I'll keep it down. I know what's good for me. A married man isn't."

"It isn't like that," he said.

"It's always like that."

"If things were different ... I can't tell you everything. I have to keep my job. It's the only leverage I have to make a difference. There's something I need to do."

"Come off it, Mr. Becker. I've seen ministers in office flings. The only thing any of them ever needed to do was get re-elected. The two I know of who let the folks back home learn they had left their wives for someone in their office didn't even get to run for the party nomination in the next election. They knew better than to try."

"I won't argue with you. Just know that I really do care for you. It isn't wise now for you to stay on my staff. I'll make sure you're placed in another office, with someone I'm sure will be good to work for."

She kept staring at him. He could not tell whether the words were sinking in or bouncing off her. After about half a minute she said, "I suppose I should walk out of here in a huff, maybe even feeling hurt. I think I'm going to wake up next week and realize you're not worth it. So buy me the most expensive cognac in this place. I saw some on the drinks menu. It's time I learned to like cognac. I didn't learn anything I didn't already know about men from you. I may as well see if I can figure out what the appeal is in high-class drinks."

22.

THE DOGS HAD BEEN FED. THE BECKERS WERE HAVING breakfast together for a change. John had decided at the last minute to stay home an extra half-hour. Arlene had made no comment. Thick toast with Seville orange marmalade for her, ham and two fried eggs for him. Coffee from a French press for both, a recent upgrade in kitchen implements and taste.

He began to tell her about his suspicions, almost surprised that he was blurting out the words while wondering if the chance to talk to her about this was really why he had chosen not to drive straight into the capital.

"I think Frank Jeffries has an interest in the Ostroski photograph collection. I mean in a handful of photos he thinks were in there. I think also he planted the idea of sending me out to Broken Pines so that he could get his hands on them while I was out of town."

Arlene bit a piece of toast delicately, keeping the marmalade from spreading on her lips, looked into the brown depths of her coffee and said, "How do you know this?"

"One of my admin assistants was assigned to sit with Ostroski as he reviewed the collection. It turns out she was also watching for Jeffries. She must have thought twice about it and told me after I got back."

"And she was really supposed to be watching for you?"

"For the government. We didn't trust Ostroski not to remove photos he might take an interest in."

"I see. This was Ginny?"

"Yes." He thought he had succeeded in not hesitating before answering in his most neutral tone of voice. Then he thought about gossip, how it spread like weeds under concrete and asphalt.

"What could have interested him about a collection of old photographs?"

"That's what I don't know. You knew Jeffries from university days. Can you think of anything from years ago that would be a reason for him to want pictures so badly? He went to the lengths of planting a spy to be on the lookout for them."

Now she turned her head up and to the side to face him, eyes narrowing slightly against the morning sunlight streaming in through the kitchen window. "Frank liked to keep secrets. I suppose you've encountered that in your dealings with him. He also tended to be involved in things you would never suspect."

"I'm given to understand that the particular photographs drawing his attention were of Hesperia Tindall."

"Ah." She waited but he made no response. "You haven't heard the rumours?"

"No."

"Perhaps gossip would be a better word. But gossip implies wide circulation. Rumour may fit better in this case."

He saw the morning light from the sun low on the horizon highlighting wrinkles around her eyes and a few strands of grey in her hair. He thought the new depth to her surface looks was attractive.

"The rumour about Hesperia Tindall," she said, "was that she was a lesbian."

It took him a few seconds to process that before he said, "And?"

"And what?"

"And why would that lead Frank Jeffries to be wondering what photographs of her were in Ostroski's collection? It's not as if he would have been posing the lieutenant-governor naked with a girlfriend."

"No. But one of the propellants behind the rumours was her tendency to display a little physical affection, even at public events. An arm around a waist. Holding hands a little too long. That sort of thing."

"That's all?"

"It could be enough for Frank. He can be obsessive about protecting reputation. He may want to destroy any kind of evidence of something he doesn't want known."

John looked at her blankly. "I don't get it. She's been dead for years. And it's not as if we're living in the Fifties or in Oscar Wilde's day. It's generally known that Billington's EA is lesbian. It's generally accepted on the inside that one of our MLAs and one of our cabinet ministers is queer."

"You may not be living in the Fifties. Frank may be, to some extent, as much as he prides himself on keeping current with culture. And there was one more thing. Hesperia was rumoured to be very close friends with George Manchester's wife. No one ever claimed to have proof as far as I know, but they were thought to be affectionate with each other. Certainly Mrs. Manchester would have been looking outside her marriage for real affection. She would have got little enough from that conceited old goat. The thought of that rumour becoming sniggering common currency would drive Frank to do anything he could think of to stop it."

"Still...."

She broke into a slim smile. "Oh John. You really don't understand, do you? Despite all your years living here. It isn't even a question of someone's attitudes being formed in the Fifties when people were desperate for a return to normal. It's about this land and about the people who built an admirable community here.

Frank's ancestors settled here in the 1890s, nearly as long ago as mine. When mine arrived, the buffalo had just disappeared four years earlier. The Natives were trying to stay alive without them and not always succeeding thanks to meanness among government officials. The Hudson's Bay Company still had a fort here and there was still some beaver trapping. But then very quickly there were cattle ranches and lumber mills and stores run by independent business owners. And railways. And courts and schools and churches. And all those things were built by people who wore long woolen coats and voluminous dresses on top of their corsets. But that wasn't all. They wore probity and rectitude on their sleeves. Haven't you seen old photographs? Their clothes symbolized their rectitude. Never mind the stories you've read about saloons, and brawling mayors and councillors. The real people who made this province were the ones who could always stand in front of a crowd of their peers and be acknowledged not only as builders of commerce but as moral leaders in their communities. That's not the stuff of the half-baked TV documentaries your department encourages. It's not anything those people who keep coming here from the East or from other countries for jobs will understand. It's something rooted in the soil and passed on from generation to generation. We don't need anything to show us or remind us what we are. We know. We can't leave that even if we wanted to, and most of us don't. And a lot of us can't accept letting anything sully that image. We've moved on from corsets but we still need the rectitude. That's why Frank is fixating on those old photos. It's even more important for him because his family were marginal farmers and members of one of the stricter churches. He doesn't want even suspicions to break out."

"And there's never been any change? Never any failure to keep living the past? Not by anyone? I can't believe it. No place produces people who are all the same."

She looked out the window, considering what to say, narrowing her eyes again to see better in the coarse morning sun.

"No. We're not all the same. We're not all obsessed with appearing flawless. Maybe even Frank is different than what he wants people to think he is."

He stared, looking for any trace of change in her expression.

"It's hard to be different," she said. "When you grow up in one place, not having a lot of communication coming in from the rest of the world, you end up believing what you've absorbed from the people around you. It becomes more than belief. It's knowing. Belief is what you rely on if you are confronted with contrary facts. You can believe yourself all the way into knowing. Then you can't admit there even are contrary facts."

She looked at him again. "That's why Frank would want to suppress any questionable photos of Hesperia Tindall. He wouldn't want any question about who we are. Or who he is. It doesn't matter if we know there are cracks in the façade. What's important is what the rest of the world sees, and what the next generation here grows up knowing."

She continued to search his face in the ensuing silence. Then she said, "I always thought you might be able to understand someday. That's why I had such high hopes when you told me you were going into Energy. You could see the bedrock there, the foundation, not just the business but the people. Do I still have reason to hope?"

"Well," he said, "you'll be seeing me sworn in this afternoon. Tell me this evening if you see I'm different now."

He rose from his chair and took his dishes and cutlery to the dishwasher. He turned to go upstairs for a shower and a change into his business suit.

She said, "What do you know? Absolutely know? You never talked much about Wisconsin even when we were first getting to know each other. What I remember you talking about more than anything else was your friend and some kind of revenge or payback for him."

"That's more a case of what I don't know," he said. "By the way, I haven't seen that young Latin American around. Did he fail his visa application as far as you were concerned?"

"He finished the work. He isn't useful here anymore."

He climbed the stairs. She poured another cup of coffee and picked up the morning newspaper, looking for the political page, the business pages and the obituaries.

The drive into the city passed quickly. He listened to the political talk episode on the CBC. The commenters were trying to make more of the expected cabinet shuffle than there was. He thought he could do a more effective job than his predecessor. Other than that, the only real effect would be to enhance Becker's status and give him more weight with other cabinet members and caucus. He could also expect a few campaign donations from drilling and exploration companies; donations were always welcome even though he probably would not need the extra funds.

He parked at the side of the Legislature Building and walked up straight to his 10 a.m. appointment with the premier. Morehead was all smiles. Waschuk was half-smiles and appraising, but Becker knew Morehead was doing just as much appraising of his new cabinet luminary. The other two new appointments were minor in comparison.

Becker accepted a coffee, brought in immediately so that it must have been ready. Morehead said, "It will be good to have you taking over. You know we're in tough with the price drop. I don't know when oil is going back up. The economists in the department say gas is a better bet but it could take two or three years for its price to recover. The job in the meantime is to keep up public confidence and keep the companies from trying to suck more money out of us when Treasury is already dry. And keep the Opposition from making any headway with the situation."

"It may be a long slog," Becker said. "We'll get out of it."

"I know I can count on you."

He smiled beneficently. "John, how's that deal with the photograph collection coming along?"

"Wrapped up as far as I know. We have all the negatives in our hands now. There's no reason to think any prints are floating around out there."

Morehead's smile faded a touch. "I ask because I hear there's still some friction with that cranky photographer. Something about him maybe taking a few pictures out of the collection, or you pressing him for some pictures that weren't found in the review."

"You seem to be well informed about some pretty insignificant details."

Waschuk cleared his throat, but his voice still sounded paper dry: "We're hoping that's what they are, insignificant. Frank Jeffries seems to think there's still potential for trouble."

"Frank watches for trouble like a Kansas farmer watching for tornadoes. He expects it. I grant that's kept him out of the soup through most of his career. I won't say he's approaching paranoia. But sometimes he worries about things not worth worrying about."

"Is that the case here?" Morehead said. "Are you sure?"

"Yes. I'm still curious about a couple of items. But they're nothing that could affect the government. I'll talk to Frank about it."

"That's good. That's all I need to know."

Becker doubted that Morehead was completely satisfied. He was sure Waschuk would not be. But he had breathing room. He went to his office and phoned Jeffries to arrange a short meeting later in the day. The next few hours passed boringly. He played his role at the swearing-in, noted Arlene's genuine look of pleasure, smiled when the cameras were on him, and chatted politely. Late in the afternoon, still in his old office before the moving crew arrived, he welcomed Jeffries and apologized for the disorganized look left by the packing,

"That's fine, Minister," Jeffries replied. "I've become used to seeing members of cabinet come and go. One adapts."

"Good to hear," Becker said. "Let's see how quickly we can adapt to this business of the photographs. I understand there are some in the Ostroski collection that you want—not necessarily for the government and not necessarily for public viewing ever."

"True. And I understand there may be some that you want."

"Then why are we working almost at cross purposes?"

Jeffries smiled with slightly raised eyebrows. "I don't know that I would say we are working at cross purposes. I would characterize the situation more as us working independently toward similar ends."

"But you'd be happy to see me out of the way while you pursue your ends."

"Not necessarily. I don't see why we should continue on separately. We're after essentially the same thing. A little pressure applied from both of us in combination could make us both happy."

"I don't see it that way," Becker said. "There's no equivalency simply from the fact that we're both interested in some old photographs. I've become convinced that the ones I'd like to see have never been in the collection. The ones that Ostroski seems to have removed recently were still in the collection by his own choice. That suggests he never saw them as particularly meaningful."

"That's just the point. The photographs I would like are meaningful to me. They are meaningful to the province. They can have no particular meaning to him. Why is he holding out? The only reason I can imagine is that he thinks he can squeeze us for yet more money."

"I don't have that impression of him," Becker said. "Not that he would turn down money. But I don't believe that is his primary motivation. He may not have a motivation other than pure mischief. Maybe he just has an instinct not to co-operate when he feels he is being forced to do something. In this case, it may be worse. He may still have a grudge against us and especially against the Culture Department."

Jeffries sighed. "He has no valid complaint. It's true we had a disagreement but that's been resolved. And he is fifteen thousand dollars richer as a result. Do you know how often I look at my budget and wish I could find fifteen thousand dollars somewhere?"

"Let's not pursue this any further. The whole situation has to be put to rest. I'd like you to drop whatever you're doing."

"Hardly a directive considering you have not been my minister for the last hour."

"Call it words of advice, and a respectful request."

Jeffries stood. He glared in a way Becker had never seen before and said, "There's only one problem with how you view this situation. I don't give a rat's ass. Minister." He walked out.

Becker began considering next steps before the door closed. Jeffries already had next steps in mind. He was prepared to act alone. He was not prepared for rapid breathing and heart palpitations that assaulted him on the way out of the building and back to his office, or for the beginnings of tears that had him looking down as he walked so that others could not see his distress.

23.

ALEX RABANI'S FUNERAL TOOK PLACE IN BRIGHT SUNSHINE
at a cemetery east of the city. Puffed clouds, white on top, grey
underneath, floated slowly across the wide sky's magisterial blue
background. The grass had faded from green to autumn tan on
the slight rise where the Rabani brothers' mother was buried. Alex
was laid to rest in an adjoining plot. A handful of people joined
George for the ceremony: friends from the office, Dominic Sandro,
Adela Morales. George gazed at the casket as final words were
said over it and it was lowered into the ground. Afterward, he
glanced at the sky. It was filling up with the kind of clouds that
herald snow. He felt lightheaded. Adela put an arm through his
as the group walked back toward the parking lot. His awareness
of sights and sounds began returning at the feel of her next to
him. They rode together in the funeral home's limousine. Then
he drove her back to the camera shop before going to his office.
He read files there.

The next day he arrived at the usual time and found Becker
waiting to see him. With no urgent business on his desk he
invited the province's new energy minister to sit in one of the

brass-studded red leather chairs meant to make clients comfortable but impress them at the same time.

"I came in person rather than calling because I wanted to be sure you understand the importance of what I'm going to ask," Becker told him. "I also wanted to see your response. I apologize for coming in so soon when I hear you just buried your brother. But I assume your coming into the office means you're ready to take on work matters."

Rabani leaned back in his leather armchair. "Go ahead."

"It's come to my attention that Mr. Ostroski took some photographs out of his collection as he reviewed them. As you know, that breached the terms of our agreement with him."

"Come to your attention? How do you know he took anything?"

"Let's not waste time. He took some photographs. I'm not interested in pursuing the matter because I don't think he took anything materially important. Nor is the premier's office interested in dragging this matter out any further. However, I believe Mr. Ostroski holds other photographs that were never part of the collection and that I have a strong interest in seeing. That is, I have a strong interest in taking possession of one or more of them. I'd very much appreciate your intervening to persuade him to turn them over to me, or at least allow me temporary access, and possibly a chance to make copies. He knows which photographs I'm talking about. If he does not comply, there will be repercussions. No one wants that. But he has to know the seriousness of the matter. I've tried talking with him personally, with no result. I'm hoping you can get him to see sense."

Rabani looked out his window at the office building across the street, wondering if he would see signs of life through the dark windows set into the dull concrete.

"I don't think I want to be involved in this. My engagement with Jack Ostroski has been completed. He's old enough to take care of himself in non-legal matters."

Becker leaned forward. "He's old enough but not reasonable enough. If he's not a client anymore, then please consider this pro bono work, a contribution to the public good. I'm not speaking lightly. If he won't co-operate, the consequences will be serious."

Rabani turned back to Becker looking as if he'd just tasted something he would like to spit out. "At every turn in this business I've encountered something that sounds suspiciously close to blackmail, on both sides. I'm fed up with it." He knew he should stop there but gave in to curiosity. "And what could possibly be so important about some old photographs?"

Becker considered the right words. "The ones I want represent things from the past that were never adequately resolved. That's how I would describe them. The ones he took from the collection may fall into the same category. I can't vouch for that. I do know all the photographs are important. The ones I'm interested in are more important. You know how crucial bits of evidence can be once they come to light. Think of them that way—pictures that can determine the course of justice."

"What if he wants money?"

"I'm prepared to be reasonable."

"You're willing to pay only for the photos you're interested in, I assume. Not for the ones that were part of the collection and that he may have removed."

"That's correct. The ones that were in the collection are secondary. No longer my concern."

Rabani sighed. "I thought that people in positions of responsibility here were mostly honourable. Business conducted on a high plane. I'm starting to think it's all pretty grubby." He sighed again. "I'll see what I can do. But I'm not going to let this turn into a never-ending back and forth. One shot."

"Thank you. You have my best wishes. Please do not characterize anything I've said as a threat when you talk to him. But keep in mind the situation is serious. It's not a whim. On a scale, it's closer to life and death."

"You've made your point. I'll look into it. Please close the door behind you."

Rabani watched him leave. He swivelled his chair and looked out again at the concrete block with windows that reminded him of sightless eyes. He had never seen people through them. Then he walked out to the reception desk and asked if Morley Jackson was in and could be interrupted. In Jackson's office he took some comfort from the alert, benign countenance of the veteran to whom most of the young members of the firm usually came for advice or encouragement.

Rabani sagged into the chair facing Jackson's desk and said, "I'm back to that Ostroski business. When I thought I was finished with it. It seems there are more photographs kicking around and they are sensitive for some reason. Ostroski probably nabbed a few out of his old collection while he was reviewing it. But he may have more that he never put in with the others. John Becker just asked me to try to pry those more mysterious ones out of Ostroski's hands. I'm not happy getting dragged back into whatever quarrel they have but it sounds like something serious could happen to Ostroski if he doesn't co-operate. Besides, I'm more curious than I probably should be to find out just what could be important about some old snapshots."

"Hmm. Did he give you any idea why they're important to him?"

"Something about justice being done. Some unresolved matter from the past. Probably a fair distance in the past. Ostroski hinted to me about a disagreement over some photographs but he wouldn't tell me anything about it. All I know is the new energy minister thinks the matter is important enough to ask me to intervene. He also talked about unnamed serious consequences if Ostroski keeps being stubborn."

"And all he said is that the photos are somehow related to doing justice?"

"He even used the word evidence."

"Well, speculation could lead anywhere. It's difficult to imagine what a government photographer could have recorded that would be evidence in a serious matter. He would usually have been working in a crowd of people."

"That's one of the things I don't get. Another is what could possibly be nagging Becker and/or somebody else in the government many years after the fact. If it involves a crime you'd think steps would have been taken long ago. If not, what could a few photographs mean? And whatever they mean to Becker touches him deeply. You know he's one of the smoother operators in cabinet. Never ruffled. Always ready to treat an opposition attack like a mildly funny joke. His face didn't look that way when he was talking to me this morning. I'd describe him as looking at least as desperate as he did forceful."

Jackson spread his hands on his desk. He moved his thick fingers as if manipulating a pliable object into an understandable shape. He stopped moving his fingers and said, "I'm just thinking of a German writer named Walter Benjamin."

"Oddly enough, I heard about him a few weeks ago," Rabani said. "I don't know much about him other than that he collected things."

"He did that too. Benjamin said there's a difference between history and what he called remembrance. History tells you what happened in the past. Remembrance involves a past event that still has to be settled. He said experienced events have a definite beginning and end. But remembered events are infinite because they are only the keys to everything that happened before and after them."

Rabani thought about that. "Keys aren't usually shared with a lot of people," he said.

He said he had taken up enough of Jackson's time, said thanks, and paced back to his office, thinking about how many people had walked along the soothingly carpeted hallway with secrets they had hoped to protect.

He waited until late afternoon to walk to the camera shop, calculating that he was most likely to catch Ostroski without customers at that time of day. The usual pieces of trash lay on the sidewalk in the light autumn breeze. Dingy and still wet from recent rain, they did not add the usual spots of colour or jittery movement to the grey sidewalk. He walked up to the familiar storefront with its thick layers of paint on the window frame, each layer cratered with its own flaked depressions. He opened the door and walked in. The door squeaked against the jamb as he pushed it shut. He heard the light tinkling of the bell that announced customers entering.

Ostroski shuffled out of the back room and behind the counter, keeping his eyes on Rabani the whole distance. Rabani smelled a hint of film developing chemicals.

"I know," Ostroski said. "I'll take the cheque over to your office tomorrow. You won't have to hear it's in the mail."

"I didn't come about the bill. There's unfinished business to take care of. Becker was in my office this morning. He's worked up about photographs he says you have and he wants. They aren't the ones you took from the collection, although the government would like to get those back. These are some private ones. He said you'd know what he was talking about."

"He asked me for some old pictures himself. I told him no. I didn't say whether they really exist."

"I don't think you're in a position to play that game, Jack. He's willing to let you keep the originals and just take copies. He said if he doesn't get them, there will be serious consequences. Not could be. Will be."

Ostroski snorted. "What serious consequences? He's going to make sure I never work for the government again? Check that my city business licence is up to date? He can shove his consequences up his ass."

"The deal you had with the government is complete," Rabani said. "But a good lawyer could probably find a way to accuse you of reneging somehow. Your taking some photos out of the collection while you reviewed it is probably a good starting point. Then they may come after your money. Or just take you to court and watch your legal bills mount up, which would not be coming from me by the way."

"Let them. I don't feel like giving him anything."

"It doesn't have to go like that. He's willing to come up with more money too. He didn't say how much but I had the impression he was talking five figures again."

"From him or from the government?"

"Does it matter?"

"It matters. It's a funny thing. I felt a little sorry for Becker. If I could trust him...."

"Trust him with what?"

Ostroski pulled up a corner of his mouth, appraising his former lawyer. He waited and the moments stretched out. At length he said, "All right, I guess you earned it, but I'm taking the full thirty days to pay your bill."

Rabani said nothing. Ostroski appeared to be reconsidering, but then started talking.

"I was in Wisconsin in the early Seventies, visiting a friend in Riverton. We heard there was trouble brewing down at the local college. I wandered down there with my old 35mm Canon. I couldn't tell you why, maybe habit. Same reason I always took the camera when I went anywhere. A couple of hundred college kids were demonstrating against the war. I guess the local authorities didn't like that, or were just scared. Of a bunch of kids. A platoon of National Guardsmen showed up on a rise in the road most of the kids were on. Nice positioning. On the high ground. Some lieutenant must have paid attention in tactics class. There was a lot of yelling going on. A couple of TV crews were there shooting, for the local evening news, I guess, and maybe hoping their footage would make it to the networks. The cameras just incited the more rambunctious of the kids. A few stones started flying. I tried to stay out of the way and started taking pictures. Habit again. Documentary images from the front lines.

"Next thing I know I see a bunch of the Guardsmen levelling their rifles at the kids. I didn't hear any orders being shouted. It looked bad, which was all the more reason to snap a few more frames. I started out with a roll of thirty-six. Then I hear shots and see rifles jerking. I'm looking through the lens at all this. I hear screaming. A girl is down. She's in a long flower-print dress and sandals like they used to wear. Blood's pouring out of her chest like a hose someone forgot to turn off. Jesus."

Ostroski looked down at the chipped Formica countertop. Rabani heard oppressive silence around them.

"I'd been taking photos of the Guardsmen. I was off to one side and in among a few onlookers who might have been college officials or professors. The Guardsmen were concentrating on the kids. If they'd seen me with the camera pointed at them they might have let loose on me too. The TV crews had been pointing their cameras at the kids when it happened so they were nothing to worry about. Hell, the Guardsmen probably thought their pictures could be useful in spreading an object lesson. I nearly got sick to my stomach but beat it out of there. When I develop the film strip I can see I caught the decisive moment, just like Cartier-Bresson said you can. You remember I told you about him?"

"Yes."

"Three Guardsmen pointing their rifles but fairly elevated. Even from the rise in the road they were going to be shooting over the crowd's heads. One had his rifle pointed straight. He was shooting to hit someone. I caught the moment the bullet was leaving the rifle and I caught his face. I never tried to look him up. I can imagine what was going through his head. He couldn't have been scared. The kids were too far away and were never going to get close enough to hurt those guys. He was mad. Could have been mad about kids throwing stones at him. I ended up thinking he had a brother or a friend in Nam, maybe still alive or maybe dead, and here were a bunch of privileged, snotty college kids making all that sacrifice look cheap. It wasn't all that way, of course. By then the war had been going on a few years. Some of those college kids had probably been drafted and served over there. They knew what they were protesting against.

"Maybe it was even simpler for the shooter. Some of those guys were just law-and-order types. I once met one who had me over to his place for a drink. He had posters of SS soldiers on one of his walls. You never know. But I ended up thinking the guy who did the shooting was gritting his teeth about snotty kids carrying flowers and smoking dope and playing guitars while his friend or brother was looking around in the dark in some swamp hoping there weren't snipers or booby traps waiting for him. You know what the capper was? I could see my old man doing exactly that. He might have fired. And I'm not about to let John Becker or anyone else get hold of that guy's picture and track him down to be crucified. Now you've got it. Satisfied?"

Rabani was not. His life consisted of asking questions. "Why didn't you just destroy the negatives?"

"I couldn't. Cartier-Bresson said a photograph can fix eternity in an instant. That's what happened in Riverton. It was too much responsibility. An armed man killing an innocent girl. That's eternity. I told you before, keeping it fixed is what a picture does. It fixes the moment. It doesn't keep the moment alive. It keeps the moment from spreading. I need a beer. Want one?"

"No, thanks."

Rabani watched Ostroski head into the back room, visualized him walking past what he called the time machine, heard the door open and close on the 1950s-era fridge and heard the bottle cap snapped off. Ostroski had what looked like a third of the bottle drained before he came back into the shop. He sat down and took another pull on his beer.

"Well, what now, lawyer?"

"I'm not sure, Jack. Why do you think Becker would go after that fellow, even if it were possible to track him down, if in fact he's still alive?"

"Becker's obsessed. I've seen that before. He won't let it rest because he can't."

"People change. What's important to them changes. He may still be obsessed about getting his hands on the photo. Taking some kind of revenge is an entirely separate step."

"Why take the chance?"

"Then there's the question of whether it really is right to protect that Guardsman. He wouldn't be charged with a crime even if a definite link could be made to him. People have to be responsible for their actions. That's a large part of what appeals to me about the law. It's a way of applying that principle of responsibility. Making the principle a reality."

Ostroski tilted the bottle for another long drink. Rabani was briefly struck by the ridiculousness of the sight of an Adam's apple bobbing up and down.

Ostroski looked at the chipped and yellowed linoleum floor and then at Rabani with an unfocused gaze: "Maybe it's the other way around. People also have to be responsible for what they don't do. That's a lot harder to pin down. Someone might have stopped something and didn't. No coming up before a judge and jury to explain that. Just something eating away at your insides for the rest of your life. You ever think that's why Becker is obsessed about this Riverton business? Maybe what's really galling him is this friend of his who got killed in Vietnam. Do you know about that?"

"No. What about it?"

"He lost his best friend. He told me this himself when he came to talk to me the other day. Didn't want the friend to go. It could have been arranged. Thousands of guys found ways to avoid being drafted. Or their fathers did it for them. Anyway, the friend got killed and Becker swore to himself someone would pay. That's a good one. One of the old bastards who got us into that mess was going to pay somehow. Now think about this. What if the guy who really had to pay—has been paying every day of his life since then—was Becker? What if he thought, still thinks, he could have tried harder to keep his friend at home and alive? Maybe he thinks he's the guilty party but he's trying to take it out on someone else. Besides, why should I try to help him with his problems? No one ever helped me."

Rabani felt his stomach tighten. His head felt light the way it had at the cemetery and he let it slump forward until he was sure he had recovered. He stood to leave and Ostroski said, "Aw hell ... I'll think it over."

Rabani said, "Thank you, Jack." He walked to the door, went out, pulled it shut behind him and looked down the pallid street. People two blocks away on the main avenue were starting to hurry back to their homes after a day at work or pick up a birthday card or newly repaired shoes before closing time.

Next morning, Adela arrived at the shop with two coffees. Ostroski said thanks and told her he would be in back working on a newly arrived Pentax for about half an hour and then going out.

She said, "You look a little funny, Jack. Is everything all right"

"I had some trouble with Becker and I'm trying to figure out what to do about it. Fixing cameras is easier than fixing people."

24.

SHE WAS BACK TO WORK IN THE CAMERA SHOP ON TIME THE
following Tuesday morning. She hadn't brought coffee. She had
her grim face on instead of the smiling one. Ostroski thought
about how many times trouble had started on a Tuesday in recent
months. The title of an old song came to mind: "Call It Stormy
Monday (But Tuesday Is Just as Bad)." Yeah, Monday morning is
a peach in comparison.

He wasn't ready for the story she had to tell him: immigration
trouble. Not just any immigration trouble. This had come out of
nowhere, and for no good reason that she could see. And it was
serious. A potential deportation order for her and her brother.
And all happening fast. She said she hoped to see if the lawyer
could resolve whatever issue the government had with her. But she
doubted they had any real issue, despite Roberto's slight brush with
the law a few months ago. She was suspicious about the coincidence
of an unwarranted immigration problem and Ostroski's problem
with a man who now was in the powerful post of provincial energy
minister. Politicians were all potentially corrupt. The smart ones all

knew how to pull strings and get things done, even dirty things. She had said that to Roberto.

He told her going to the lawyer was probably the best idea. Get him to look into both ends of the business—take on the federal officials but also talk to Becker. Afterward, he telephoned Rabani, explained what was happening. He said if it came to that, he might trade the Riverton photos in exchange for keeping Morales and her brother safe, but the photos should be held in reserve until they were clearly needed.

Rabani called Becker's office and learned how difficult it was to reach a cabinet minister, even on what he described as urgent personal business. The minister was away talking to oil and gas executives, he was told. Then he was coming back to the capital but would be leaving the office immediately and had left strict instructions not to be bothered until the next day. Rabani thought about staking out evening commuter flights at the mid-city airport but did not want to appear desperate. A short window of time the next day would do.

Becker had far different things on his mind. After an inconclusive meeting at which he heard about what he'd expected on regulations and royalties he stopped at a high-end jewellery store. He bought an AA-grade ammolite pendant set in gold for an anniversary present. Not the most spectacular gem that he could have bought but one he knew Arlene would appreciate; it came from near her family's ranch in the southern foothills. He had already done some research after hearing about ammolite and been amused to find it fit his impression of the province. The rainbow-hued stone was actually a fossil. In jewellery it was almost invariably set as a thin veneer attached to a backing material like slate. Everything valuable in this place comes from dirt and usually still has a bit of dirt attached to it, he thought.

Back in his office two hours later he was told about the urgent request to meet with George Rabani and resigned himself to what would probably be another exercise in frustration. But you never knew. Something could come of it. Just better not to build up hope. He decided to set aside ten minutes after lunch the next day. He walked out to his car, noting the chill and the telltale puffiness in the clouds. On the way home he listened to a classical music program rather than his other usual choices. Mozart suited his mood. He planned to take his wife out for dinner but then return home reasonably early.

In the middle of town, Rabani packed a thick file into his briefcase for further reading after supper and decided to stop at the Czech bistro on the way home because he knew he could get a fairly light meal there. He was not officially on a diet, but still....

Back in his apartment later, he decided the file was too thick to handle in his reading chair. He took it to his oak table and placed it under the hanging lamp. He had worked through about ten pages when a loud insistent rapping on the door interrupted him. He opened it. Adela Rosales stood in the hallway, her mouth partly open and her eyes looking filmy with gathering tears. He quickly asked her in and before he could invite her to sit down or ask what was wrong, heard her say, "I'm afraid for Roberto. I think he is going to do something stupid and dangerous."

The story spilled out in short bursts. Roberto knew about Becker's approach to Ostroski and about the implied threat in his warning of consequences for failure to give him what he wanted. When he heard about the threat to his and his sister's immigration status, he had flared up but quickly gone cold and sullen. Now she had found a note from him saying he was going to "take care of" the persecutor. If he did not come back, she should know that he loved her and had always appreciated everything she had done for him. She knew he had access to guns.

"Just a minute," Rabani said. "Someone in my office spends time with people in the government. He may know how to get in touch with Becker." He called Morley Jackson, who had Becker's private phone number and address in his private files. Then he called the number but got no answer.

"I'll have to go out there," he said. "I'll take Jack with me. And maybe someone else from the office. Do you know Jack's number? I keep it at the office but I don't remember it."

He dialed Ostroski's number and arranged to pick him up in a few minutes. He asked Adela to go home and stay there just in case Roberto showed up again. Then he found Harry Asher in the office. Asher had just finished articling. He was solidly built, strong and young. Rabani thought he would be cool under pressure, and would provide muscle if needed. He made it plain he was asking something that was probably dangerous. Asher said he was used to frozen hockey pucks flying around his head and big bruisers trying to knock him around.

They were on their way to the acreage within minutes. Rabani explained what the Morales boy might be doing and why. He drove fast but stayed within twenty kilometres an hour of the speed limit to cut the chances of being stopped. At the acreage, they stopped at the driveway entrance to check the number on the gate and discuss whether to drive in or walk in. They quickly decided they were likely already visible if Morales were on the property. They pulled up to the three-car garage, and stepped out. Gravel gave way slightly under their shoes. The dogs started barking behind the wire fence surrounding their long run.

Rabani called out "Roberto" twice, loud the first time and as loud as he could the second time. They stopped moving and listened through the barking for any sound breaking the silence of the chilled night air. Rabani noted there was more light than he had expected. He looked up and saw a full moon looking as white as winter snow and thought, "Full moon, great. It's crazy time."

Now Ostroski called out: "Roberto, it's me, Jack. If you're there, come out so we can talk to you." No answer. "Or stay put if you want and we can talk to you where you are." More moonlit silence broken by sporadic, less frenetic barking.

They discussed what to do. No lights were on in the house. The doors were locked with no damage indicating forced entry. They were sure a cabinet minister would have better locks than the kind that could be opened by a credit card. There was no sign that Roberto was nearby. Leaving did not seem like a good idea. Calling the police was a sensible option but Rabani and Asher both had reservations. They knew about the recent formation of what were called SWAT teams. Ostroski told them heatedly it was out of the question. Too many rifles. Too much darkness in which a random gesture might be taken for a threat. Then there was the stress the appearance of what looked like paramilitary might put on Morales, who was not only extremely agitated but probably having flashbacks to his days as a child soldier in the Central American jungle.

"He's still just a kid," Ostroski said. "They'll kill him. God knows that may even be what he wants. I've seen enough kids killed. You call the police over my dead body."

They decided to wait. They stood at one side of the car, keeping it between them and the dogs. The barking died down although the animals were still pacing around their enclosure.

Several minutes later they heard engine noise and the crunch of tires on gravel and saw headlights glaring at them. Not knowing whether it was Morales or the Beckers or someone else, they stayed where they were.

"Roberto wouldn't have a big sedan like that," Ostroski said as the dark vehicle pulled to a stop a few car lengths from them. Becker and his wife opened their doors slowly and stepped out onto the gravel. Becker started to ask who they were but recognized the lawyer and his troublesome client.

"What are you doing here? What's the meaning of this?"

The three men were already closing toward the couple, loosely arranging themselves in a protective triangle. Rabani said, "You have to get into the house, Mr. Becker. Mrs. Becker. Please. You could be in danger here. I'll explain. But first get into the house."

"The only danger here is the one you're in," Becker said, glancing at Asher, whom he did not know, and turning back to the others. "Trespassing. Coming close to using force to push us around. What the hell is going on?" He spoke to Rabani but looked at Ostroski.

They heard a loud, percussive pop from the woods and then howling from the dog run.

Roberto Morales's voice came out of the darkness: "I know you like your dogs, gringo bastard. You have time to say goodbye to them. First the dogs, then you."

"We have no choice now," Rabani told the others. He turned back to the Beckers and said, "Get in the house. Now. We'll try to talk him into giving up his rifle. But call the police in case we can't handle it." He looked at Ostroski, who was looking into the woods and breathing harder.

Arlene Becker walked quickly to the back door, reaching into her purse for the key. She opened it. Ostroski told them to turn on only what lights they absolutely needed and to stay away from the windows. Another explosive puff of noise popped from the woods. They heard more howling and now saw two shapes lying in the dog run. Ricky barked repeatedly and strained at his leash. The two remaining dachshunds darted back and forth. The Beckers hurried into the house, Asher going with them rather than leaving them on their own. He waited until the brief phone call to the police ended. Then he explained that a young man named Roberto Morales had snapped after being told that Becker had arranged to have him and his sister kicked out of the country.

"What? I never did any such thing. Where would he get an idea like that? What makes you think that's why he's out there shooting at us?"

Rabani and Ostroski slowly moved toward an area they calculated was between Roberto and the dog run. Rabani felt more alive and more afraid than he could remember ever feeling. He was glad someone closer to Morales was with him.

Ostroski called out loudly, but avoided shouting and tried to keep his voice as calm as possible: "Roberto, this is no way to solve anything. Please stop this. Come to the edge of the woods where we can see you, put the gun down, and come out to talk to us."

The voice in the woods came back. "Time to talk is over. That cockroach is trying to ruin our lives—me and Adela. I do not even know why. Only that he wants something from you. Why don't you give him what he wants?"

"I think I'll do that, Roberto. I'm sorry. I didn't know it might come to him using Adela and you to get to me."

"He's talking to us even if he says he doesn't want to," Rabani said quietly. "See if you can wear him down."

Ostroski began talking again. He tried the obvious points first. Nothing would be solved with more shooting but he could probably get Becker to back off the immigration complaint by giving him what he wanted. Adela should be remembered; she was going to get dragged into a police investigation and things would be worse rather than better. There was still time to stop before anyone got seriously hurt. The dogs were just dogs. He held off warning that police were on the way.

Inside the house, Asher said, "At least the shooting has stopped for now."

"There's going to be more if the police show up while that boy is still out there with a gun," Arlene said.

"Can't be helped," Asher said. "All we can do now is hope George and Ostroski can talk him into coming out before they get here."

"No," she said. "That's not all we can do. I know what's behind this. I can guess with a high probability anyway. And I know he won't hurt me. I'm going out to talk to him."

John grabbed her by an arm. "No. That kid is crazy. You're not going out there to get shot."

She fixed her eyes on his. "He won't hurt me, John."

"What does that mean?"

"It means he's a boy looking for someone to accept him. He's still hoping I will. I won't. But he doesn't know that. There's no reason to see him hurt or possibly killed. Especially when I think Frank Jeffries caused this mess. He's capable of setting someone up to die."

"Jeffries?"

He loosened his grip. "Frank has his own reasons for squeezing the photographer," she said. "Have you forgotten? Didn't you realize how much it meant to him and what he is capable of doing?

Let me go. I won't stand by and watch blood shed when I know I can stop it."

Asher moved between her and the door. "I don't know who you are," she told him, "but if you stop me from putting an end to this, I will make your life a living hell. And if that means nothing to you, ask yourself what living hell you will be in if that boy and maybe some other people die and you have to live with knowing you stopped me from preventing a tragedy."

John said, "Arlene." She looked at him and saw tears welling up.

Asher hesitated but moved aside. "Be careful," he said. "If the situation breaks down, get behind the biggest tree you can find out there. If he starts coming for you, run as fast as you can and stay in as much darkness as you can."

She opened the door and walked into the driveway.

The two men outside heard her footsteps behind them. "Get back inside," Rabani hissed. "Why are you out here?"

"I'm going to bring that boy out here before he kills someone or gets killed himself."

"What? You have to get back inside. He may be here to kill your husband. He may be just as happy to shoot you."

"You're standing here and he hasn't shot either of you. And get your hand off me. How do you suppose he will interpret your trying to manhandle me? He likes me. Maybe not as much as he once did, but I'm sure I'm safe with him."

"A hundred per cent?"

She thought for a second. "Close enough to that." And she began walking toward the trees.

"Goddamn," Ostroski whispered. "I hope she knows what she's doing."

Arlene walked past the first few trees and stopped. The two men could still see her despite some branches and slim aspen trunks in the way. Her head was a pale halo above her black coat.

"Roberto," she said, "I'd like to talk to you."

There was no answer.

"I know you're angry and I know why. I can tell you there is no reason to hate my husband. He is not trying to get you and your sister deported."

He spoke now and she tried to place his voice in the trees. It sounded nearby: "I did not come here for lies."

"It's true. My husband is not doing this to you. I know who is. It is someone else in the government."

"Same government. Why should I care? And why should I believe you? Anglo bitch trying to save her gringo husband so he can keep buying her nice things. Go back. I did not come here to hurt you but I will. After I kill your husband's precious dogs."

A shot filled the quiet of the night. The dogs barked as a bullet pierced the wooden wall of the shed. The men in the driveway and in the house gasped and started. She turned quickly and shouted, "It's all right. He's not shooting at me. Stay back."

She turned back to the dark trees and said, "Roberto, are you doing this only because the immigration people are making trouble for you? Or because I sent you away?"

"You? Why should I care about you? You are too old and too stupid."

"You're right. I'm old. Maybe I'm stupider than I think. But I never lied to you. Did I? I never gave you a reason to believe I cared for you. Only that I appreciated the way you did your work. And when you asked about more I gave you an honest answer."

He made no reply.

"Isn't that right? I never lied to you."

"You don't think I am worth a lie. I am just an immigrant making your property look better and worth more money."

"You're a human being with a sister who loves you and a life still before you. You have a friend behind me in Jack Ostroski. He doesn't want to see you hurt. I don't want to see you hurt. And I have never lied to you and am not lying now. My husband did not set the immigration people after you. Please. Put down your gun and come out. People care about you. All you've done is create a disturbance and kill some dogs. You will be charged with crimes, but we will make sure you have a very good lawyer. I will pay. Please, it's not too late."

Long moments of silence answered her.

"Roberto?"

She heard a rustle of dry leaves. Twigs cracked as he walked out from the trees, only about ten metres away. He had a rifle in his right hand. He dropped it as he came closer. Rabani and Ostroski walked slowly toward him.

"If you are lying ..." he told her.

"On my mother's grave," she said, "I am telling you the truth. My husband is not persecuting you. We will all help you."

Becker and Asher had watched from a window. They came out the yard door and walked deliberately up to the group at the edge of the driveway. Asher placed himself, as unobtrusively as possible, in a spot where he could tackle Morales if the kid changed his mind and went for the rifle. Roberto glanced at him. Asher did not move further. He saw a boy, but a boy used to fighting and aware of the importance of positions.

Rabani told him, "Roberto, you know you can't just walk away from this. Police are on their way. Please co-operate. With all of us here to watch, you will be safe. I'll get a friend who's a top criminal lawyer in the city to speak for you tomorrow and begin work on your defence."

Morales said nothing. He looked around at the group, one by one. Staring at Becker, he said, "I killed two of your dogs. A third one got lucky. I am not sorry."

Becker said, "They're dogs. They are not as important as my wife, or you." Arlene's breathing stopped for a second. She resisted an impulse to look at her husband.

Flashing lights pulsed from the end of the driveway. The police arrived. They emerged from their two vehicles with rifles pointed. It took a minute to assure them all danger was over. They handcuffed Morales somewhat roughly but he was apparently used to such treatment and did not object or try to pull away from them.

The officer in charge had one of his men pick up the rifle from the edge of the woods and said a forensics team would arrive at first light to search the grounds and complete the investigation. One of the police stationed at the end of the driveway came up and spoke to the officer. He said two television news vans had been stopped just up the road. They would be kept away until the investigation was complete.

When the preliminary questions were over, John took his wife's hand. "How are you feeling?" he asked.

"Shaky," she said, "but I'm relieved that no one had got hurt. I'm sorry about the dogs."

She paused as if remembering something and said, "I heard the police say the TV vans will be held away from the property. You'll certainly have to face cameras in the next day or two. You know you can't comment on any criminal proceeding. But you can present a calm and authoritative face. The image is what counts. You're not just a cabinet minister anymore. You're going to be a recognizable person on television, someone people know is important and know they can probably trust. Being energy minister is important. This is when you really become part of the province."

He was at a loss what to say to that. Years of work had built up to a few hours at Broken Pines that made him a presence in people's living rooms and dens. Now a few minutes of fear would make him an even bigger personality, a constructed personality that had little to do with how he felt as a real person. And he was not sure that being better known made people inclined to trust him.

"I want to go check on the dogs," he said.

He found Gretchen and Heidi dead on the ground, thankfully both shot in mid-chest and likely dead within seconds if not immediately. The others slouched in a corner of the pen, looking at him inquiringly. He thought about finding a shovel and burying the two dead ones immediately but could not bring himself to it. He stroked their heads and carried them one at a time into the shed, covering them with a tarpaulin. Rabani and Ostroski, finished with the police, came to express their regrets.

Ricky the Doberman paced over to them hesitantly, sniffing. Mitzi, the dog Ostroski had kidnapped, waddled up and looked at him. He wasn't sure it was the same dog, and he wondered if she were looking to be petted or sizing him up as an enemy. Then she approached and lay down beside him. The other dog hung back and then approached him in short steps, stopping at each move forward to snarl at him with intermittent barks. Becker told her to quiet down. She stopped moving and resorted to a low growl.

The two men left through the gate and walked toward their car, where Asher was waiting for them.

Ostroski said, more to himself than to Rabani, "Goddamn dachshunds."

25.

RABANI DROPPED OFF OSTROSKI AND ASKED IF ASHER WOULD mind stopping several blocks away on the north side so that he could tell Adela Morales what had happened and what to expect from court proceedings. Asher said that would be fine. "Sounds like it's close to Dominic's. Care to stop in for a brandy and coffee? I could use a little calming down before going home."

Rabani said that sounded like a good idea. He found the building and went in alone to knock on the Morales apartment door. Adela opened it but he could see another Latin-looking woman standing several steps behind her.

"Roberto is in police custody but he's safe," he said.

"Thank God."

"He didn't hurt anyone although he did shoot two dogs. He'll face some charges related to firearms. I'm going to line up a very good defence counsel. It will be hard to avoid a conviction but a relatively light sentence is possible. There will almost certainly be no evidence of intended harm to humans. Plus there are the mitigating factors of the immigration ploy and of Roberto's psychological stress stemming from being a child soldier."

Adela took it all in. Then she introduced the friend who had kept her company through the harrowing night, Rosa.

"Rosa has a friend named Ginny Radescu who might be able to explain some of what led to this."

Rabani took Ginny's name and phone number and drove off for a drink with Asher at a bar across the street from the Italian grocery store. He did not normally go to a bar with anyone. They spoke about hockey and cars and the variety of their clients. Rabani talked about the couple he had met with a parrot. Then he talked about a thoroughly unexpected experience he'd had while waiting in line late in the summer to renew his driver's licence. A Sikh with a turban and a white beard trimmed to a sharp point had struck up a conversation with him. He had initially expected talk about the weather but the old gentleman began talking about literature. He admired Thomas Mann and asked if Rabani had read *The Magic Mountain*. Rabani said no and the gentleman said it was a true masterpiece. Then the line moved forward and Rabani picked up his new licence. "That's one thing about this place," he said. "You never know what could happen here. Sometimes it's nothing like what you'd expect. People surprise you." They talked about anything except what they had seen and felt earlier in the night. Their mutually unspoken understanding of what not to talk about would prove to be the beginning of a long friendship.

He arrived at the office in mid-morning next day. He began by arranging for defence counsel for Roberto Morales, then surveyed what he had waiting on his desk and decided in what order he should tackle it. Concentrating on work helped him calm down further after a fitful night. Early in the afternoon he received a phone call inviting him to the premier's office next morning at ten. Henry Waschuk was on the line, saying only that the meeting involved both the Morales and Ostroski situations. On an impulse, Rabani asked if he could bring Asher, who had taken part in the previous night's events. Waschuk asked if that was really necessary. He said it was not absolutely necessary but highly desirable.

Early in the evening he visited Adela again. She told him Rosa and Ginny would like to meet him at a nearby café. He went there and saw them seated at a table over coffee. Ginny had inquiring eyes. She told him a story of two powerful men in government both wanting something out of the old photo collection but both wanting something different and working at cross purposes.

"I get along with Becker but Frank Jeffries gives me the willies," she said. "There's something about him. He can say something ordinary to you and it can sound like a threat."

Rabani was intrigued at the way she half-laughed at points while telling a serious story and the way she looked at him as if he were interesting. He said his thanks and went home to fit together all the pieces of information, the ones he had so far.

In the morning he and Asher were shown in immediately to the premier's office. Morehead and Waschuk were there. So was John Becker. More surprisingly, so was Arlene Becker. After introductions, Morehead said he realized that Jack Ostroski had an interest in the matter as well but he and Waschuk had decided not to bring him in because of the possibility of unexpected reactions. At ten on the dot, Frank Jeffries entered the room. He hesitated at the door, scanned the faces in the room, lifted his chin, walked in, and sat in the chair that Waschuk indicated for him. It resembled all the other chairs in the room except for the leather work model behind Morehead's desk—well padded, upholstered in a thick fabric coloured with subdued candy-striped pastels.

Jeffries sat back in it, legs crossed, corners of his mouth turned up sardonically. He had heard about the shooting incident and suspected his attempt to put pressure on Ostroski by threatening the Morales woman with deportation was somehow linked to it. That had been unfortunate. He had been sure his plan would work and now was extremely worried that the scheme might fall apart. He had spent the early part of the morning convincing himself that he could find a way to salvage it. He had spent years salvaging bad situations—the unrecognized and unappreciated guardian. The most important thing by far was to keep the entire controversy out of public view. He had to keep everything out of public view—the reasons behind the incident, the Tindall photos, and himself. The public gaze was uncomprehending and pitiless. It burned like the sun.

Morehead made sure names were exchanged, then moved briskly to the point of the meeting. "Frank, there's been a lot of trouble about the Ostroski photo collection."

"There certainly has."

"It's going to end today. I know you've had a hand in the situation. You also seem to have your shorts in a knot over a few pictures that you think were in the collection and that you want back.... Well, is that right?"

"Inelegantly expressed, but substantially correct. I should add my concern is not personal. It's for the good of the province."

"We'll get to that. Was it also for the good of the province that you asked an old friend in Ottawa to lean on a brother and sister named Morales for some phony immigration violations? And that the purpose was to put pressure on Ostroski to cough up the pictures you wanted?"

"You seem to know the answer to that already," Jeffries said. He was almost thrown off balance by the unexpected question but recovered in a split second and offered a condescending smile. Morehead grimaced in exasperation. He was smart enough to know, however, that Jeffries was deliberately provoking him, hoping to trigger an outburst that would throw the meeting off track and perhaps even end it early and in confusion.

Waschuk's dried-paper voice, much louder than a whisper this time, intervened: "We know you did it. We know who in the immigration executive in Ottawa you've had past dealings with. What we don't know is why you're rocking the boat over a few pictures, apparently of Hesperia Tindall. Half the population doesn't even remember her. She was just another lieutenant-governor. What's your interest in old photographs of her?"

"Rocking the boat?" Jeffries leaned forward, his mouth tightening and eyes gleaming behind the wire-rimmed spectacles. "You, all of you, have no idea. No idea what's at stake. You've heard—or have you heard?—could you be so oblivious?—the rumours about Hesperia."

Waschuk had heard, but wanted everything in plain view. "What rumours?"

"You know what rumours. That she was a lesbian. Scurrilous certainly. True? I have no definitive proof although I'm almost certain of it. But I know she was sometimes careless in the way she acted at public events. She offered displays of affection, physical contact, that could easily be interpreted as supporting or even confirming the rumours. And I know that an official photographer hovering around the fringe of most government events would have captured some of those moments. Inadvertently at first, no doubt. Perhaps deliberately and mischievously for some time afterward. He may even have photographed moments she thought were private, perhaps even a kiss, for example. Do you know what letting such photographs out in public would do to our reputation? We would become a national laughingstock. Our image has been one of people who are rough and ready, not effete and confused. We can't allow a scandal that would make us lose our standing, that would have people question who we are. Not to mention what would happen to the government's support among religious communities."

Asher stifled a comment he was ready to make about the way a lesbian of notoriously starched manners could enhance a "rough and ready" image.

Jeffries had been talking directly to Morehead. Now he stared around the room, gazing into each face with an acid certainty that he was dealing with people too slow or too careless to understand the gravity of this crisis.

Morehead said, "Let's take this slow, Frank. You're talking about photographs taken at public events. Nothing like a private detective peeping in through a window at a bedroom. How damaging could anything be?"

"You are in this office in part because you know how to manipulate public opinion. And you ask me how damaging a mistaken impression about a serious matter could be? Besides, until I see those photographs, I have no idea how innocuous they are."

"And who would really care aside from a small fringe of people? We're not in the Fifties anymore."

"This is not something that can be written off with cheap talk about decades and their supposed character," Jeffries said. "You have no idea what you're dealing with. God help me." His breath was starting to heave. His eyes glittered behind his spectacles and he began darting glances at the impassive faces around the room.

Morehead watched the signs of stress building and said, "Let's try to keep calm, Frank. You're still determined to get your hands on that handful of photographs?"

"I certainly am. There is no one else I can trust. None of you appears to have a full grasp of how much is at stake. Are you all imbeciles? Don't you know? It's bad enough to have Hesperia Tindall exposed as having relationships with other women. The worst is her relationship with Mrs. George Manchester."

He looked again at all the impassive faces staring at him. "Do you not have any conception what that would mean? Scandal. Laughter across the country. Who knows what kind of reaction from Manchester himself. All our standing and self-respect destroyed. The world is full of little minds waiting to grasp any excuse for the pleasure of belittlement and scorn. You have no idea of the degradation. Or do you not care?"

Jeffries leaned back in the chair again, gasping, looking around at the apparently uncomprehending tormentors and waiting for the next assault.

Waschuk's voice rustled across the room: "One of the reasons we wanted to get the Ostroski collection in hand was that we had a lot of trouble resulting from the purchase of the Briller collection. It was badly handled and overpriced. Frank, did you have a prior relationship with Anthony Briller?"

They saw Jeffries slightly tilt his head back as he focused on Waschuk. "I knew him, of course. He was a leading figure in the province's cultural community."

"That's not the kind of relationship I'm talking about. Did you have a personal relationship with him? One that might even be called intimate?"

Jeffries coloured now, the pastiness of his face oddly coming close to a normal flesh tone, and a vein began to bulge on his forehead. "What are you insinuating?"

"I'm asking a question. Since you seem uneager to answer that one, how about this? When you were a professor at the university, did you have a relationship with any of your students, particularly a student named Melnychuk, who later killed himself?"

Jeffries snapped his gaze to his left and glared at Arlene. "You," he said in a hoarse gasp. "You're behind this." He was hissing now. "Is this your idea of revenge?"

"No, Frank. Management."

Jeffries stood up and took a step toward her. Asher had been standing next to the wall beside a seated Rabani. He sauntered toward Jeffries, who was saying, "You think you know about management. Someone who would marry a nobody American economist. You're as blind as the rest of these malicious fools. Worse. You're a traitor." He looked around again. "I'm the only one who really belongs here. You are all traitors. Now you want to be assassins too. You want to destroy me."

His last words rose in pitch as if asking if something unbelievable could be true. His breaths were coming even faster now. "But you of all these people are the most brutal and treacherous," he said to Arlene, taking another step toward her. He saw Asher ranging within reach. "Who are you? What do you want?"

"I'm just a junior lawyer who works with George Rabani," Asher said. "But I'm an old hockey player. I played in bantam with two young guys, good guys. They became alcoholics. One died a couple of years ago in a car accident. The other still lives here, going to

AA meetings when he isn't falling off the wagon and scraping by when he could have had a good life. He told me last year why the two of them began drinking. He said he still blames himself for what his coach did to him and our dead friend."

"Get back from me, you thug."

Asher whacked him on his left ear with an open hand. Then he whacked him on his right ear with a closed fist, hard enough to hurt Jeffries and cause him to stagger but not hard enough to knock him down.

Becker stood up looking as if he might intervene.

Rabani shouted, "Harry."

Asher turned and said, "Don't worry, George." He walked slowly back to the wall, looking at it as he said, "Two hits. One for each. It isn't much but it's some measure of justice."

Jeffries shuddered and sank back into the chair. His formerly reddened face was rapidly turning pale. He looked at Morehead. "Is this why you brought me here? To be assaulted?"

"I didn't see any assault, Frank. I doubt that anyone here did. I brought you here to explain why you were making trouble for two innocent people. That's going to stop. I also brought you here to tell you I expect a letter of resignation on my desk by noon. A short one. One of the security staff will accompany you to your office in case you need anything. If you need any boxes to pack personal belongings you can call building maintenance, but that's the only call you will make."

Jeffries' face was crumpling now. Tears welled up in his eyes. The others watched him, wondering whether they were tears of frustration or of mortal anger.

"You'd let those photographs end up in who knows whose hands? When they're already in the hands of someone who's shown he's willing to indulge in blackmail. I'm innocent. I'm innocent. You aren't merely condoning thuggish behaviour. You are, you are … you are conspiring to drag me through the mud, to drag this whole province through the mud. The province and all the people who love it and understand it and are truly part of it, those who have always remained true to it. Not like any of you. For something that couldn't be helped. A minor lapse. Something contrary to our true character. It's an outrage. It's indecent."

"No one will publish any photos, Frank," Morehead was keeping his voice steady, trying to calm the situation. "And no one will talk about you. We're clear on that, right?" he said as he gazed around the room, the question sounding more like a warning. "We're trying to run a scandal-free administration here. There won't be any scandal because of any photos, and if I see your letter of resignation by noon there won't be any scandal in your leaving. I'll issue a statement thanking you for many years of fine and loyal service. Don't look for another job, though. Take up golf."

Jeffries pushed himself out of the chair, his mouth hanging open. He closed it, glared around the room half-blinded by tears and walked unsteadily to the door. He opened it and left. Morehead said, "I think that concludes our business here. I have a delegation coming in to see me in a few minutes. Thank you all."

The two lawyers returned to their office together. Asher said, "It's funny. Jeffries seems to think most of us don't really belong here. Not even some of us who were born and raised in this province. But now he's being excluded from his idea of a private club, too. Who really belongs here?"

"Who belongs anywhere?" Rabani said. "After the accident that left him brain damaged, my brother felt that he was something of an outsider. He lived in a different world much of the time. Yet he was a fixture in the lives of people who knew him. He was part of a small family that way. At least he was for me once I'd accepted what happened to him. He was a fixture in that little business community where he sold his smokers. And, I suppose, in the downtown library. He still felt alien. Maybe we all do in a way. We all fit into different kinds of communities, yet we all have a core within us that remains hard for others to know and hard for us to express. And at the same time, maybe most people's private inner life is much like that of others. Who knows? Maybe that's what binds us, a common experience of feeling uncommon. Life is movement and change."

"You've got that right. There's only one place I know of you can find certainty. A grave."

"I wouldn't go so far as to count on certainty even there, Harry. You go along thinking you can trust something and one day the bottom drops out on you."

"No point in counting on that. One thing I learned playing hockey: play like you expect to win until you don't."

"And then?"

"Play the next game."

Asher was silent for a moment, then said, "Do you think that old stick Tindall was really getting hot and heavy with Manchester's wife?"

Rabani answered, "There are some pictures I'd rather keep out of my head. Anyway, Tindall is dead now and Manchester's wife is so forgotten she may as well be. For that matter, Manchester liked to keep the spotlight on himself so much that she was hardly ever more than a rumour. I wonder what it's like practically being a ghost before you're dead."

They walked up a hill from the legislature, anonymous grey office buildings several storeys high around them. The dreary sameness was interrupted here and there by parking lots and a Smitty's restaurant.

By the time they reached the top of the hill, Jeffries was in his office. He pulled aside the vertical blinds on his window and looked out at the bridge. It was a short walk, he thought, and a short climb over the railing. He could fall like an angel.

He looked at the papers on his desk. He did a quick mental inventory of the personal belongings inside the drawers. No, he decided. They would not win that way. There should still be a way to redeem the situation, to continue protecting what needed protecting. Ending his life would be seen as an admission of guilt. "I'm innocent," he breathed.

The Beckers were sharing a quick coffee in a corner of the nearly deserted legislature cafeteria. John was looking at Arlene as if they had just met. He noted small things about her: a few creases at the corners of her eyes, two lines across her brow, finely manicured fingernails shiny with a clear polish, the just-right look of her navy blue suit, a blank expression that yielded nothing but that seemed built on something immovable rather than masking emptiness.

"Did you tell Morehead about that kid, what was his name, Melnychuk?"

"Yes. I telephoned him yesterday while you were outside fixing up Gretchen and Heidi's grave."

"You seem to know a lot about Frank Jeffries."

"I know what he was. I know what he is now. He was ambitious and successful and often dangerous before. He was insidious and immoral in ways I somehow did not recognize. Or perhaps I simply refused to recognize it, couldn't believe it. Now he's still those vile things but he will no longer be successful. And he will no longer have enough power to be dangerous."

"What did you mean by management? Not revenge, but management, you said."

"Growing up on a cattle ranch you learn to face realities, John. A spring blizzard comes along and kills some of the stock. Newborn calves get scours and some don't survive. A cow gets sick or badly hurt by something out on the pasture and has to be put down. Horses are worse. They're surprisingly fragile for an animal that size, always getting sticks puncturing their hooves. Or they get their skin torn on a loose wire or nail and develop an infection. You want to save them all but some you can't. The ranch is better off if you close the book on them."

"And the revenge?"

"If I'd wanted revenge on Frank Jeffries I would have taken it long ago. That doesn't mean I didn't admire him once. I didn't after I'd grown up."

Becker decided to leave it at that. He looked into the muddy swirl at the bottom of his coffee cup. He looked around the cafeteria, all brown wood and beige fabric, the walls covered with a similar beige paint, innocuous strips of wallpaper and some of the endless store of landscape paintings constantly going in and out of the government's art warehouse. The paintings invariably showed mountains or empty prairies. Each one looked like the cry of a painter saying, "Here. Here is what this place is really like. The way I see it is real." And maybe some of them did capture some essential aspect. But there were so many of them, so many paintings that what the artist hoped was unique got ground down into the generic and hackneyed.

"Do you manage me?" he asked.

She pursed her lips and looked at him with the same blank expression. He thought she looked tired. "I've been under the impression that you've been managing me."

He felt the weight of the brown and beige surroundings, all the decoration and furniture in the room calculated to be unnoticed but coming together in an oppressive artificial unity, a relentless vision of mute acceptance.

"If I ever did, I apologize," he said.

"Hypothetical apology accepted, on the premise that I needed one.... Now let's move on."

"To what?"

"You're going to be minister of Energy. That will make you one of the most important men in the government. You will be one of the few faces that people recognize from being on television regularly. That will give you a certain power of persuasion, a weight beyond being merely a cabinet minister."

"A television star. A face that people will remember as long as the sponsor is satisfied with the ratings. Until they're bored."

"It's the world we live in now, John. More the one that you grew up in than I. My family's world was the land. Things last longer out there. Still, here I am in the capital, wife of a cabinet minister about to become a much more important member of cabinet. You will have somewhat more influence than before. I'll have marginally more influence on the symphony board. And who knows? Maybe you will have enough influence to support regulations that keep sour gas plants from being built right next to some of the ranches down south. The families have kept the land pretty much as it was a hundred years ago. You can ride out on the grass and see exactly what people saw when hardly anything was there except deer and elk and a few grizzlies."

He studied the varnished top of the small wooden table. The sheen had worn dull over the years, but the varnish, polyurethane he assumed, had been applied so thickly that it would still protect the wood for years. He looked at her medium-brown hair, carefully cut, held neatly in place by some means about which he never inquired.

He said, "How did you get Morehead to arrange to get rid of Jeffries so fast?"

"I didn't have to persuade him, if that's what you mean. He was a football player. He knows that players who underperform or might embarrass the team should be cut. Professional sports are a bit like ranching that way. Emotion is good, even necessary. Sentiment leads to mistakes."

Becker considered that. He glanced up at the round clock on the wall. "I'll have to be getting up to the office," he said.

"I hope you enjoy the new surroundings. Will you be home for dinner?"

"Yes, probably about 6:30. I was thinking. We haven't been out for an evening walk in a long time. I should take the dogs out after supper. It will be easier with just the three of them. Would you like to go too?"

"Yes, I'd like that."

26.

RABANI FELT WEARY. THE TWO FILES ON HIS DESK BULGED with details. Lifting the top of the folder on either one seemed like it would take too much effort. The papers inside the folders seemed crammed with the thousands of words and with the freight carried by the words: irritations that people had let drive them half-wild, carefully hedged representations of fact, citing of precedents, suitably disguised ill will, muted bursts of outraged innocence—all presented in a voice of reason.

He decided to leave them for next day, not even take them home. He took his grey wool overcoat from the small closet built in beside the oak bookshelves, walked down the carpeted hall that felt like an airlock keeping out the chaotic world, told Julia he was gone for the day, and walked out onto the street. His head quickly felt cold in the moderate wind. It crossed his mind that he should buy a woolen peaked cap, one that would go well with his coat.

A panhandler with a deeply creased face and a damaged, blood-shot eye looked in Rabani's direction but he slightly shook his head; he did not want to encourage people to hang around the entrance to the office building with their hands out. He walked slowly along the grey sidewalks, peering occasionally at store windows with early Christmas sale displays. In mid-afternoon there were few other pedestrians. Diesel buses roared by him regularly. He turned up the quieter street leading to the camera shop, looking into Sunrise Coffee and seeing only two strangers talking across a table with coffee cups and empty plates.

The street looked windblown as usual. The recently planted line of green ash trees between the sidewalk and the curb looked like stubborn hope. He walked, the only human figure on the entire block, to the aging storefront. He pushed the door open and heard the tinkle of the bell announce his arrival.

Ostroski came out from the back after several seconds. His usual sardonic smile was missing. He eyed Rabani warily, like a driver sizing up a cop who had pulled him over for a reason that wasn't clear.

"Must be dull days at the law office," he said. "It's only a little after three. Or are you doing your own bill collecting these days?"

"Tying up loose ends."

He let the comment hang as he surveyed the shelves. He saw names like Pentax, Canon, Leica, Olympus, even Kodak, and an old Royal typewriter. He saw Kodachrome and Ilford film boxes, and other small boxes that he thought probably held some kinds of lens filters, and two old leather camera cases.

"In the market for something?" Ostroski asked. "Lots of good used cameras here. They'll do the job right. Taking photos can be a satisfying pastime. As for film, I'm partial to the Ilford black and white. The Kodachrome can't be beat for slide film. But if you want colour prints, get in touch with an outfit called Seattle FilmWorks. They sell a film stock that's really 35mm movie film. Instead of a negative it creates a positive image. They'll give you a slide and a print both. High-quality stuff. Bright colours. Long lasting."

Rabani looked at two famous prints on the wall that he knew to be the work of someone named Ansel Adams. One had a moon in it. The other had slim aspen trunks and one aspen fully out in leaf, all of them shining ghostly bright against a dark background. He took his time turning to Ostroski.

"Has Adela told you the immigration problem has been sorted out?"

"Yes. She's relieved. It's the only time I've ever seen her looking like a nervous wreck, even though she has plenty to worry about. She told me it didn't matter so much about her but it would have been really bad for Roberto."

"Did she also pass on that a deputy minister in the provincial government named Frank Jeffries was behind the whole business?"

"She mentioned that. I don't know how he got involved like that, why he'd mess around with people's lives, especially people he doesn't know."

"It's a long story, although the kind you'd be interested in because he was obsessed about old photographs too. Particularly the kind you spirited out of the review room."

"You're telling me I'm responsible for that whole mess?"

"No, I'm telling you John Becker was not. I'd like to know what you've decided about giving him the picture, or pictures, of the shooting in Wisconsin."

"I haven't yet. Haven't decided that is. Maybe I should give it to him. He's just a guy trying to get a handle on a lot of things in his life. I guess I caused him enough trouble. Besides, I know it's too late for him to do anything to the Guardsman. My friend in Riverton tracked that guy down about five years ago. We decided not to make trouble for him. He had two kids. Besides, going after him would have made trouble for us too. A few days ago I got in touch with my friend and asked if he knew whether the guy was still around Riverton. He is. Most of the time in a wheelchair. He has one of those diseases that eat away at your internal wiring. It's hereditary. Maybe that's why he hated people enough to shoot them."

Rabani kept a straight face. He had practised law enough to know he should probe every statement. "Is that the truth or are you just putting me off the track?"

The impish glint reappeared in Ostroski's eyes. "You keep asking questions you'll end up never believing anything," he said.

"Yeah? Well try this question, Jack. Why do you keep telling me old secrets? It's been like that since I took you on as a client. One revelation after another. They never end. It's like peeling an onion. Except I have a feeling this onion has something at its core. And all the outer layers are a way to deflect attention. Or to give yourself something to talk about without talking about what's really bothering you."

"The only thing bothering me is my lawyer, who doesn't know when the business he's handled for me is over."

Rabani leaned toward the counter, breathing in a scent of dust mixed with film chemicals and straightening up because he didn't like it.

"You said an interesting thing the last time I was here. Something about people being responsible for what they don't do as well as the actions they actually perform. You said things you don't do can eat away at you as much as regret for things you've done. I know a little about that, Jack. I know what it's like choosing not to be there for someone who needs you. I did that with my brother after he was hit by a car and suffered brain damage for the rest of his life. After a few years I smartened up and went back to him. But I've felt guilty ever since and last week I buried him after another accident."

"So Adela told me. I'm sorry. Feel bad for you."

"Thank you. I wanted you to understand that I know what you're talking about. What I want to understand now is how you know about it.... How do you?"

For the first time since they had met, Rabani saw shock in Ostroski rather than the usual irritation or amusement. "How do you know, Jack?"

"You're my lawyer. Were. All I have to tell you about is what's landed me in trouble with the police or with someone who's suing me. I haven't been to confession since I was fourteen."

"You've never given information to me easily. Now you come up with the story behind a highly sensitive photograph just like that?

I don't believe it, and I don't believe that's everything. Not after what you said about people finding that what they fail to do eats away at them. People are more alike than they think. I thought for years my clients could tell me a lot about people and maybe even about myself. This time I looked at myself and decided that what I saw told me a lot about you. How do you know, Jack? How do you know about not doing something you should have done and paying for it the rest of your life? And what does that have to do with the picture Becker is after?"

Ostroski stared at him without a twitch. Rabani kept on: "One thing I've learned through being a lawyer is that there's almost always a reason for the things people do, even the things that don't make sense. You see people talking to themselves on the street, you see them wearing garish clothes they think are normal, you see them do any of a thousand things, there's usually a reason."

Ostroski sighed and stood up. "I need a beer. You're having one too, whether you want it or not."

Clinking sounds angled out of the back room. Ostroski reappeared with a bottle in each hand and gave one to Rabani before sitting down. They each drank, the gesture an unspoken seal on an unspoken agreement. Ostroski began talking without preliminaries.

"I was an infantry private in Korea. This was late in '52. The war was getting close to the armistice but we didn't know that. We never knew anything except what we could see in front of us. Not that another half-year in Korea could have been called a short time. We're walking up a dirt road, keeping an eye on the hills around us. A corporal comes back down the road in a hurry. He says he's going for a medic. A sniper's hit a guy in his squad. He sees we're carrying a machine gun and says he thinks the sniper is in a shack beside the road and a machine gun could probably take care of him. We move up fast, but being careful so we don't get hit ourselves. Then we set up the .50-calibre. You know what a .50-calibre bullet can do? Even one of them?"

"I don't know much about guns, Jack."

"Be happy you don't. One of those guns can turn trucks into wrecks. If someone is in the truck one of the slugs can take off an arm or a face. A Korean shack wasn't going to protect any sniper. We're looking for good cover but in a spot with a clear field of fire. We find a little rise and set up the gun."

He paused, then went on: "I think I see movement beside the shack and it doesn't look like someone wearing a uniform. Something about it looks like a woman. But I don't say a thing. Not a thing. About half a minute later we're ready. I think again about speaking up. But by that time I'm so worn down by the whole shitty experience, by Korea, I'm not volunteering comments let alone volunteering for patrols. The gun starts firing and blowing chunks off the shack. I hear what sound like a few short screams. A dwarf runs out the front door. A dwarf in peasant clothes. He falls down right away. We move up carefully for a look. There's no sniper. There probably was one but he's taken off out the back way long ago. There's no dwarf either. Just a little boy. We've just shot the hell out of a woman and three kids."

He was staring at the countertop. Rabani thought he was seeing who knew what ghosts in the Formica pattern. He looked up at Rabani and said, "Shot them for nothing, in a war that meant nothing. And I could maybe have stopped it but didn't. Because I did nothing. And there was no camera to fix that moment. It's going to go on for eternity. My eternity anyway." He ran out of words. Rabani said nothing, sure that whatever he found to say would be fatuous or somehow ignite anger.

They finished their beers in silence.

After awhile, Ostroski said, "You want to know why I wouldn't give Becker that picture? I lived with my pain. Why shouldn't he live with his? I told you, people think photographs capture memories forever. They only capture a moment. If you look at them long enough they make memories dissolve. I live with my memories, why shouldn't he have to live with his?"

Rabani kept silent. A question was not likely the end of what someone had to say.

"Besides," Ostroski went on, "it isn't just what happened in Korea. It's Gloria Sandring. Remember I told you about her? I don't have pictures of her either, just what I remember about her. Becker is the sort of guy she found a lot more attractive than me. Another Chad Jenner. Maybe he doesn't have big money but he has the looks and the smooth way about him. He has a position in society too, even if being a politician isn't like owning some big business. Not that he needs to own anything. He married into that."

Rabani took that as an opening. "Whatever you think of him, he's not a careless rich boy. Can you see Chad Jenner ever obsessing about a friend who died in Vietnam or a shooting of a girl at an anti-war demonstration? Jenner probably never had a friend who got drafted. As for Becker's marriage, from what I've seen it's no bowl of cherries. A guy who's devoted to his dogs the way he is? And marrying into the local aristocracy? You may think you're joining something when you sign up for that. But you're never really accepted. There's always a limit. It's like someone marrying the queen of England. You get a title, you get duties and recognition, you may even be regarded as royalty, but you never become king."

Ostroski blew out a breath that pushed out his lips. He looked up at the Ansel Adams print with a half-moon shining above a massive rock face.

He said, "This is a hell of a place, you know that? You come here and think someday you'll belong but you find out that you're living beside people who know something you don't. You ever have the feeling that you're in a strange place? Like it looks familiar but you're not really sure and not sure how you fit in?"

"Not me personally. I know my brother felt like that," Rabani said.

"Yeah? The people who feel like they belong, they live by some secret code. You have to figure out what it is, and then you have to accept it."

"I don't think it's all that different from a lot of other places. Moving to another country is never easy. There's always a local culture that isn't written down anywhere. It's more difficult to learn than the local language. It's a different kind of language, built partly on behaviour and partly on memories."

"Well, maybe they have a point at that. You hear people complain that foreigners come here and won't leave their old quarrels behind. Some of them going back hundreds of years. You ever see one of the movies they made of *A Christmas Carol?* The ghost of Jacob Marley wandering the earth dragging chains behind him? Something like that."

"You know, I worked a couple of summers on a garage building crew when I was going to law school. One of the crew leaders told me one day he'd been living on his own since he was seventeen. He said his father kicked him out of the house. His father told him he was old enough to live on his own and he should come by and visit now and then, like at Christmas. When this guy asked why, his father told him, 'That's what my old man gave me so that's what you get.' All sorts of people around you looking like they lead normal lives and an untold number are dragging old burdens around with them. If it isn't family history, it's national history. My family comes from Sicily. Countless invasions over thousands of years. All that blood and tumult. In the end the place became unique. A byword for crime and poverty, sure. Also a place where everything mixed together and became a new kind of life. You can have a good life there. But some of the people still have a tradition of vendettas."

"You know what all the places like that have in common?" Ostroski said. "All those stories they're trapped in are old. They live halfway in the past. Maybe if they had more pictures of how things really were they could stop carrying pictures around in their heads."

"I don't know, Jack. I'm not a photographer, just a lawyer."

"I'll think about it. About Becker and the pictures he wants. Not Jeffries though. He and all his bunch will have to live with the memories, even if they don't know for sure which of their memories are real."

"I'll see you around, Jack. Thanks for the beer."

Rabani walked out into the cold street. He decided to check back at work rather than going to his apartment. He wanted people around him so he walked back to the office on the main avenue rather than on one of the less travelled avenues north of it. The sun behind him began finding openings in the lead-coloured clouds sliding out of the west in ragged bands. The low light of late autumn reflected off a new building that had just been finished that summer. It was a departure from the usual grey concrete and dark green glass. The whole seven-storey building was clad in a copper-gold glass that reflected bright rays of sunshine. It looked like a dream of prosperity, an illusion that hope could always be made real in this land of never-ending memories and endless new optimisms.

He rode up the elevator to the office and the deep green hallway carpets that felt a little like a cushion of air. Inside the office, he slipped off his coat and sat down in his chair, thinking he could spend half an hour reviewing one of the two files he had left behind, and then go out for supper. He reached for a folder and stopped. Without putting his usual thought into it he picked up the phone and dialed Adela's number. He was surprised when she answered and even more surprised when, after a second of thinking it over, she agreed to go out for supper with him.

They talked and occasionally laughed. They both stayed away from worrisome topics. He told her how his first car had been a used 1976 Ford Pinto and he had been scared of stories about exploding gas tanks but it turned out he should have been even more scared about weak engine timing belts and rust-prone fenders. She told him she had been intrigued by the notion of making banana bread. When she was a girl, someone had always done that for her. She found that the most difficult part was judging when bananas were soft enough for baking but not yet collapsed into an unappetizing brown mess. "They're like people," she said. "You want them mature, but not collapsing into a soft middle age. Ripe but not turning into mush."

They went for a walk afterward and kissed in an empty corner park. They drifted toward his apartment. His biggest surprise of the evening came when she agreed to go up with him and they quickly began making love. It was the most physical affection he'd known in three years. She stayed until one in the morning. She came back once in early January, the coldest week of the year. By then he realized that what he liked about her best was the sound of her voice.

27.

THEY MET ON A SUNDAY AFTERNOON FOR A WALK ALONG the riverbank. It was the last week of February. The weather had warmed up but was still wintry. Ice on the river was covered now by deep snow. The snow bore tracks where deer had sauntered out of the willows and poplars in the safety of darkness. The deer had wandered out where the surface was still firm and smooth. Near the far bank a narrow stream of open water ran downstream from a drainage outlet. In some places, ice piled up in chunks like boulders on an avalanche slope.

Fluting whistles of chickadees pierced the air as sharply as the slivers of sunlight dazzling about them. They looked up at the bundles of black, grey and white hopping from twig to twig and looking back at them.

"Chickadees were the first birds I truly noticed when I moved here," Adela said. "They look so friendly."

"They are," Rabani said. "I've walked down here on weekends when I needed a break from work and there was no one to spend any time with. The chickadees are always here. They're always curious about you, which is something a lot of people can't manage."

He was happy that it was warm enough not to have the lenses of his glasses fog up. They were a week old, with frames of thick black plastic instead of the tortoiseshell look he had favoured for years. Rabani liked the idea of going into courtrooms and into client meetings looking a little more aggressive than he had in the past; still, he counted on strong preparation rather than on the projection of a useful image.

Adela had noticed the change, not so much of looks as of tone. She did not talk about that, though. She talked instead about the book he had lent her, the autobiography of Clarence Darrow. He had told her that reading it was one of the main reasons he had gone into law.

"It's different from Agatha Christie," she said. "Christie made up a world full of nicely placed facts and big emotions pushing against each other in tightly contained spaces. Darrow's world was full of rock-solid principles and factual uncertainties, contested in a wide-open social setting. The crimes in those settings often reflected the struggle of big conflicting interests in the surrounding society. Some could even be described as a struggle of alienation against settled order."

"That's true," he said, which was a way of saying he liked hearing her think. "Darrow's world had verdicts but often no absolute certainty about what had really happened. The appeal of Christie's fiction is the knowledge that one will get to the bottom of things."

"Yes," she said, "the appeal of knowing."

The sidewalk had been swept clear of snow. They did not have the familiar crunching squeak under their boots but they did have the radiant glitter of the low February sun and the delicate ridges of snow on tree branches to marvel at. He waited for her to take a glove off her hand and hold his, as she often did when they walked along this pathway, looking down at the frozen river. He thought their hands were magically a perfect fit.

"I'm going to stay with the firm," he said. "I may even make a lifelong career there. The senior partners, one in particular, are good men, all worth knowing and learning from. Some of the new associates are promising talents and good company. But I've been changing my mind about what sorts of cases to take on. This city, the whole province, has more rottenness in it than I imagined. Like waking up one morning and finding your bananas have turned squishy and brown," he joked. "I think it's time I accepted that. Maybe what my colleagues call the garbage cases are worth taking on. They're as real as the higher-status ones. Maybe I can learn more from them."

She said nothing for about half a minute. Then she said, "You will make a good lawyer, George. I think it is a career that will suit you. And this city suits you. You will probably be a senior partner yourself one day, perhaps sooner than some of your colleagues."

He kept walking, looking at the bright snow on the tree branches and the occasional chickadee twitching its head to study the passersby with its bright eyes. But he felt a hollowing in his chest, a sudden and certain sense of relegation, of being placed on a shelf from which there would be no return.

"I'll just keep doing my job," he said. "It's the most interesting thing I can think of."

They reached a small observation platform and crowded to its wooden railing to look out over the silent valley. That was when she told him she had given notice to Jack that she would be leaving the city in mid-March.

"I am moving to Chicago," she said.

He could not immediately find words.

"I have a chance to work in architectural restoration there," she said. "They are beginning to restore truly beautiful buildings from the first forty years of this century and even some from the last of the nineteenth. It's what I was trained to do and want to do."

She did not stop to wait for anything he might say. "Nothing like that will happen here. Here they think a city is a place to build structures fast and pull them down not long afterward to make room for new ones. They think they acknowledge the past if they keep a little stone from an old façade on the front of a new building. Or maybe they put a fresh coat of paint on one of the big advertisements that used to be painted on the sides of old brick warehouses. It's true that Chicago has more money to make preservation and restoration possible. Very rich families and businesses have started foundations with enough grant money at their disposal to make such work possible. But here? I don't think money can ever make a difference. Here there is no will."

He finally found a voice and said, "What about Roberto?"

"We have talked," she said. "He will stay here. I think he likes it. He likes it now even more than before his encounter with authority. He said he felt fairly treated. And he felt he had friends looking after him. He likes construction work too. That's what he will do. He said he may decide to become an apprentice in one of the trades. Carpentry and electrical installation both interest him. I think Jack will look after him as well as Jack can look after anyone. I hope you will keep in touch with him, too." She turned to look at him with the last statement. A request? A polite acknowledgment? Something close to a direction? A hope sent floating into the winter air?

She turned back to the river and said, "In any event, he will be better off staying here than dealing with the American authorities after his legal experience here and with his background."

"Separating still seems like a difficult way for a brother and sister to proceed."

"Do not forget that we were separated for two years when he was abducted by the guerrillas," she said. "And I was much older. We enjoyed each other's company but we were never as close as many siblings. Even here, when we ended up living together again, he and I were living quite different lives."

"Different is not the same as separate."

"No, but I think perhaps this is inevitable. Now I will live in a city where people want to preserve architectural evidence of the past but see those buildings as a departure point for new ways of expressing who they are, and what their community is. Roberto will build new structures. But he will do that in a city that always tears down its old ones. Perhaps the achievements of the past are never thought to be good enough. The visual evidence steadily disappears. It is removed quickly and replaced quickly. People here seem to think that is the way to build the future. I think it is a way to keep forever building a future that forever recedes from view. You think you are leaving the past when you take down all the old buildings. But you keep living the memory of old dreams, hoping the next building will be the fulfillment, the one that will finally get you to the future."

"You make it sound glum," he said. "Not even tragic, just glum."

They were both looking at the river and the snow-frosted trees on the other side. A couple in puffy jackets, he in red and she in white, stood talking on the far bank, looking quite small, too far away to hear.

"I hope you will find someone to keep you company," she said. "I know there are women who like you. That friend of my friend Rosa, the one named Ginny, she told Rosa she liked you."

"I liked you," he said.

They walked back to his car and he drove her to her apartment. He wished her good luck with her new life and she wished him good luck with his career. She kissed him on his right cheek and slipped out of the car seat and onto the sidewalk, so quickly he had the impression of a blur. They never saw each other again.

Midway through March, he was walking along the thickly carpeted hallway toward his office one afternoon when a door opened and Asher stepped out, his overcoat on and a briefcase in his hand.

Rabani broke into a smile, surprising himself. "Hello, Harry," he said. "You had a good day?"

"Progress on all fronts. You?"

"My two top cases are coming along nicely," Rabani said. "One should be wrapped up in a few days and the other in a couple of weeks. I'll probably spend some of the evening in the office going over the files. The first case will be in the judge's hands. The other is probably headed for a reasonably amicable settlement."

"You should remember to save time for company some evenings," Asher said. "Preferably female."

"I intend to work on that. You know, I'm changing course with the kinds of cases I handle. The partners had me lined up to take on some important new commercial work but I've been losing interest in that field. Commercial cases more and more seem artificial. That drawn-out business with Ostroski's photographs opened my eyes to what's underneath what passes for high society in this place. It's a densely intertwined and often unseemly world. That could be interesting to explore. I'm going to start taking on the cases that none of the partners want to touch, messy things like divorce and fraud."

"Are you sure?" Asher said. "There could be a fine line between interesting and depressing. It could also put you on a very slow road to a partnership. It usually pays to keep one eye on the future."

"True," Rabani said. "But in this town, probably in this whole province, the future often seems to be jumping out of reach. Like it's running away from the past and the past never gives up or lies down to rest. Be careful the past doesn't catch you someday, Harry. It's a dangerous thing around here. Sometimes you can't recognize it until it's all around you."

Asher smiled. "I never believed in ghosts, George. But I'll keep that in mind."

Rabani thought he had time to drive over to the camera shop on the way home. It was late enough in the afternoon that he would find a parking spot with no problem. He pulled up on the street opposite the little storefront and noticed how small and sparse it looked. Not desolate and bare. The sign over the window gave it a spark of life—but, what to say, a modest life, careful, watchful, yet insistent on its own small space. A sparrow in a park full of crows and magpies.

Ostroski was behind the counter reading a photography magazine. He looked up as the door opened and said, "Hello, lawyer. Here to hand deliver my receipt for paying the bill?"

"That's only for clients we can expect to be repeat customers," Rabani said. "How are you making out these days?"

"Personally? Fine. If you're asking how I'm going to get along without Adela to help out, I've got a kid coming in from the photography class I teach over at the college. A couple of them can take good pictures but he's interested in learning how to do basic repairs, too."

"That's good. And Roberto?"

"I see him from time to time. He promised to drop in once every week or two. So far he's kept his promise. We go out for burgers or something. He has a bigger appetite than I do. How about you?"

"There's never any shortage of work for a lawyer in this town. Especially now that I'm switching into the messier side of the work—divorce, business partners suing each other, that sort of thing."

"I was thinking more of your social life. You can't work all the time. You going out on a date some night with that Ginny Radescu? From what I hear, she could be fun."

"That's the impression I got the one time I met her," Rabani said. "Yeah, I think I'll see what she's like."

"She used to be involved with Becker, you know?"

"That's my understanding. I thought he'd be one of my divorce cases. I guess not, though. He strikes me as a guy who never managed to settle down. Now he has."

"He was in here a few days ago."

"Oh?"

"Picking up a few negatives. I decided to let him have those photos I took in Riverton. He didn't want me to make any prints, just the negatives. Didn't want to use the loupe to inspect them closely, either. Said he'd probably look at them someday."

"That's good, Jack."

Ostroski put down the magazine and looked around the shop. "Well, what the hell, he doesn't seem like such a bad guy, really. Even offered to let me have one of his dogs if I wanted it. He said that one he calls Mitzi likes me. What would I do with a dog? And a dachshund. I'd rather take my chances with that Doberman he keeps."

He opened his hands and looked at the palms and tilted his gaze back up at Rabani. "You know, I have a bunch of other old pictures around here. I took some of Adela once. She didn't like having her picture taken but I got her to stand outside in the sunlight and behind the counter here when I was testing an old Leicaflex. You could have any of them you wanted."

Rabani had time to think as Ostroski was finishing the offer and answered without hesitating: "No thanks, Jack. That guy you met from my office, Harry, told me he doesn't believe in ghosts. Think I'll try to see if he's right. Can I let you know if I change my mind?"

"I'll keep them nicely stored."

Rabani shuffled to look up at the black and white prints with a ghostly moon and strangely luminous aspens and said, "Well, I just dropped in to see how you were doing, and check on Roberto."

He started walking out and heard Ostroski say, "Okay. Don't be a stranger."

Then he drove to the observation point overlooking the river valley, where he saw the ice had started to thaw and break up, just as it did every spring.

TWENTY-FIVE YEARS LATER

THE SMELL OF FURNITURE IN A STRONGLY HEATED ROOM oozed up around Rabani, along with the leftover aromas of chicken soup and some kind of sandwiches. The staff were clearing away the last of the lunch clutter. All the chairs at the lunch tables had arms and all the stuffed couches and seats around the sides were covered in floral print fabric. He saw Ostroski sitting in an armchair in a corner talking to a woman with thinning whitish hair and thick spectacles with translucent cream-coloured frames. He walked up and smiled a hello.

"Hi George, this is Hazel," Ostroski said. "I've been trying to get her to model for me because I think her cheekbones would photograph well but she says it might lead to hanky panky."

"Oh you," Hazel said. Rabani thought her tone of voice contained an unresolved mixture of delight and annoyance.

"Excuse us, please, Hazel," Ostroski said. "Time for gin rummy. Have to keep the brain cells firing."

They moved to a card table, Ostroski walking stiffly but at a good pace. His hands were getting a little stiff too but he could still shuffle if he did not try to rush.

"What's new in the world? All we ever get to see of it in this place is the evening news, and I don't trust any of that."

"Not much. The usual. You'd probably be interested to know, though, that phone manufacturers are squeezing high enough resolution into their camera feature this year that they expect a lot of people will forget about having separate equipment and just take pictures with their phones."

"Hmmph. They'll think they're taking pictures. I'm not surprised. Getting rid of Kodachrome was only the first shoe to fall."

"Anything new here?"

"You'd never guess. John Becker is one of the inmates now. He checked in three weeks ago. Still has most of his marbles but they're starting to fall out of the bag. Just gets a little vague now and then. I suppose he can hang on well enough to talk to for another six months, maybe a year if he's lucky. I don't know if you'll see him today. He likes a nap after lunch."

"I suppose he's here because his wife died several months ago."

"Looks like it. His kids aren't eager to have him living with them. He says he wasn't eager to impose on them anyway. They're all well fixed enough to go their own ways. His wife sold the family ranch and there weren't many other relatives to split it with. Funny thing. She used to make a big deal about preserving the ranch way of life down there. You used to see her in the papers talking about how it was the heart of the province. But he said she had it in her will that a block of the land right up against the foothills should be leased to a wind power company. She wanted the rest sold to a nature conservancy."

Rabani considered whether to pick up a discard or try his luck from the top of the pack. He turned a card from the pack and said, "She was a realist. She knew you can hang onto the past for a long time, or let the past hang onto you, but a long time is not forever."

Voices rose on the other side of the room. They looked over to see a small family group around one of the other residents. A woman in a striped dress had a cellphone out and was taking snapshots with it.

"Phones," Ostroski snorted. "Any old camera in my shop would have taken better pictures. The digital cameras have a lot going for them, I'll admit. When the staff here found out I made a living as a photographer they got me to take pictures of birthdays and things like that. They lend me one of those pocket-size digital cameras. It's a long way from a good 35mm with Kodachrome or Ilford film but you can take as many shots as you like and you can see what you have instantly. That makes you less careful, of course. But every professional photographer threw away a lot of exposures. One of the secrets of the trade was to keep taking a lot of pictures. You looked for the one or two that would stand out."

He was getting wound up now. Rabani didn't mind. He had come to enjoy the grumpy lectures.

"And those phone cameras are too handy, too accessible. You see relatives coming in here and using them all the time. I read about people taking pictures of themselves and everyone and everything around them and putting them on the Internet. I see in the paper once a week a full page of pictures that people have taken of food. You wonder how you see so many fat people around these days when they're taking pictures of their food instead of eating it. They don't have a clue. They don't realize that when they record everything in their lives they're not saving it, they're throwing it away. They're making everything forgettable the instant they live it. Who knows? Maybe they don't even live their life, just see it through a little glass screen. People constantly taking pictures of themselves like they're television stars. And they don't realize television dissolves the past, chews it up. Hell, the TV's on in here most nights. You know what I see? The same thing over and over. TV finally used up every idea any writer or director ever had. Now they just keep remaking the same shows with different names and different characters. Even the stars aren't stars anymore. They're just a bunch of factory workers no one remembers the week after their series is cancelled."

"You finished?" Rabani said.

"Sure. Gin."

Rabani wasn't surprised. Ostroski was in the home because of arthritis and a weakened heart, not because he had lost his ability to count cards and talk at the same time. Rabani shuffled the deck and Ostroski said, "Speaking of gin, how come you never married that woman?"

"Ginny? I don't know. She never pressed the issue. I thought about it off and on. Then we ran out of time. Too used to not having to trip over someone else in the apartment now. We still see each other a lot. Sometimes we stay over at each other's places."

"I think I'd have married her. Maybe doing that would have been a mistake, maybe not. You can't go through life without making mistakes. I look back and think about all the things I would have done differently if I'd been as smart as I am now. I used to regret most of them. Now? I see people taking pictures like they have no choice. I read about insurance companies bribing people to install devices in their cars to let the companies keep track of how they drive. I read about experiments with driverless cars. I hear about younger folks buying nothing but premade dinners and getting wrapped up in social causes that don't mean much. All those causes do is keep them from paying attention to things that really count. From what I hear about computers you don't even have much choice there. You buy Microsoft or Apple, and then you're stuck with buying everything else from the same company. Now I hear the big outfits don't even want to sell you stuff, they want you to pay a monthly subscription, like you're on the hook forever at a company store. Fridges that spy on you. I look back and think we didn't have a lot of the conveniences people have now but at least we had freedom."

"You're getting ornery in your old age, Jack."

"I'm working at it. Got to keep your mind occupied somehow in this overheated birdcage or it'll turn to mush. Time to take a walk after this hand?"

"Yes, I have some time. I have some refreshments in the car so we won't get dehydrated."

They drove to a small unnamed park area overlooking the river and strolled slowly to a bench where they sat down and opened two cans of beer that Rabani had selected because the labels could easily be mistaken for something non-alcoholic.

Ostroski took as long a sip as he could manage and smacked his lips. "Ah," he said. "Thank you, George. The doctors and the dietitians who keep trying to tell me how to die don't know how this tastes on a summer day. They probably stick to that stuff they call energy drinks, or broccoli juice. We get enough broccoli at dinner in that place." He took another sip. "Goddamn busybodies," he snarled.

Rabani smiled at the thought of how much his friend sounded like a short-tempered dachshund.

He looked at the river, knowing Ostroski was enjoying the sight of the placid, multi-coloured surface with the deep currents underneath, flowing between the willows and cottonwoods year after year. He looked up at the clouds, endless white puffs of cumulus sliding across the austere blue sky, and wondered what dreams he could make of them or what memories they could stir.

DISCUSSION QUESTIONS

1. What images decay in the course of this story? Do some images not decay and, if so, what makes them different? Do the effects of images that decay and those that resist decay differ?

2. George Rabani becomes a link between a number of quite different characters in the book. Does he have a strong personality of his own and how does his personality allow for him to interact with the other characters?

3. Is Jack Ostroski fundamentally a sympathetic and likable character or not? Would you want to spend any time with him?

4. This is a book about place as well as about characters. The setting is not meant to be a mirror image of Alberta but is obviously in the same location. In what ways does it look like Alberta to you? Are there ways in which it does not?

5. Jack Ostroski argues that photographs are a way of forgetting rather than remembering. Is he right or wrong? Or can they be both? Why?

6. Most of the characters live with memories, often memories they regret. Some may even have lives shaped by those memories. Is that unusual or is it a common condition experienced by most people?

7. Ostroski ends up saying people had more freedom in the analogue days than during the modern digital days. Is he right? Is there a similarity between that freedom and Alex Rabani's living without much memory? Is Alex's state a loss or a freedom?

8. Differences in social class seem to underlie some of the characters' attitudes and some of the events in the book. How important are these differences? Do they reflect real life as you know it?

9. Some of the characters feel at home in the place where they live, some do not, and some keep insisting it is their home when they may not actually fit in. For example, Arlene Becker and Adela Morales have strengths that may not be immediately apparent and opposing views of the place where they live. How do their experiences alter how they view the city in which they live? To what extent is feeling at home anyplace you live a result of objective circumstance, and to what extent is it a result of your own perceptions and adaptability?

MARK IS A WRITER LIVING IN EDMONTON, ALBERTA. Originally from Hamilton, Ontario, he began working as a journalist in Regina in 1973; moved to Edmonton in 1978 to join The Canadian Press as a reporter-editor; became provincial affairs columnist at the *Edmonton Journal* in 1987; and was publisher and editor of an independent political newsletter from 2005 to 2013. He has since been a freelance editor and written novels, the first being *Where the Bodies Lie*, which was shortlisted for the 2017 Crime Writers of Canada Arthur Ellis Award for best first crime novel. He edited a collection of speeches by former Alberta lieutenant-governor Lois Hole, titled *Lois Hole Speaks*, and wrote two books about Alberta politics, *The Klein Revolution* and *Alberta Politics Uncovered*, the latter winning the Writers Guild of Alberta Wilfred Eggleston Award for non-fiction in 2005. He enjoys the work of many authors, including David Adams Richards; his favourite authors of mysteries/thrillers include Ross Macdonald, K.C. Constantine, Nicolas Freeling, Dorothy Sayers and Josephine Tey.